PICO'S CRUSH

CENTRAL GALACTIC CONCORDANCE BOOK 3

BY CAROL VAN NATTA

CHAVANCH PRESS

WWW.CHAVANCH.COM

PICO'S CRUSH
Copyright © 2016 Carol Van Natta
First Ebook Published January 2016
Published by Chavanch Press, LLC
ISBN: 978-0-9831741-6-5

Cover design by Gene Mollica Studio
Edited by Shelley Holloway
Author website: Author.CarolVanNatta.com

DESCRIPTION

* * * * *

A galactic security specialist expects a quiet vacation visit to his daughter's college campus. Instead he finds himself in battling for the safety of the students, with old friends and an ex-military squad-mate fighting at his side. Can they find a cunning serial killer before he finds his next target?

When ex-military sniper and current personal security specialist Jerzi Adams visits his daughter Pico's quiet college on the paradise-like planet of Nila Marbela, he doesn't expect emergency evacuations and rogue robots. Nor does he expect to renew a friendship with former squad-mate.

Explosions, sabotage, and assaults used to be Andra De Luna's daily routine, but she gave it up for a professorship at a prestigious university. Now she's flung back into that world, with an entire floating campus of students to protect.

When the hunt for a cunning serial killer leads Jerzi's old friends Luka and Mairwen (Overload Flux) to town, there's trouble in paradise as the body count starts to rise. Either the world of academia has gone from merely cutthroat to downright deadly, or more sinister forces are in conflict, with the campus as a battleground. Without an improvised miracle or two, no one's going to make it out alive.

* * * * *

CHAPTER 1

FOR PARADISE, IT sure as hell rained a lot.

Jerzi Adams hunched his shoulders forward and tried to keep the warm, torrential rain from drenching every square centimeter of his new corporate suit as he half ran toward the huge, rounded entrance to the lecture space in the Optimal Polytechnic Chemistry building. It was supposedly the tallest building of the four clustered on the anchored ovoid disc that made up this part of the famous floating campus, but he couldn't see anything but gray shapes. The only available parking for his flitter had been on the east end of the floater, on top of the Materials Science building.

The wind drove the drumbeat of rain in waves of white noise. The remnants of the late-season typhoon hadn't been expected to extend so far west, and he hadn't brought rain gear. The permaturf walkway was so waterlogged, it felt like slogging through a shallow swamp. He was glad he'd fished his all-terrain boots out of his luggage, even if they didn't go with the corporate look.

A quick glance at the building name above the oversized, half-round doorway confirmed he was finally in the right place. The doors irised open on his approach, and he hurried through them. He was immediately assaulted by a wave of sound even louder than the rain.

The student event was supposed to have been held outside in the central commons area, where everyone could enjoy the famous tropical ambiance that drew students like a magnet to the city of Tremplin and the O-Poly University. The unexpected rain had forced the school to move the exhibits and scientific demonstrations for visiting parents and sponsors into the lecture hall. It was a frenetic bazaar of human voices and whirling technology, of chaotic motion, and bright kaleidoscopes of clashing colors demanding attention. Display tables were jammed into haphazard clusters with no obvious order. Despite the heat and humidity, or because of it, he detected whiffs of smoke and chemicals, from sulfur to cloying citrus and everything in between. Easily several hundred people were squeezed into a space intended to hold maybe half that.

Somehow, despite the oppressive din, he heard his daughter Pico's voice.

"Dad! Dad!" From the swell of humanity, a petite figure emerged and ran up the wide ramp toward him, waving. She was wearing a sleeveless, fitted white-and-red jumpsuit and matching boots, reminiscent of a combat mech-suit liner, and her midnight-blue hair with silver tips was in pigtails, but he'd know her energetic grace and wide smile anywhere. "You found us!"

He grinned and started to open his arms, then changed his mind and stepped back. "You'll get wet. I'm soaked."

She laughed and threw herself heedlessly into his embrace, squeezing tightly. "We're all wet. The rain surprised everyone. That's why they made us move everything in here." She pulled away and grabbed his hand. "Come on, the solars are over here. Nice suit, by the way. Earrings, too." Turning back to the pandemonium, she shouted, "Valenia! He's here!" Several people turned to look. Her voice was surprisingly loud for someone who looked so dainty.

Pico led him into an alcove that had a bank of a dozen solardry units. He tapped the control panel, and the unit began evaporating away the moisture at an alarming rate. It was airfoil-loud and too warm, but it was efficient. He smoothed his hair so it would dry flat. Pico crowded close, using the edge of the field to dry the front of her. The industrial-strength solardries made sense, considering Nila Marbela was a watery planet and the sprawling O-Poly campuses were on natural islands and man-made floaters in the equatorial zone.

The dry cycle finished just as Pico's roommate and best friend, Valenia Tamheurre, joined them. She was a head taller than Pico, and dressed like a fashion designer's prototype tester, all rippling pastel pink ruffles and winking fairy lights, but Jerzi knew she had a good brain hiding under her poof of pomegranate red, waved hair. She was carrying a cheap, nova-bright orange umbrella, the kind tourists bought as souvenirs.

He greeted Valenia, then put his arm around Pico's slender shoulders. "Did I miss your team's presentation?" He knew she'd collaborated with several other students for their exhibit, but she'd been secretive about the details. He'd missed too many of the milestones in her life.

"Yeah," Pico said, "but so did everyone else." She sighed disgustedly. "Apparently, there's a rule against launching rockets in the lecture hall."

Jerzi tried to keep a straight face. "How shortsighted of them not to have designed the space for such harmless activities."

Valenia laughed. "That's what Professor De Luna said, except I think she used the words 'crazy stunts.'" She glanced at the huge, ornate clock on the wall. "I'll be late if I don't leave now, and the kid pawners will complain. It was nice to see you again, Mr. Adams." Her precise diction and accent-free Standard English were a credit to her private education, because he knew her wealthy family's primary language was Afro-French.

"I'll be there at six," said Pico. "I'll bring your long coat if it's still raining."

"You're the best friend ever," said Valenia with a smile. She took a deep breath, powered the umbrella to full, then headed out through the door and into the rain. He hoped her umbrella lasted longer than his had.

He frowned as the doors irised closed. "Maybe I should go with her."

Pico shook her head. "It's daylight, and she's just going to the other end of the floater. She'd have asked if she wanted company."

She grabbed his hand again and started leading him down the ramp into the crowded hall. He was comforted by her easy affection. It had been a lonely nine months only seeing her on delayed holo.

"Kid pawners?" he asked, raising his voice to be heard over the sudden rising whine of a miniature toroidal engine, fortunately tethered.

She veered closer so he could hear her. "At the childcare where Valenia volunteers, some parents drop their kids off like they're boats to be docked. She calls them 'kid pawners' because they're always pawning their kids off on someone else."

Jerzi hid a wince. Dhorya, Pico's mother, had accused him of that more than once. His military service as a ground-pounder gunnin and civilian private security career had kept him away, leaving Pico and Dhorya alone to deal with her nasty Sankirna family for long periods. He and Dhorya had both been too young and so very naïve about what it would take to raise a child, even one as remarkable as Pico.

"Hey, P.A.!" A slender young man whose hair and skin were so pale, he was nearly albino waved his arms frantically. "We got the Decas-Yee reaction to work above three hundred K and in full G!" He pointed to a floating holo display. "We already won a POGS prize. Do come see!" His accent said he'd been raised on Albion Prime, or close to it. Few could outdo the exclusive planet for over-the-top pretentiousness.

Pico smiled but didn't stop plowing forward through the crowds. "Can't, Sully. Places to be, rockets to launch. I'll see it later."

"We could stop…" began Jerzi.

Pico shook her head and increased her pace. "No, or we'd be there the rest of the afternoon. Let's find Professor De Luna, then see if she'll let us escape this madhouse."

Jerzi couldn't agree more. Even though he had plenty of experience with crowds, he didn't care for them. Give him a nice, high vantage point above the fray any day, like the almost invisible ledge high on the north wall. Probably a support for the room's audiovisual functions, though he couldn't see where to access it.

He had no idea how Pico, who took after her short, slender mother of Asian descent, could see where she was going, but she'd always had a superb sense of space. She'd never gotten lost, even when she was a child, barely able to walk. He was content to follow, using his larger physique to help part the crowds for her. He saw almost nothing of himself in his daughter's appearance, but they thought very much alike. She was a lot smarter than he was, though, enough to get into a prestigious school on a scholarship. If it hadn't been for the military, he'd have no advanced education at all.

As they rounded a table with a clump of chattering students gathered around it, he saw a flutter of a holo displaying a green and gold prize seal, like the one Sully had been bragging about. "What's a POGS prize?"

The crowd thinned for a bit, and Jerzi consciously relaxed his shoulders. It was hard to remember he wasn't there to provide personal security for a public figure. He was just on vacation, visiting his kid. Adult kid, he reminded himself.

"POGS stands for Parents, Obligates, Guardians, and Sponsors." She gave him a cheeky grin and squeezed his hand. "Since you're a 'P,' I'll send you the ping ref so you can vote for my team's excellent project."

He started to tell her to send the code to her mother, too, but thought better of it. Pico didn't like the reminder that Sankirna money was the only reason she could afford to share an apartment near campus and eat without needing a food service job. It didn't thrill him, either.

"The POGS prize is mostly a popularity contest, and faculty votes get extra weight." She pointed a thumb back over her shoulder. "Sully sounds rich, but he isn't, he's just brainy. His experiment partner's family is name-on-a-building rich, and she's brainy enough to let Sully do the work. Funnily enough, they win something every time her family makes an appearance."

Jerzi detected a bit of defensiveness in her tone. "Scholarship students don't win very often, I take it." She shrugged a shoulder as if she didn't care.

He assumed a mock enforcer look as he leaned in and whispered, in his best heavily menacing Slavic accent, "Tell me who is in your way. *Zajmę się tym.*" He flexed his arm and shoulder muscles, as if he was the evil crew enforcer in a thriller.

Pico snorted with amusement. "I'm pretty sure the school has a rule against 'taking care of it.'"

Jerzi crossed his arms, pushing out his triceps with his fists, then shrugged with elaborate carelessness. "Accidents happen."

Pico put her small hands around his left biceps and kneaded, a throwback to when she was a child and fascinated by his well-developed upper arm muscles. "I miss you. I'm glad you could come."

"Me, too." They edged around a group of people standing in front of another student table. It felt like they were going in circles. "Are we there yet?"

She rolled her eyes. "Creaky, Dad."

"Wait until you have children," he said archly.

Pico grabbed his wrist and pulled him around more tables. He found himself cataloging the distance and paths to the nearest exits out of habit, and sternly told himself to stand down. He really needed to get a life outside of security work and time at the gym.

Finally, Pico stepped up to a table pushed up against a two-meter wide, square pillar.

"*Voilà!*" She opened her arms at a wide diagonal, presenting the display, entitled "Domestic Launch." The carefully arranged items looked like they'd been salvaged from the recycle bin, but he realized after a moment that was the whole point. Everything on the table was commonly found around the house, but combined correctly, made an effective propellant for the rocket, which was a simple sink hose caged with rigid screen mesh, with a flat-bottomed cone for a fuel chamber and a standard wirekey for ignition energy. The direction was controlled by adapter wings from a child's rocket ship toy, and didn't rely on anything with motors or anti-grav tech.

"It's really clever. How did you come up with it?"

"The projects on the 'recommended' list were boring, but none of us could afford to buy the materials for something more fun. We kind of made this up as we went along."

A pretty, dark-skinned woman approached Pico from the other side. "Ms. Adams, have you seen... oh, pardon the interruption." She smiled at Jerzi. "I'm Professor Chandravarthi, in the Chemistry Department." She pointed to the temporary nameplate pinned to the shoulder of her sleeveless, multicolored top that stopped at her flat midriff and gave a slight bow, then turned to Pico. "Do you know where Ravlenko's and Bando's teams ended up?"

Pico started to point, but was interrupted by what sounded like an overstressed teakettle and a flurry of conflicting orders. It sounded close.

"Kill the power!"

"Flood the chamber!"

"*Duck!*"

Jerzi stepped closer to Pico and put himself between her and the noise. The earsplitting, rising pitch whistle abruptly cut off. He waited for an explosion, but none came. A cloud of bluish smoke billowed out and dissipated. After a tense moment, everyone nearby seemed to relax.

Chandravarthi heaved a melodramatic sigh. "Mr. Ravlenko's team, I presume." She set off toward where the noise had come from, muttering darkly as she left. "Everything will be fine inside, they said. Mustn't disappoint the POGS, they said."

Pico poked his chest twice. "Hovering."

"Sorry," he said, backing up, but he wasn't, really. Protecting her was in his DNA.

A frown crossed her face as she ducked away, but it quickly transformed into a smile. "Professor De Luna! Come meet my dad."

Jerzi turned to see the famous professor of materials science who had inspired Pico to declare a study focus for her certificate. The woman was a little taller than mid-height, conservatively dressed in a long-sleeved, high-necked, dark jacket with half-tails, and her dark hair was scraped back away from her striking face. If she wore makeup on her light brown skin, it was subtle. She seemed familiar, somehow.

"Professor Andreina De Luna, this is my dad..."

"Commander Crush," she said with a lopsided smile. "It's a small galaxy."

It was the use of his old unit nickname and her soft Spanish accent that finally sparked his memory. "Subcaptain Lightning. It certainly is." Delight bloomed in him, and he grinned and held out a fist to her, thumb up. She bumped his knuckles twice with a fist of her own, once straight up and once turned sideways.

Pico looked back and forth at them, owl-eyed. "You *know* each other?"

Andra nodded. "Five years together as gunnin in the CGC Ground Division, Command's Forward Intelligence Unit Zulu Six Echo." She winked at him. "Your father was the best sniper we ever had."

Jerzi felt himself redden, as if he was suddenly twelve years old. He ducked his head to hide it. "Thanks."

He looked at her more closely, trying to reconcile the brash, volatile, very unconventional officer he'd known in the military with the sedate, contained woman in front of him. She was the picture of a dedicated academic, though her straight pants didn't quite hide her muscular legs, and he suspected her shoes were more practical than they looked.

She'd apparently been thinking along the same lines. "You sure clean up good, Adams. Nice suit. Must have given the designer fits with all those extra muscles." She winked at Pico, who smirked back.

He had no idea why women were interested in what he wore, but no way in hell was he getting into a discussion about clothes. "Materials science, huh? That's what they're calling boom-down these days?"

Andra's eyebrow twitched. "*Claro que sí.* Of course. Sounds more dignified in the college brochure."

"What's boom-down?" asked Pico.

"Munitions. Explosions," said Jerzi.

"Just a flyby to see your daughter, Commander?"

"Visit and a short vacation. It'd be longer if it wasn't seven transit days from–"

"And who do we have here?" The resonant voice came from behind him. He turned to see a tall, very sharply dressed man with a wide, professional smile that almost reached his brilliant green eyes. He looked to be in his late fifties, though if he followed regular health maintenance protocols and good body-shop work, he could be twice that age. His face was too thin to be called handsome, but his tanned skin was as perfect as his full head of wavy blond hair, tasteful ear jewelry, and skin art in geometric ovals.

The man caressed the gold, glowing nametag on his chest pocket. "Master Benedar Vestering, Department Leader for Materials Science." His naturally rich voice rang with pride bordering on condescension.

"Adams." He tilted his head toward Pico and gave her a quick smile.

"Peregrine Adams is my daughter."

Vestering's smile faltered as he stared at Jerzi. "You're not, eh, that is, you don't look like a Sankirna." There was a hint of accusation in the tone.

Jerzi felt his face freeze. "No. Were you expecting one?" Surely Pico would have told him, but maybe she didn't know about it.

"Oh, no," said Vestering, brushing invisible lint off his tunic hem. "I just happened to see a tuition transfer this morning for a Peregrine Adams from a Sankirna account. It's an unusual name." He looked down at Pico as if seeing her for the first time.

Jerzi felt Pico's hand slip into the crook of his elbow, causing him to automatically fold his arm to support her. "*Chodźmy, tato. Coś jest śmierdzący tutaj.*"

She was rarely that overtly insulting, so she apparently knew Vestering didn't understand Polish. While it was true that something was stinking, Jerzi didn't want to encourage her rudeness.

Vestering's professional smile returned. "Such an expressive language, Russian."

Jerzi patted Pico's hand and smiled indulgently. "Yes," he said, "it certainly is." Out of the corner of his eye, he saw Andra cover her mouth and turn her head away to cough. He remembered she'd always been good with languages.

Vestering might not speak Polish or Russian, but he appeared to suspect they weren't being respectful, even if he couldn't pinpoint the specific offense. His disgruntled gaze landed on Andra. "I don't care how popular your Practical Applications class is, it's not rigorous educational practice." He waved an arm toward the improvised rocket display. "Encouraging *this* kind of childish nonsense isn't preparing your students for anything but a career in a shady jack crew."

Jerzi wondered if Vestering thought there were aboveboard jack crews that engaged in punching and hauling cargo from space stations and interstellar freighters.

Pico let go of Jerzi's arm to step closer to Andra, then gave Vestering her best wide-eyed, innocent look. "Really? Will they have a booth on recruiting day? I'm told they pay very well."

A couple of nearby students tittered. They looked away fast when Vestering shot them a glare.

He frowned at Pico, clearly not sure if she was needling him or if she was really that naïve. Her petite frame and doll-like features often caused people to underestimate her. He opened his mouth, then closed it as he glanced at Jerzi, finally recognizing he'd either look like an idiot or a bully if he engaged. He turned to Andra. "I'll be at the presenters' station, if anyone *important* is looking for me."

He straightened his nameplate and brushed his tunic flat, then smiled and waded into the crowd.

Andra sighed and put her hand on Pico's shoulder. "You shouldn't have baited him. Now that he knows who you are, he could make your life difficult in a hundred little ways."

Jerzi wanted to chime in and agree with Andra, but held his tongue. Pico was adult enough to make her own decisions, and only experience would teach her how to pick her battles. A lecture from him wouldn't change anything. Besides, he wasn't exactly innocent.

Pico looked briefly mutinous, then sighed loudly. "Point taken."

Jerzi wished he could take credit for her mature behavior, but she'd always been a good kid, even at her most rebellious. He was grateful she respected Andra enough to learn from her.

"I was hoping to find the rest of your team," said Andra. "I'd like to reschedule the launch next week."

Pico looked around and shrugged.

A young woman with shaded, sea-green hair and pearlescent blue skin appeared from around the pillar. "Hey, Pico, did you hear when Ravlenko's phase gate failed?" She slowed to a more sedate pace when she saw Andra. "Heyo, Professor D." Her tight sarong dress and elevated sandals were glowing. She looked like she was in costume as an alien sea creature, complete with what may have been gill slits on her neck and upper chest and actual webbing between her fingers. He'd heard about the "native" body mods that were all the rage on Nila Marbela, designed to make people look as if they'd evolved locally, instead of settling on it like every other terraformed planet in the Concordance. She was the first he'd seen up close.

Andra nodded. "Ms. Grien."

Grien leaned in toward Pico, as if speaking confidentially, but didn't lower her voice. "Their mix chamber nearly launched itself through the east wall. Bet he's sorry he didn't get *you* to check his calcs this morning. Now that whole area stinks, like they all ate at the Death Court."

Pico shook her head. "Anyone could have checked his calcs."

Grien snorted. "Yeah, but it would have taken them two days with a math AI to do it."

Pico frowned and dropped her gaze.

"'Death Court'?" asked Jerzi, nudging Pico's shoulder with his arm.

"Food court." She pointed vaguely toward the west. "Replicators, pouches, junk food, failed experiments from the Chem lab."

Andra smiled. "So, Jerzi, what are you doing with yourself these days?"

Jerzi smiled back. "I'm in the Personal Security Division of La Plata Security and Investigations, in Etonver on Rekoria."

He didn't expect her to recognize the company. A lot of larger security firms had their headquarters in Etonver because of its anything-goes policies for buying and carrying weapons, and its hundreds of martial arts studios that made it an attractive home base for mercenary companies.

"He's the assistant director," said Pico. He was warmed by her pride, but he wished she hadn't mentioned it. Providing bodyguards and security drivers for celebrities and visiting dignitaries wasn't nearly as impressive as the title implied.

Recognition dawned on Andra's face. "La Plata. Isn't that where Dom DeBayaud went after he got out? Is he still there, too? And is he still cohabbed with that crazy woman?"

Jerzi shook his head. "No, he died in an accident about four years ago." It had been much more complicated than that, and had nearly cost Jerzi and his friends Luka Foxe and Mairwen Morganthur their lives, but "accident" was the official public version the lawyers agreed to.

"Dad just got promoted," added Pico.

Jerzi tilted his head toward her and smiled. "My publicist."

Grien, who had been fussing with something under the table, stood and put her arm around Pico's shoulders. She turned wheedling eyes on Andra. "Can we start packing up? Since we can't launch or anything?" Pico followed Grien's lead and did her best to look pitiful, but her mouth quavered as she fought off a smile.

Andra shook her head regretfully. "That will be up to Department Leader Vestering."

Jerzi gave Andra a questioning look, but she shook her head minutely, meaning she didn't want to discuss it then. Funny how with some people, unspoken connections were never lost, just paused. He'd missed that.

Grien made a disappointed whimper and sat on the edge of the table. She took off one of her sandals and stretched her blue toes, which were webbed like her fingers.

A sudden, sharp percussion of an explosion echoed in the lecture hall, accompanied by a vibration through the springy silcrete floor. A second, deeper explosion followed, shaking the floor and walls, accompanied by the sounds of things falling off tables.

Grien scrambled up from the skittering table, bouncing one-legged as she tried to put on her sandal. "What the hell?"

Jerzi got a whiff of acrid smoke and looked around, then up. Smoke was pouring from the high ceiling vents on the western wall.

Fire-suppression spray triggered, covering everything in a fine, powdery mist, but the smoke kept coming. A stuttering alarm began to sound.

"Fire!" someone yelled. Panic spread, and the crowd started to move. It was going to get ugly, fast.

Chapter 2

JERZI LOOKED AROUND. They needed to get to a wall. They were in the middle of too many people and nowhere close to an exit.

Pico tried to help Grien, but they kept getting jostled by people who were passing by, trying to find a way out, and the chemical mist was making the non-skid floor slippery.

When a bigger man nearly ran Pico down, Jerzi scooped her up into his arms, and looked for options.

"The pillar," ordered Andra. She shoved the display table aside and quickly herded Grien toward it. "Put your back to the pillar." Grien looked pale, and flattened herself against its surface.

Jerzi carried Pico there and let her down. "You, too," he said, and she nodded, her eyes round with nerves, but her expression determined. He was proud of his kid.

He edged toward Andra, but not close enough to get in her way. "Stay or go?"

A young, dark-skinned woman tripped in front of them, terror in her eyes. He and Andra each grabbed an arm and lifted her to her feet.

"Let go of me!" she screamed, kicking at Jerzi's knee and twisting out of Andra's grip. They both let go at once. She stumbled forward, then picked up speed. "Norro, wait!"

Jerzi forgot about her and turned to watch for new threats.

Screaming and shouts punctuated the sounds of tables skidding and toppling. His lizard brain was telling him to run with everyone else, but years of experience said it had to be done smartly, with a goal in mind. He suddenly realized he was wet, and he looked up. The ceiling was obscured by smoke, but he could see a watery mist drifting down. On his sleeves, and wherever the mist fell, a pale pink foam began to form.

"Seawater," yelled Andra. "Catalyzes the suppression chemicals."

Everywhere he looked, people were scrambling and running, some with purpose, some in fear. The exit markings were being obscured under the pink foam, but Jerzi had already memorized their locations.

"Stay or go?" he asked Andra again. She knew the environment far better than he did.

"Go." She looked back at the girls behind them. "Grien, lose the shoes. Pico, help her stay upright." Andra paused to wipe foam from her face, grimacing. "*Espuma maldita* tastes like crap. We're going with the flow, but angling toward the north doors." She pointed toward them. "Work through the crowd, but don't go against the flow. Stay together."

A loud, stuttering alarm started up, apparently intended to tell occupants to evacuate. More than a little late, in Jerzi's opinion.

Andra waited while Grien finished tying the straps of her shoes together and slinging them around her neck. Jerzi mostly kept his eye on the crowd, but he saw Pico grab an umbrella from the display table.

By tacit agreement, Andra took point, followed Grien, then Pico. Jerzi took the rear, using his bulk to protect them and his height to watch for potential trouble in front of them. They moved at a fast walk and let others run past them. The annoying pink foam broke down when trampled, but it clumped and obscured obstacles. Several small, mobile obstacles turned out to be cleaning robots. At a guess, someone forgot to override their normal instructions to automatically deploy in the event of a major spill.

Up ahead, he saw a knot of people start to form around some unseen problem. "Left! Twenty degrees!" he shouted to Andra. She veered that direction immediately, and Pico and Grien followed. Grien slipped and slid several times, nearly taking Pico with her. Pico put one arm around her friend's waist, to help keep her on her feet.

The loud alarm stopped in mid-stutter, replaced by Vestering's voice, booming over the noise.

"Attention. Please continue to exit the building. A minor lab accident on the second floor has been fully contained. There is no fire. There is no danger to the building or the lecture hall. The safety systems are doing their jobs. Head for the nearest exit in an orderly manner. Emergency responders are outside waiting for you, and will direct you where to go."

His tone was the perfect blend of authority, confidence, and reassurance. He might be a jerk, but he was excellent in crisis communications. He repeated his message three more times, each time sounding warmer and calmer, making it sound like the evacuation was just a realistic drill.

It worked. People began to slow down and started paying attention to their surroundings.

Jerzi was impressed, despite himself. He half expected to see a Minder Corps crowd-control team, but a minor local panic was beneath the notice of the Citizen Protection Service. Just as well. No one he knew would enjoy the notice of the government's minder testing, elite military operations, and covert operations agency.

Their little band was about twenty meters from the wide-open exit when more trouble started, in the form of what looked like a homemade, meter-tall combat robot that glowed orange-red. Whether from a flawed design or damage from the foam, it was ramming into people from behind, knocking them aside or to the ground, then using its treads to roll over them. When an angry young woman kicked it aside, it responded by deploying a plasma loop and administering a burn and a shock that felled her where she stood. Two people dragged her out of the way as it tried to climb her body. It spun again.

"That's Dortief's Doomreaper," said Pico. "The black beads are motion sensors." Its bulging round chassis was studded with them. "It goes for any movement under about forty centimeters."

Andra pushed Grien toward the exit and urged her to keep going, then went back to rejoin Jerzi and Pico to see what the trouble was. She muttered in Spanish, probably colorful curses. "I told her not to bring that thing."

A young woman with hair in long braids tried to edge around the bot, then screamed when it started lumbering toward her.

"Everybody freeze!" ordered Andra. Her command voice compelled compliance, even from civilians. "Movement at knee level and below triggers its combat sequence." She stared at it a moment. "We need tables to box it in." She pointed to three people on the other side of the bot. "You, you, and you. Tell the people behind you we need four tables. Don't turn around, just tell them."

An older man in a green, casual suit kept glancing toward the exit, then slowly started edging toward it. The bot spun toward him. The man started running, and the bot made a beeline for him. Other people in its path started screaming and backing up, and running into other people.

"Stay still!" yelled Andra.

Jerzi jumped into the clear circle, knowing its plasma loop was going to hurt like hell if he couldn't avoid it. He delivered a solid side kick to the bot, causing it to skid sideways, then leapt back toward Pico and Andra as it spun quickly toward him. He froze. It was hard not to flinch when it came closer, but his tactic seemed to have confused it. The plasma loop retracted, but the bot slowly drifted closer. He hated that Pico was in the line of fire, too.

Andra scowled at the robot and muttered, "And me without my shockstick."

Despite the tense situation, Jerzi smiled. The mugger's weapon of choice had been one of Subcaptain Lightning's favorite accessories, but it wouldn't go well with her conservative professorial attire.

"What if I break the safety off my umbrella and knock the cap off?" asked Pico, pointing to it with her chin. She'd wedged it between her arm and her body.

Andra gave her a crooked smile. "Good thinking, but you'd have to bend the ribs together, and you'd need micro forcewires to kill the power limiter series, like the stasis box we took apart in class. It's only good for one shot." Her expression turned innocent. "Not that I've ever done anything like that."

"Three tables coming through," shouted a man's voice from behind the crowd.

"We need a fourth," shouted Andra. "Don't break the line until they're all here."

The robot was indecisively rocking back and forth about a meter from Jerzi's legs. He tried not to think about it and kept his gaze on Andra and his daughter.

Andra eyed the robot. "We'll have to distract it, no matter what."

Pico touched his arm and Andra's. "Dad and I can do this." Her voice was barely audible. She held up the umbrella and gave him a meaningful look. It only took him a moment to realize she meant she was willing to use her hidden micro telekinetic talent to do what Andra had described to turn the umbrella into a one-use shockstick. He slightly raised an eyebrow, asking her if she was sure she wanted to take the chance. She nodded once.

"Yes," he confirmed to Andra. If push came to shove, he'd take full credit for Pico's actions. Let them try to prove it wasn't his own negligible talent, which heretofore had only been good for targeting his long sniper shots.

Andra gave them each a considering look, then said, "Do it. Ribs first, then the cap, then the safeties. Limiters last." Her unquestioning trust was a warm relief.

Since Andra was far enough back to move freely, she directed the people carrying the tables to get into position behind the people stuck in the ragged circle around the robot. Jerzi bent the umbrella's ribs up into a bundle, using the hem of his jacket to protect his hands against the sharp edges. It took longer than he'd have liked because he could only use his upper body to do it, since his legs had to remain frozen. Next, he removed the cap, again relying only on his arm strength to twist it off. He started to slip it into his pants pocket, but it made the cloth shift, which caught the attention of the robot.

He swore under his breath and froze.

Andra glanced at him, then came back around to him and held out her hand. He carefully gave her the cap, which she put in her jacket pocket.

Pico had already disabled the safety and slid aside the access plate on the umbrella's shaft. They were lucky it was a good quality umbrella, intended to be serviced, instead of the cheap tourist kind. She stared at the exposed circuitry for a moment, then her eyes drifted a little, signaling she was using her talent. He was pretty sure she was out of practice, since she'd made the decision to hide it, or more accurately, deny it. He knew she'd deliberately failed CPS talent testing, and why, and it broke his heart that the result wasn't what she'd hoped.

From behind him, two women came up carrying the fourth table Andra had asked for. She directed them and the others where she wanted them, explaining her plan to corral the bot.

Jerzi saw that his position was a problem. "Put the table behind me," he said. "I'll jump over."

"You won't make it," said Andra. "That thing's fast." She glanced at the rigged umbrella in Pico's hand, his position, and the robot. "If you're willing, I'll use you for a scaffold to hit it from above. I mass about sixty kilos these days."

He shook his head. "Give me the umbrella and I'll do it." He didn't want Andra or Pico anywhere near the plasma loop.

Andra rolled her eyes skyward. "*Caramba*, deliver me from white knights." She took a deep breath and blew it out testily. "I know the bot, and I know how to use the stick. It's too dangerous if you miss."

Damn, but he hated that she was right. With bad grace, he nodded. "What do you need me to do?"

She kicked off her shoes. "Lift me up to your shoulders, Commander Crush." She reached across and tapped his right shoulder, smiling. "I'll try not to step on anything important."

"Thank you," he answered with a reluctant grin. She'd have to come at him from the side, or the bot would detect her motion. He slowly flexed his knees as much as he dared, watching to see if the bot noticed, then held out his hands.

"Tables up," she ordered, her voice carrying easily. "When I say go, put them down in front of the people in the robot's view. As soon as the tables are in place, duck as low as you can behind them, and make sure the tables stay upright."

"Pico, hold the umbrella for me here." She moved Pico's arm into the position she wanted it, then turned back to him. "Ready?"

He tensed his leg muscles as she moved back two steps, then launched toward him. He grabbed her waist and lifted her onto his shoulder. She spun her legs across his upper shoulders and twisted. He fought to stay rock solid and absorb the momentum.

She grabbed the shockstick from Pico's outstretched hand as she straddled his shoulders. "Go! Tables go!" she yelled.

At the flurry of movement, the bot spun, and the damp plasma loop crackled with power. One of the men holding a table dropped his end too fast, leaving several people vulnerable.

The bot started to glide toward the movement, swinging the plasma loop forward.

"Jerzi," warned Andra, but he was already moving. He grabbed her ankles and lunged toward the bot. He felt her weight shift as she took her shot. The bot spun toward the original threat—Jerzi's nearest leg—and lashed out with the plasma loop.

Andra's shockstick delivered a satisfying arc of power directly to the bot's foam-logged power port, but it wasn't in time to stop the charged loop from hitting his calf muscle.

He grunted with the burning pain but held his position and hung onto Andra's legs. The bot momentarily hissed and glowed blue, then with a loud thunk, went dark. A weak cloud of smoke rose, accompanied by the acrid stink of scorched circuitry.

"Down, Jerzi," said Andra, patting his left arm. He let go of her legs so she could slide down the side of him. He supported her hips to help steady her as she hit solid ground and bent her knees to absorb the impact.

Ragged applause sounded, and Jerzi looked around in surprise.

The people behind the tables, both students and older men and women he took to be POGS, were focused on Andra, but he was apparently included. Andra gave him an amused smile as she stepped forward and bowed once. "Good work, everyone. Leave the tables, and let's get out of here." She pointed toward the exit with the blackened, warped umbrella.

Jerzi surreptitiously examined his aching calf, wincing when he saw the pant leg was singed and burned into his flesh. Probably better to leave it as is until he could get to a medic. He hoped they were waiting outside as Vestering had promised. He'd make Andra go first, though. The flame-red skin on her hand from the wild energy discharge probably hurt a lot worse than his leg.

CHAPTER 3

ANDRA KNEW IT was crazy, but she felt like the afternoon's events had been the start of something. She wished to hell she knew what, but she was no minder forecaster, able to predict the future from seemingly random facts. Most likely, it was just that the familiar, reassuring presence of Jerzi Adams reminded her of the countless intelligence missions they'd been on, where her instinct for trouble had saved their asses more than once. It hadn't saved Da'vin Quillier, though, which is why she'd stopped paying attention to that nonsense.

She wiped the accumulated mist off her forehead as she watched the medic fishing through the hole in Jerzi's ruined pant leg to firmly apply a large burn patch. Jerzi was seated and chatting amiably with his animated daughter, as if they were in a body-shop spa. He was still better at hiding pain than anyone she knew, including elite Jumpers who ate pain for breakfast. She remembered asking once if it was because he didn't feel it. He'd laughed and said of course he felt it; the trick was to focus on the things that didn't hurt. She'd never gotten the hang of it, and she'd really tried.

The commons area between the buildings was filled with students, faculty, parents, and a respectable number of emergency response personnel who insisted on seeing every single person who had been in the Chemistry building at the time of the explosion. Five floors' worth of students, staff, and faculty was a lot of people, even on a light class day. At least they hadn't had to evacuate the Materials Science, shared labs, or Math buildings, too. The manmade ovoid floater was only one and a half kilometers wide on its long axis, and in Andra's opinion, overbuilt.

Unsurprisingly, the responders and uniformed security personnel all appeared to be Optimal Polytechnic staff. O-Poly was fanatical about maintaining its reputation as the perfect paradise school, and keeping internal problems private. The downside was that it was taking forever to get everyone reassured, treated, and/or released, depending on what they needed, and gently pressured to sign a liability waiver.

Andra checked her wristcomp. It was only late afternoon, but it already felt like it had been a very long day. She'd lucked out and snagged a spot on one of the benches that ringed the tall sculpture in the center of the floater, next to an older man and his wife. Her back was sore from helping carry dozens of tables inside earlier because of the rain, and despite the medic's burn patches, her left hand still ached from the energy backlash from the rigged umbrella when flatlining the rogue bot. Pain patches were better than nothing, but she missed the talented minder healers who'd been on call after military operations.

After they'd gotten out of the building, she'd entertained herself with thoughts of dismantling the damned bot piece by piece, which had kept her from growling at the steamy weather or the soggy turf that overwhelmed her sensible heels. She envied Jerzi and Pico their boots. Father and daughter may not have looked like they shared a gene pool, but their mannerisms and habits were strikingly similar.

Ordinarily, Andra would have slipped away to visit the gym or sparring studio to work off her current bad attitude, but Vestering had pinged her to see him before she left, and she hadn't found him yet. First, she'd wanted to make sure Jerzi got treated, and the stubborn man had insisted she go first. She couldn't pull rank on him anymore, so it had been easier just to comply, but it hadn't helped her temper any.

Jerzi stood and thanked the medic, then looked around until his eyes lit on her, and she waved. He and Pico threaded through the milling people. He was carrying his jacket, and his thin, white undertunic was plastered to the exquisitely sculpted muscles of his chest and shoulders. It looked like he'd erased most of the body art he used to wear with such pride, but he'd added a close-trimmed beard along his jaw and under his chin. It wasn't the prevailing fashion, but it added maturity to his boy-next-door face. The tiny banded diamond earrings, high on his ears, were new and suited him. She was wryly amused to see that he was still blind to the admiring looks from both men and women. Including hers, a sly little voice in her head pointed out. She ignored it for the nonstarter idea it was. She didn't mess around with married people.

Just as he and Pico got close, Romila Chakravarthi appeared out of nowhere, making a beeline for Andra. "Thank the stars above I found you. Can you believe it? Another 'accident.'" Romila squeezed herself onto the bench, oblivious to the annoyed grunts from the bench's other occupants.

"Are you all right? I heard you got hurt." She put her arm around Andra's shoulders and hugged tight. "You poor thing. Come home with me, and I'll share some really good chems that will make you forget all about this."

Andra laughed. "Thank you, but no, I *like* my brain cells." Romila, her Chemistry Department colleague for the Practical Applications class, had contacts in the chems and alterants industry and often had exotic, and sometimes untested, samples. She patted Romila's knee and stood up. "I'll be fine."

Being fussed over made Andra twitchy. She'd had enough of that from her four older brothers who'd tried to appoint themselves as her protectors, jailers, and relationship arbiters. It had, however, taught her skills in getting out of inconvenient custody situations.

Romila stood as well. "I could give you a ride…" She trailed off when she noticed Jerzi. She smiled and held out her hand. "I'm Romila. May I help you?" Her provocative tone suggested she'd like to help him into her bed.

Jerzi blinked, then glanced toward his daughter.

"He's with me," said Andra. It was easier than explaining.

Romila made a surprised sound. "Well, then, I won't keep you." She left quickly, and Andra sighed. She'd somehow hurt Romila's feelings, and would have to grovel tomorrow.

Their little group stepped off the walkway onto the soggy permaturf to make way for a grounded medical evacuation capsule.

"What was that about 'another accident'?" asked Jerzi.

Andra started to say she'd tell him later, but she knew him well enough to know he'd worry about it. She tilted her head to suggest they step farther away from the rest of the crowd. Pico followed. They ended up under a broad canopy tree, where it was muddy, but private.

"Ms. Adams, pretend you're deaf for the moment. In the last month, the accident rate in the Chem labs has increased significantly. I asked Romila's opinion, because she knows the Chem labs better than I do. I figured she'd tell me it was nothing, but instead, she put together a pattern that seems more than random. Outside of the usual student experiments that go awry, big equipment suddenly needs recalibration, small appliances fail, and an entire storeroom of organic scaffolding kits went bad. Last week, eight ortho-phase replicators went missing all at once. I can't imagine there's a huge blackmarket for them." A heavy drop of water splashed down Andra's neck. No wonder they had the tree to themselves.

"Most of it seems to happen to the labs on the third and fifth floors at night, when the labs should be empty. Today is probably just an ordinary accident. Romila would probably tell you it's sabotage, but the woman loves drama."

"What does campus security think?" asked Jerzi.

Andra frowned. "Security is handled remotely. Romila and I brought it up at the joint faculty meeting last Friday, because Lavong—he's the manager for all the labs on this little floater—was ignoring us. He said he's handling it, and said no one would get a lab if they were shut down for security investigations." She snorted. "Romila thought he was trying to intimidate us. I think he was gassy."

"Uhm, Professor De Luna," said Pico, "I think Mr. Vestering is looking for you." She tilted her head toward the man who was bearing down on them. He looked dyspeptic, but that was his usual expression when dealing with her. When he saw who she was with, he frowned and stopped a few paces away, on the edge of the permaturf.

"Did all of your Practical Applications students make it out of the hall?" His sharp tone implied it was her personal responsibility to track all twenty-five of them, and never mind the dozens of students from her various Materials Science classes. She forced her tense shoulders to relax.

"I haven't spoken to the emergency commander yet. Have you?" He was the administrator in charge; she was the lowly professor, as he so often reminded her.

His lips tightened in annoyance, and he started to speak, then glanced again at Jerzi. His gaze dropped down to Jerzi's burned pants. "I heard you were involved in trouble with an uncontrolled homemade combat robot."

Jerzi started to answer, but Andra cleared her throat loudly and shot him and Pico both a look telling them to stay out of it.

"It was nothing," she interjected firmly. "It was taken care of." The last thing she needed was Vestering tormenting the young woman who'd built the robot, or asking about the improvised shockstick.

"I'd hate to have a guest or a student bringing unwarranted injury claims against the university," he said, eyeing her burn-patched hand. In other words, keep their mouths shut, or he'd make trouble.

"I'm sure it won't be an issue," she said calmly. She was less worried about Jerzi and Pico than she was about whatever story Romila would soon be embellishing. Her wealthy family background insulated her from some of Vestering's power games. Andra still had to work for a living. "Is that all you needed to see me about?"

Vestering frowned. Someone behind him in the crowd called his name. Andra couldn't see who it was, but he was clearly happier to see whoever it was than her. His smile lit up as he rapidly left and headed toward the crowd.

Pico turned to watch him go. "Somewhere," she said acidly, "a stinking goat is missing its misbegotten male offspring. Or not missing him."

Andra snorted and tried not to laugh. It was bad to encourage Pico's antipathy toward the head of the department. "We'd better get out of here while we can." She turned to Jerzi. "Commander, do you have a way off this little slice of paradise?" She circled a finger to indicate the whole campus floater.

"I rented a flitter." He smiled as he shook out his jacket. "Better than I have at home."

Pico made a rude sound. "That's because he takes the metro when he's at home. Etonver traffic eats hot death."

Andra laughed. "Nothing wrong with public transport."

As Jerzi struggled to pull on his damp jacket, Pico suddenly looked alarmed and activated her percomp. "I totally forgot the time. I have to meet Valenia at six and go with her to Hospitality Services class."

Jerzi nodded. "I'll fly you…"

"It's on the mainland campus. We'll never make it. It'll be faster if we take the water taxi. Traffic control gives them priority." She keyed something on her percomp's holo display. "I'm sending you the apartment access codes so you can get in." She jumped up and kissed Jerzi on the cheek. "We'll be home by eight." She took off toward the east like she was fluxed for interstellar transit.

Jerzi laughed as he smoothed his jacket. "I guess I'll have to trust the planetary satnav not to send me on the scenic route."

They began walking toward the main east-west path on the commons. The crowds were starting to thin out at last. As a small blessing, the misty rain had stopped, but Andra didn't trust it to stay that way. She wanted dry clothes, a beer, and to put her feet up, but she felt bad about leaving Jerzi to fend for himself. "This is what passes for winter here, so it'll be dark soon. How about you give me a ride, and I'll help you find Pico's apartment before you drop me off?"

Jerzi looked up at the stormy sky. "If it won't be too much trouble, I'd appreciate that."

The Jerzi she'd known eight years ago would have refused the help, still determined to demonstrate his competence. To be fair, back then, she'd not only have refused help, she'd have taken offense that someone had even offered. She guessed they both had less to prove these days.

They moved around the clumps of people at a purposeful pace, and soon arrived at the far east corner of the Materials Science building, where he'd stacked the flitter. They rode the lift to the airpad, then used the control kiosk to tell the stacker which flitter slot was his. Once it delivered his flitter, Jerzi unlocked it with his biometric and passcode.

"Ooh, a Pazorbaal DF." Andra stroked its sparkly, lava-red exterior and whistled. "The security business must pay better than I thought."

He keyed the doors open. "I wish. Oh, it pays better than the military—what doesn't?—but the nice woman at the rental counter gave me a free upgrade because they ran out of the compacts."

"Lucky you," she said as she slid into the wide front passenger seat. She liked riding in luxury when she had the chance. "The professor business doesn't pay enough to afford flitters, either."

He powered on the console, sent their destination coordinates from the percomp he pulled out of his coat's chest pocket, then fiddled around with the controls while they waited for the traffic control system to sync. He grinned at her. "This will be a novel experience, letting the TCS do its job. Etonver allows everyone to operate manually, so they do, meaning ground and air traffic are hell, even in the dead of night."

She'd forgotten how enjoyable it was to be around someone who delighted in the things that most people took for granted or became jaded about. He probably had no idea how much his presence had anchored their unit. They'd all been so young and idealistic back then.

"What does Dhorya think of Etonver? I think I heard she and Pico moved there with you a few years ago. It must be nice to finally be together."

His face lost all expression. "She and I are divorced. She moved back to Vaylamoinen two years ago."

Andra winced at the tightly controlled emotion she heard in his voice. Obviously, the divorce hadn't been his idea. She reached out to touch the back of his hand. "I'm sorry. That must have been hard for you." She didn't try to hide her respect for his loss or her sympathy for his pain, because that's what gunnin did for one another. Only a fellow gunnin would truly understand. Losing a loved one was the worst.

He turned his hand over to squeeze her fingers briefly before letting go. "Harder for Pico. Dhorya said some unforgivable things to her before she left. In a few years, I'll probably feel sorry for her, because she's never going to be happy with what she has or where she is, but right now, I'm still mad at her."

Andra had a momentary impulse to give Jerzi a hug and tell him… she didn't know what. She rubbed her palms on her thighs. "I know what you mean. I was furious with Da'vin for accepting that final mission right before our wedding and getting killed."

He jerked back in his seat and stared at her in shock. "What?"

It was her day to put her gravity boot in it, apparently. "I'm sorry, I thought you knew. It was five years ago, back in '36. A year after you left the service." She breathed through the familiar weight that bottomed out in her stomach.

"What happened?"

At least the distance of time and a complete change of career had made the story easier to tell. "A jack crew was selling shipkillers and munitions on Penrius D'Or's space station. High Command said it was a small op and ordered a fast takedown. Da'vin and I were about to take leave for the wedding trip, and Da'vin felt guilty about leaving the unit shorthanded, so she volunteered for recon. I wasn't letting her go without boom-down expertise, and Shinn took comms. The jack crew was small, all right, but the whole station was corrupt. We got caught trying to get the hell out. Shinn and I made it because Da'vin sacrificed herself for us."

Jerzi met her gaze and held it. "I'm sorry for your loss, Andra." His voice was quiet and sincere.

"Thank you," she said, and took a moment to acknowledge his respect, which meant a lot more than the plethora of platitudes she'd heard at the time or since. She quirked a smile at him. "It was one hell of an engagement party, though, wasn't it?"

The corners of his lips curved upward. "Legendary. Dom DeBayaud talked about it for years. Of course, that may have been because, when he passed out after his marathon with the exciter twins in the low-G sex room, someone deep-inked a large, fluffy pink kitten across his ass cheeks."

Andra laughed. "Did he think you did it?"

"No, he knew I didn't. I'd already left by then, on my way home. He suspected everyone else, including the joyhouse owners, at one time or another." Jerzi's smile grew wistful. "He was a good friend, and I still miss him."

The center console chimed to let them know the traffic system was ready for them and displayed a thirty-second countdown.

Andra secured the seat webbing across herself and gave Jerzi a thumb's up sign. He did the same, then eased the flitter out of the stacker and into a hover. He grinned when the traffic system took control, and leaned back in evident satisfaction.

Andra let herself be talked into spending the evening with Jerzi, Pico, and Valenia. Ordinarily, she'd have turned down the offer, to avoid any appearance of favoritism, but Pico, clever young woman that she was, had stocked the apartment pantry and cold box with quality ingredients, and Jerzi had offered to cook. He'd always been a damn fine cook.

Afterward, Jerzi had insisted on flying her home, and she'd agreed. It would be impossible to get an autocab on the night before the Winter Solstice holiday, and the rain had returned. She still wasn't used to winters without cold weather.

"If you don't mind my asking," said Jerzi as he set the flitter's console to display a holo of their progress through the traffic, "how did you end up here, of all places?" The holo's light gave his face a tinge of blue, as if he'd done one of the locally popular "native" body makeovers.

She gave him a sardonic smile. "You mean, how did a ground-pounder gunnin like me make full professor?" She held up her hand to still his protest. "I know you don't think like that, but you'd be surprised at how many do."

"Like Vestering?"

"No, he thinks I want his job." She shook her head in disgust. "Too political for me."

She put her foot on the soft seat and rested her elbow on her knee, enjoying the freedom to sprawl in an upscale flitter, instead of being jammed in, packing-case tight. "Like a lot of kids, I wanted to be an exploration spacer, so I got my B-level certificate in xenogeography. Once I actually met some of them, though, I couldn't see being stuck on a ship with a bunch of arrogant wankers for years at a time. When I talked to the military, they liked my experience with explosives and recruited me for Forward Intelligence."

"Oh, that's right, you worked summers at a mine. Minerals, or metals, wasn't it?"

"Yes, rare earths," she said, surprised that he remembered. "While I was in the unit, I went for a C-level in materials science so I could blow up more things. After Da'vin died, I buried myself in courses for D-level, so I'd have career options when my contract was up. Too many memories to stay in the military, and absolute zero interest in going home."

"And teaching?"

She shrugged. "I like it. I've always been seduced by the potential I see in others." Including what she'd seen in Jerzi, when they'd served together, but the galaxy would have to stop spinning before she'd admit that. The second cold beer she'd had after dinner had already made her too talkative.

"Pico says you're a good teacher, and she's picky. Comes from growing up in University Town, I think."

It was a good bet. When the unit had been stationed there, practically every block had a private school or training center. The competition was fierce.

"She's a good kid…uh, person. Now that I know who she is, I remember her from when she was a child. Wise beyond her years."

The flitter banked left and descended to a lower level. Jerzi rotated the holo so he could better see the angle. He'd always been good at finding his way around.

"She was born that way." Jerzi smiled ruefully. "Most days, I think she's more adult than I am."

"Oh, please," Andra scoffed. "You settled down a lot sooner than the rest of the unit, much to everyone's dismay."

Jerzi made a rude noise. "Dismay, huh? That must be why you all gave me so much shit about wanting to get married."

That was the Jerzi Adams she remembered, so good-looking and so good-natured, and a bit of an idiot.

"We were jealous of you, *compadre*. Most of us could barely figure out how to have sex with someone more than once, much less a relationship." She waved her fingers toward herself. "How do you think I got the name Lightning? Never strikes in the same place twice." What could she say? She liked men and women, and she liked sex with either. "And there you were, being a husband in all but name, and a father. And if we didn't want what you had, we wanted *you*. Why do you think we called you Crush?"

"What?" He stared at her with blatant astonishment, then shook his head. "You're chemmed."

"No, I'm not. The day you saved Dhorya Sankirna from that clusterfuck of drunken spacers, you were a goner. How could any of us compete with a rescued princess who made you feel like the white knight?"

Andra realized the alcohol was loosening her overly-candid tongue way too much. She reached for a safer subject. "You, uhm, still lift weights, I see." He was even bigger than when he'd been at her engagement party. His discipline, and determination to do it without body mods or sports chems, had gotten him teased mercilessly.

He shrugged an impressive shoulder. "Keeps me grounded. Sometimes my brain won't turn off."

Andra laughed. "I sync that. I run most mornings and try to hit a sparring studio at least once a week. Keeps me from hitting *los burros* at work."

"Speaking of jackasses, what's the deal with your boss?"

She snorted. "The O-Poly regents liked my 'real life story,' meaning they thought it would be good publicity, so they hired me for one of Vestering's faculty slots outside of the normal process, and waived the probation period. He was going to dislike me anyway, but then I committed the sin of succeeding with a tedious lab course he dumped on me as a way to get me to move on."

"The Practical Applications course?"

She nodded. "Romila was new in the Chemistry department, and she and I were in the same boat. Her department leader hated the 'baby' courses and dumped them on noobs like her. You know me, I love a challenge, and Romila was game, so we requested the same lab space and time period, and let the leaders think it was their idea to combine our courses for the next year and give us an extra budget to come up with a new curriculum."

Jerzi laughed. "Which, of course, you'd already done."

"*Claro que sí.* It went so well that now they're pushing Vestering to open a second segment of the course he wanted to delete."

"Don't underestimate sore losers," said Jerzi, frowning. "A zifthead at La Plata tried to assault a friend of mine because he lost out on a promotion, then claimed she tried to stab him."

She repressed a loud sigh. What was it about her that made people like Jerzi, or Da'vin, for that matter, think she wanted or needed protecting? She'd had far too much of that from her family.

"*Burros* are everywhere, Commander Crush," she said, looking pointedly at him.

Jerzi glanced at her. The flitter's arrival signal sounded. He took control of the flitter and eased it down onto the rooftop airpad.

He met her gaze with a contrite look. "Sorry. Pico calls it hovering."

It was hard to be mad at Jerzi for long. His heart had always been in the right place, even if he sometimes didn't think.

"Forgiven." She swung a mock punch to his upper arm. "But next time, I'll kick your ass."

He met her smile with a challenging grin. "You and what platoon, gunnin?"

She unfastened the safety web. "You bring your analog railgun? 'Cause that's the only way you'd rank me."

"I did. Pico said O-Poly has a range."

"Yeah, but it's way too short for your purposes, and caters to noobs. Tell you what, I'll take you to the longest range in town if you spot me two shots." She waited to see if he took the bait.

"I'll be spotting you absolute zero, Subcaptain," he said, and pointed to his eyes. "I know you still have oculars. Saw the reflection rings when we were getting in the flitter." He smirked at her.

She laughed and held up her hands in surrender. "Okay, okay. Even up." She leaned forward to open the door.

He touched her forearm. "Before you go, tell me what you really think about the accidents in the labs."

She sat back. "They feel fishy to me. Students can be careless, but not all of a sudden." She frowned. "I've been keeping an eye out, but I don't have a good a reason to be nosing about the Chem labs. I wish I could tell you something more definitive."

Jerzi looked thoughtful. "My security credentials are only good on Rekoria, and I'm not an investigator, but I've helped a friend do security assessments, so maybe I could look at the facilities."

Andra considered his offer. It would be good to take action, if only to rule out her suspicions. It might also reassure Jerzi that his daughter was safe. "Okay," she said. "Since you're a parent, I can take you on a tour of the labs after my nine-o'clock Materials Science B-level class, which Pico is in, the day after tomorrow. We can go to the range after that, if you'd like." A yawn caught her by surprise.

"That works for me. Let's exchange ping refs so we can sync up for the tour, then go get some rest."

After he took off in the flitter and she let herself into her apartment,

Andra found herself humming as she prepared for bed. A friendly competition with someone who she didn't have to be on guard around would be a pleasant change from the petty intrigue and backbiting of academic politics. It didn't hurt at all that Jerzi Adams could wear a full-body piety cloak and still look like a galaxy-class fitness model.

CHAPTER 4

DIXON DAVIDRO LEANED back in the creaky chair and put his feet up on the floating desk, in part to keep it from creeping slowly toward the door as if it had somewhere else to be.

The huge panel on the far wall displayed a mesmerizing real-time view of the gas giant planet around which the Gulkaiyr Free Space Station orbited. The only thing free about the space station was its name. The view wall was the single amenity that made the modular rental suite worth the outrageous price. Space stations across the galaxy had a captive customer base, especially for layovers while waiting for the next ship out. Gulkaiyr was a rarity, a space station with no habitable planet in the system, so they upcharged for every possible thing beyond artificial gravity, breathable air, and potable water, the bare minimum required by Central Galactic Concordance law. The Citizen Protection Service was paying, of course, but it was a point of pride that his official expense reports were always conservative.

Gulkaiyr Station's primary appeal, besides being the only transfer hub at the edge of the Mizero Void, was its perennial failure to keep accurate records of credentials and ship registries. It was a good place to lose any pursuers, and made an excellent rendezvous location for his staff. He'd sent his newest contractor, a telepath, for a cleanup job, and it would be better if he wasn't tracked back to their group. Dixon had won Xan's undying loyalty by saving him from a total flatline session with a CPS minder enforcement team, owing to Xan's habit of indiscriminately rooting in the minds of others for sexual memories.

Of course, some of the austerity of his temporary accommodations could be sourced to Mr. Renner, who stood quietly in the corner, looking thunderous as usual. The marvelous analog collar around the man's neck had audibly ratcheted tighter a few minutes ago, and a small rivulet of blood snaked down his impressively muscled barrel chest. The buildup of scars meant the collar's razor-sharp edges cut into them more often, especially if Renner tugged at it.

Unfortunately, Renner couldn't be controlled by the usual methods, including any drugs Dixon had ever found. Not even Neirra, Dixon's former pet healer, who could use her top-level talent to craft individually tailored drug protocols, had been able to develop a regimen that worked on Renner for more than an hour or two. After yet another nearly successful escape attempt by Renner, Dixon had worked with a fixer to devise the ingenious mechanical collar that tightened every hour unless reset, and only Dixon could do it. A side benefit was that Renner took his security responsibilities very seriously, since Dixon's demise would be a death warrant for Renner as well. It was too bad that it had to be that way, but even after twenty years of service, Renner still hadn't accepted that his destiny lay with Dixon. Some people were just too stubborn for their own good.

The source of Renner's present irritation seemed to be the hallway door Dixon had left open, since he didn't want to be popping up and down letting his assistant Lamis, or the rest of the staff, in and out of his temporary office. It was a station upcharge to add biometric access so they could come and go at will, and no one else had any reason to bother him. He would have put Renner on door duty, but he upset the rest of the staff.

Dixon activated the percomp on the back of his wrist rather than his earwire. He preferred normal conversation over subvocalizing into his earwire. It was more civilized. "Georgie, my pet, have you any recommendations for me yet on the problem on Nila Marbela?" Another little problem that the CPS needed handled. He planned to see to it personally, since a week in a tropical resort would be a vast improvement over where they were now, and the less said about the frigid, flat city of Chagha'an Fodoli on Sanangerel, where he'd been last, the better.

"Dixie! I'm glad you pinged. Do you want me to come and tell you? My room is too bright. Or I could bring the new small comp into your office and set it up on the desk. It's pink, but I could change it. Or I could make a nice report with data tags and send it to you. Or I could–"

Dixon interrupted Georgie's rapid-fire delivery. "A report would be perfect, Georgie, and thank you." They were going to have to go back to the old control drugs for Georgie. Forecasters didn't usually need them, but Georgie was a special case.

Dixon smiled. All his staff members were special. He had a gift for finding the value in minders who had been neglected or disdained and giving them opportunities to shine. It was win-win: He took care of them, and they took care of him.

"Do you want the report now?" asked Georgie.

"Yes, please." Dixon infused his voice with the warmth that Georgie responded to best. "You've been very good today. Why don't you find Auntie Lamis and have her give you a nice green pill?"

"Okay, Dixie. Did you say you wanted the report now? I could read it to–"

"I'd love it if you'd send it to me, Georgie."

He waited until he saw the report in his dataspace, then pinged Lamis to give Georgie two green pills. He needed to sleep off the effects of the experimental control drugs, and given his present condition, he'd be awake for days.

It was annoying to have to adjust Georgie's drugs by trial and error. Once again, Dixon wished he hadn't allowed Neirra to retire to a rustic planet's spaceport, but her mind and health had deteriorated beyond repair. A year ago, she'd gotten very sick, and hadn't been able to heal herself as usual. She'd gone downhill from there. He used to call her crazy just to tease her, and unfortunately, the description had become all too accurate. Because she was his first pet—one he'd inherited from another handler—and because he'd loved her in his way, he'd granted her request to retire. It saddened him that the consensus of all the other healers and minders he'd taken her to said she only had a few more months to live. He thought even Renner might be missing her.

Dixon opened the report and tried to pay attention to it, but Georgie's jumbled mind had made for a jumbled report, and Dixon's thoughts of the current special project kept intruding. He excelled at handling problems that required finesse and creativity. True, he'd had to have one of his staff permanently retire the first-generation subject he'd been mentoring, but all the other subjects had needed to be put down, too, and his had lasted twice as long as any other in the program. The CPS project leads had rewarded him with his choice of a third-generation subject. If he did as well this time, he might be able to move up his personal timeline for achieving a top leadership position. The hidebound CPS needed creative people like him to shake things up and find new ways to use minder talents for the good of the Concordance.

Enough daydreaming, he told himself. He dropped his feet from the desk and focused once more on the report, only to be interrupted when

Taliferros Radomir walked in. He was a high-level shielder, able to protect himself and anyone near from minders, and forcibly contain most telepathic and telekinetic minders so they couldn't activate their talent. Since Dixon wasn't a minder himself, he always tried to keep a shielder on staff.

Radomir was feeling relaxed and confident. It was subtle, because Radomir was a slight, ordinary-looking man who cultivated a mild manner, but shielders often forgot to contain their body language along with their thoughts. Unfortunately, Radomir's demeanor corroborated the information Dixon had received from Renner.

He hid his disappointment with a smile as he invited the man to take the other chair in the room. When one of his staff strayed from orbit, it was his failure as much as anyone's. "What can I do for you, Mr. Radomir?"

Radomir glanced at Renner in the corner behind him, then smoothed his coattail before perching on the edge of the seat. Dixon knew without having to look that Renner's expression had gone from unpleasant to downright menacing. Renner had more than once said he didn't trust the shielder.

Radomir placed his palms flat on his thighs. "It's coming up on three years of employment. I'd like the opportunity to become a CPS employee, as you promised. I believe I have provided more than satisfactory service in the contracted tasks you've assigned me."

Dixon casually crossed his legs. "Yes, Mr. Radomir, you do enjoy your work. Unfortunately, you occasionally enjoy it too much. Such as the day before yesterday."

Radomir frowned. "Attention to detail is important, Mr. Davidro. You were very particular about wanting it to look like a vehicle accident."

"Yes, that was well done. Pity you weren't as careful with the young man." Dixon shook his head. "Really, Mr. Radomir, a meat-processing facility?"

Radomir kept up his mild, puzzled look for a long moment, then relaxed and uncaringly shrugged a shoulder. "I was pressed for time." He'd grown more susceptible to the control drugs starting about a year ago, to where he now needed injections every other day to stave off the excruciating and fatal effects of withdrawal. Neirra had tailored the drug formulation specifically to Radomir. Only Dixon knew the recipe, and he only kept a tiny supply.

"Besides," said Radomir, "you didn't say I couldn't, and we were leaving." Radomir had the nerve to smile, like a five-year-old who thought himself clever.

Dixon allowed some of his exasperation to show. "That is *not* our arrangement for reward outings, Mr. Radomir. You tell me when you're feeling constricted, and I help you find a suitable outlet. I know your favored type of playmate and your preferences in playrooms. You do not impulsively take a random small, blond man from the street, who happens to have a wealthy, powerful family, then ask forgiveness later." He stared pointedly at Radomir. "You *did* come to ask for forgiveness, didn't you?"

Radomir dropped his head and assumed an apologetic mien, but Dixon saw the flash of unrepentant defiance in his eyes as he did so.

Children. Dixon was dealing with children. He clasped his hands together and rested them on his knee. "I am everything that is reasonable, and I try to accommodate my staff in their needs, but your extracurricular indulgence is becoming an uncontrollable habit." Dixon sighed and caught Renner's eye. "Mr. Renner, I'm afraid Mr. Radomir needs remedial education."

"How long do I have with him?" The gleeful intent on Renner's face sent a shudder through Dixon, though he hid it.

Radomir's face paled, but Dixon gave him credit for not wasting everyone's time with excuses or promises. Radomir's punishment would be Renner's reward. Dixon preferred when all his staff got along, but sometimes, their conflicts proved useful. Dixon didn't know why Renner hated Radomir more than the others, considering Renner already hated the universe and everyone in it.

"No more than thirty minutes, shall we say?" Dixon looked at the time. "When you come back, I'll loosen your collar."

CHAPTER 5

ANDRA WAVED AT the holo display, with the six constructs still rotating.

"Any questions?"

Some of the B-level Materials Science students in her class of thirteen were making notes, and a few were looking at her as if she'd suddenly sprouted wings. Even Ms. Pharday, who was usually sleep-drooling by then, looked awake and nonplussed.

Andra had purposefully raced through the required demonstration. The students were supposed to spend half the class period "gaining an understanding" of atomic geometry and crystal structure by constructing base element cubes and hexagons with floating attractor balls. It was an insultingly boring exercise that repeated their homework. Usually, Andra just gritted her teeth and did it, but this time, she'd been inspired by the excitement in the lecture hall two days ago to create a more interesting demonstration. It wasn't worth the fight with Department Leader Vestering to substitute her exercise, but nothing in the rules said she couldn't make an addition.

"If you haven't already, pay attention to the atomic radius and molecule boundary ratios for the three basic structures." It was as close as she could come to warning them it would be on an upcoming "unannounced progress check" without getting in more trouble with Vestering. Why the man imagined that secret telepathic minders would read test answers from faculty minds but not his was anyone's guess.

"So, how many of you got foamed on POGS Day?"

They all laughed, and most of the class said they had.

"Who can tell us what made the foam?"

They looked at each other, or the ceiling, as if it was printed on the extinguisher nozzles. One student finally spoke. "The fire suppressor is hydrophilic. The salt in the seawater mist made it dissociate the long-chain polymers."

"Thank you, Mr. Truòng, close enough." She added a construct to the holo display showing the formula and complex molecular structure of the suppressor. "Its chief advantages are that it's cheap and non-toxic to humans. So what were the problems with it? Besides ruining a lot of shoes, and not everything looks good in pink."

The students mentioned the slippery floor, the fact that it obscured the exit indicators, and that the application took too long.

"Good," said Andra. "Now let's come up with ideas for a better solution. If we like it, we can make it the class project for this progression."

Twenty minutes later, the class voted unanimously for the project. Andra was happy to see her students actively engaged, and at nine in the morning, no less. Vestering could micromanage the rest of the curriculum to his heart's content, but he had no say over the class project, as long as it related to materials science. Especially if she submitted the abstract quickly and quietly, before he could claim it was too close to another project.

Since they'd done all the scheduled work for the day, she let the class discussion wander into a discussion of possible projects for the next POGS demonstration, which wouldn't be for another six months. The Mat Sci and Chem programs had a friendly rivalry as to the best project, according to some unquantifiable "splash" factor they set for themselves.

It reminded her that she needed to schedule the launch of the improvised rocket on next Monday afternoon, the lightest day for classes on the floater. Designing and constructing it had been a team effort, but she knew it had been Pico Adams's idea that sparked them. Most of Andra's students were so focused on the theoretical that they forgot about the real universe and how the work they did affected it, but Pico was firmly grounded in reality. Andra was glad Pico had accepted her invitation to join the program. She was good for the class, whether or not she knew it, just like her father had been good for their old unit.

As if that thought conjured him, Jerzi Adams slipped in through the open door and took a seat in the back of the room. Pico acknowledged him with a quick nod. Guests weren't unusual in class, so it wasn't remarkable. Or wouldn't have been, if Jerzi weren't such a well-built, handsome man, and her students weren't young and overflowing with hormones.

It was amusing to watch as awareness of him spread through the room. If Andra was being honest with herself, she'd noticed, too, especially since his black, sleeveless shirt with a red V-shaped yoke clung to every sculpted centimeter of him. A vast improvement over the business suit he'd worn two days ago.

"We have five minutes left," she announced. "Open forum, but it must be related to materials science." She leaned on the corner of the podium and crossed one ankle over the other.

Mr. Vandeerink raised his hand. "I read there's a new power source for cybernetic implants that's supposed to last decades. How did they stabilize the rho-hexquadium?"

Andra shook her head. "High-energy physics is out of my star lane."

"What I want to know," said Ms. Grien, "is why it's taking the Citizen Protection Service so frecking long to approve the power source for use in Jumpers." She crossed her arms peevishly, and her cheeks turned purplish under her blue skin. "Protecting them, hah! My uncle has to go in about every year to get his replaced."

Ms. Chao sneered. "Everyone knows the CPS has a fatal case of 'not invented here.'" She was apparently in one of her mad-at-the-world moods. "But realistically, they can't afford another public relations disaster like the Mabingion Purge. 'Accidentally' killing a bunch of minders was bad enough, but if the new tech started killing Jumpers, the newstrends would go supernova."

Ms. Dortief, of combat robot infamy, snorted. "Every big institution has that problem. My family's been trying to get new floater tech approved by the city of Tremplin for six years."

Andra cut her off before she could start in on her family's list of grievances, of which there were many. "Materials science," she reminded them.

Unexpectedly, Ms. Pharday piped up. Apparently, today's class had been interesting enough to keep her awake. "I saw a special on the history of ancient projectile weapons, and this sharpshooter said something about keeping a log of 'cold-bore shots.' Why would they need that? Wouldn't the cooling array keep the barrel at a stable temperature?"

Andra couldn't help but glance at Pico, suspecting a setup, but Pico looked as surprised as Andra was. She shot Jerzi a questioning look, asking if he was willing to step in. He smiled but shook his head.

"Interesting question. Old-time projectile guns had round metal barrels, and the bullet was essentially exploded out of it. The only controls for projectile velocity were knowing the material properties of the projectile and the propellant, and practical experience. The energy release and the friction generated intense heat, which slightly deformed the barrel. If you had to make your first shot count with a cold gun, you'd have to account for the difference when targeting, because most of your practice shots would have been with a warm gun." She resisted the impulse to look to Jerzi to see if she got it right.

"Did you ever shoot one of the old-time guns?" asked Pharday.

"Nope, I was just a simple gunnin." She'd have to explain that outright lie to Jerzi later. "Okay, that's it for today." She pointed toward the still-spinning holo diagrams. "Make note of the ratios, ladies and gentlemen."

The students packed up and trudged, walked, or launched out of the room, according to their nature. Pico spoke briefly to her father, then headed out for her next class, leaving Andra alone with Jerzi. She was about to swear innocence in the gun question, when Vestering entered the classroom. He was smiling widely, which alarmed her, until she saw the woman who followed him in.

"Professor De Luna," said Vestering with believable warmth, "Regent Quan asked to see you." Andra didn't have to be an empath to know that Vestering was unhappy about it.

"Hello," Andra said, glad to see Jerzi tactfully slipping out the door behind them. He didn't need to be catching Vestering's eye again.

Quan smiled and moved closer. "I know you're busy, but since I was in the area, I wanted to tell you we've heard good things about your Practical Applications class." Her English had a distinct Mandarin accent. "As I was telling Mr. Vestering, we need more synergy across the departments." She waved toward the holo display of spinning molecules that Andra hadn't yet turned off.

"Thank you," Andra said with a smile and a slight bow, because the woman meant well. She had no idea Vestering saw all other departments as the competition. Not without reason, considering O-Poly's budget process was secretive and chaotic, fluxed one session with donations and flatlined the next because of reduced enrollments.

Quan captured one of Andra's hands in both of hers. "I was hoping you could come to the little monthly soirée the regents host for special patrons five days from now, on Monday afternoon. We have a family foundation interested in sponsoring a materials sciences project lab. We'd like them to meet and get to know our faculty, so you're more than just names and credentials in a brochure."

Vestering's jaw clenched before he caught himself and stepped back, out of Quan's view. Andra covered her surprise by pulling her hand away so she could turn and switch off the holo display. "Thank you for the invitation, but I have a makeup class that afternoon." She hadn't officially scheduled it yet, but close enough. It was against university policy for the regents to require professors or teaching staff to do fundraising, but it didn't mean they didn't exert pressure to "volunteer."

She disliked being shown off like the newest pet-trade fantasy animal, and detested schmoozing. After discussing the weather, about which there was precious little to say in a tropical paradise, late-season typhoons notwithstanding, the conversation usually turned to local politics, which she didn't follow, or questions about her military service, which she couldn't answer. They never wanted to discuss teaching or materials science.

"Oh, well, perhaps next time," said Quan. Her bracelet percomp lit up, and she glanced at it. "Please excuse me, but I must take this." She tapped her earwire as she turned and left the room. She moved surprisingly quickly for such a short woman.

Vestering started to follow, then turned back. "Do I need to remind you about the university's curriculum approval procedure again?"

"As it happens, I reviewed it just yesterday," Andra said evenly.

Vestering's expression tightened in suspicious disbelief. He pointed to the space where the holo had been displayed. "That wasn't the approved diagram."

She switched on the holo. "It is, actually." She pointed to the new molecule. "I merely overlaid a real-world example for comparison." She removed the extra layer before he could get a good look at it. She wouldn't put it past him to derail the students' project just to make her look bad.

If they'd been alone, he might have pushed the point, but Quan was pacing just outside the round doorway as she subvocalized with whoever had pinged her. Vestering's mouth twitched in patent annoyance before he smoothed his expression into warm professionalism, then strode confidently toward Quan.

Andra quelled an adolescent urge to gesture rudely as he left. Instead, she turned off the holo and removed her content from the controller's local dataspace. She wished she'd thought to warn the students to keep their project confidential until she could get it registered. Sometimes, academic maneuvering was more cutthroat than any jack crew.

Andra busied herself straightening up the room and organizing her sling bag until Vestering and Quan were long gone. Not knowing where Jerzi had hidden himself, she pinged him that the coast was clear and waited for him in the hall. After she took him on the official tour of the chemistry and materials sciences labs, she was looking forward to spending the afternoon with someone who didn't have an agenda, other than to kick her ass at the shooting range.

She smiled. Well, he could try.

CHAPTER 6

THE GUN RANGE was less humid than the outdoors, but not by much. Jerzi pulled the sweaty cap-and-visor off his head as he rolled over on the gun range's platform pad to watch Andra shoot. She locked her Hellrim analog combat rifle and ignored the attached scope in favor of using her ocular implants to eye the target, eight hundred meters away. Her implants connected to her gun's onboard systems and gave her a visual readout. Most of her face was hidden by her protective glasses, but his angle gave him a full view of her form. The bright gold knit tank and tiger-print leggings suited her better than the subdued clothes he'd seen her in at the university. Her standing stance and technique were as unconventional as he remembered, but she'd reliably hit the center ring of the small target with twenty-nine out of thirty shots. Average shooters couldn't have hit any of the rings at five hundred meters.

She flexed her knees, started to inhale, and took the shot. Two seconds later, she smiled and turned to him, looking smug. "Even up, Commander. Your shot."

He sketched a salute, then put his cap back on and lowered the visor as he rolled back into position next to his custom Ishum Mark 30 Gamaura railgun. Its manufacturer designed it to be used with high-tech scopes, sophisticated targeting systems, and smart-powered projectiles, but he'd customized it to also handle bullets with no built-in AI, and he practiced with it regularly to keep up his skills. Technology made it possible for average shooters to be effective, but when technology failed, so did they. His Forward Intelligence unit had relied on sniper support that always worked, not just when the equipment did.

He took a slow, deep breath, then let it out just as slowly as he loaded and locked the single projectile into the chamber. Out of habit, he visually checked that downrange was clear, though it was unlikely anyone would be there, because the only other shooters in the facility that afternoon besides himself and Andra were two quiet older men. Nineteen hundred meters downrange, tiny target rings lit up, only visible through his scope of custom-printed and tuned glass. He'd made longer shots without tech systems, but not often. He nudged the projectile velocity higher, but still subsonic.

His attention was pulled when he heard a half-mumbled song to his left, which made him smile. Andra was famous for using distraction techniques to win. He remembered she'd once put ice cubes down Dom DeBayaud's shorts during a sparring session. She'd hidden the ice in her bra and waited for just the right moment. He'd been the brigade's reigning middleweight freeform champion, and it was the only time any of the unit had ever beaten him.

He let the memory slide away as he leveled the gun again and looked through the scope. He wasn't liking the recommendation from the new targeting system he was trying out. It felt loose to him, as it had intermittently since they'd been there. He let his eyes lose focus as he reached out for the target with his small telekinetic talent, then adjusted the gun's power and angle setting manually. With his talent still on the target, he took the shot. He watched until it hit, then allowed himself a slight smile.

"Dead center," Andra said beside him. Her ocular implants were as good as a spotter's scope. She bowed low to him with a sweeping arm gesture. "You are still the wizard."

Jerzi grinned. It felt good to be praised for something other than his muscles. "You did pretty good yourself with your old Hellrim."

"Thanks." She knelt to lay her rifle in its open hard case. It was a marked contrast to her soft gun bag, which was so obnoxiously bright and floral that civilians probably took it for a simple gym bag. "I've been thinking about what you said about the security of the labs being hit and miss. I know I said it was probably just the feast-or-famine funding cycle the university seems to operate under, but now I'm not so sure."

He pushed up to his knees and sat back on his heels. "Why?" He wiped his hands on his gray cargo pants. He was glad he'd chosen to wear a sleeveless shirt, because the gun range was bordering on hot. He was more acclimated to Etonver's cooler weather.

"All the new security measures you noticed are in the Chem building. I vaguely remember hearing about thefts, but why are the new camera eyes only on the third-floor Chem labs, and why does only the Chem building's freight lift need a key and a code? New sponsors like their names on visible things, not boring security systems. And if they had a new co-sponsored project to protect, the university's PR machine would be burning up the net to get the word out."

He shook his head. "You're the D-level professor. I'm just a simple gunnin with an A-level in general studies. What would be worth stealing? Is there anything that can only be accessed by the Chem building's lift, maybe on the fourth or fifth floors?"

"That's just it. You saw how the buildings are connected by the donuts." That was the nickname for the curving, translucent walkways on each floor that interconnected three of the four buildings on the floater. "All the labs have valuable goods, and all the other freight lifts have no security at all. The only thing preventing thieves from taking Chem lab stuff to the stairs and the other lifts would be laziness." She frowned. "The building airpads are wide open, and the stackers are free for public use."

"Maybe they're adding security in phases, or maybe they're protecting something else." He frowned. "I wish I could be more help, but it's not my area of expertise."

She smoothed back a lock of hair that had escaped from the loose pony tail she now wore, instead of the slicked-back, tight knot that seemed to be her professional look. "I know more than I did before, so you were plenty of help." She made a face. "Probably not how you planned to spend your vacation time, so thank you."

"Well, no, but the range time is a fair trade." He glanced at the readout on his Ishum and saw it was close to five thirty local time. He debated taking more shots to narrow down the potential problem with the targeting system, but decided it could wait. He started to power down the gun, then had an idea.

"Do me a favor?" he asked. "I think this targeting system is bad. Could you set it up for a shot, then see what your oculars tell you?"

"Sure."

She stood and stepped into his lane behind him. He duck-walked sideways a couple of steps so she'd have room to lie down prone on the pad.

She turned her head to look back at him. "Sorry, I don't know how the system works."

He rocked forward to kneel behind her. He put one arm on the pad near her shoulders and leaned over her to point to the controls as he named them. "Distance, gravity, curvature, wind, angle, projectile velocity."

It suddenly came to him that she was warm, and close, and she smelled good. Really good. He reared up and sat back on his heels before she could notice he was sniffing her hair. He flushed as he looked up at the ceiling. He needed to get a life.

No farking way was he ruining a renewed friendship with Andra by having sex with her, then leaving on the next interstellar transit. He'd never been that kind of man, and he didn't think she was that kind of woman, at least, not anymore. Not to mention, he wasn't sure she even saw him as a potential lover, or would be interested in a relationship with someone who wasn't as smart or educated as she was.

The truth was, now that he was no longer married and could acknowledge it, he'd felt an instant connection with Andra De Luna from the first day he'd met her. They just… synced. Even though he hadn't seen her in five years, it was still true. That kind of friendship was as rare as order in chaos, and should be cherished. His stupid hormones could take a hike.

"The targeting system is definitely off," Andra said. "Furthermore, it's not consistent. I tried the same solution twice, and got two different answers." She raised herself to her knees.

"I was afraid of that. I bought it just before I left, so I haven't played with it until now." Jerzi dusted his hands off on his pants. "I'll ask Pico to check the math in the AI. Might be a rounding error."

He hit the shutdown sequence of the Ishum, and closed and stack-locked the three projectile cases. He'd only brought simple projectiles with him because Nila Marbela banned AI bullets for civilian use, and it hadn't been worth applying for a security-professional waiver. He pulled off the suspect targeting system and tucked it in its case, then separated the glass scope and put it away as well. He wasn't usually sentimental about guns, but this one had survived a crash landing on an uncharted planet and saved his life a few years ago, so he was fond of it. He pushed it into his soft-sided, dull gray, flexin-lined gun bag. He liked it because it looked more like it held a vacation trip's worth of dirty laundry, rather than a very expensive, customized sniper rifle, various scopes, and enough ammo to take out a space platoon.

Andra stood and went to pack her rifle in its case. "Hey, want to take a few last shots with my old Lipara?" She pulled a smaller case out of her gun bag and peered through its clear lid. "Looks like I only have about twenty flechettes, though. I keep meaning to get a new box."

"Sure, if you let me pay for what I use." He got to his feet as she powered down and packed her Hellrim, then opened the small case for the Lipara. He used her lane's wallcomp to order the target to move closer. "What, about ninety meters?"

"Better make it eighty," she said as she unfolded the hand weapon's grip. "The flechettes are heavy, and the range charges extra if they have to dig them out of the floor."

He programmed the distance and told it the type of ammo, then stepped back. She pulled out a mostly empty case of twelve-centimeter flechettes and selected one to load. She confirmed the target distance on the wallcomp, then glanced downrange. She casually held the gun up with her left hand and pressed the trigger. The gun coughed quietly. The wallcomp dutifully reported a dead-center hit.

He laughed out loud. "You evil, evil woman," he said. "You played me."

She maintained an innocent look for about two seconds before she grinned wide. "Oh, yeah." She waggled her eyebrows and whispered. "Gotta make up for your mystical teke targeting talent somehow."

He was surprised, and yet not, that she knew about his minder talent, such as it was. He fought to keep himself from tensing up. "How long have you known about it?"

"Known? Not until just now. Suspected it, though." She bent down to pick up the box of flechettes. "A gunnery instructor I knew believed all the best snipers she trained were low-level telekinetics that minder testing hadn't detected. Not that she said anything, of course, because they'd have had to transfer to the CPS Minder Corps, whether they wanted to or not." She fished a flechette out of the box. "Even during combat, when nothing else was working, you made miraculous shots look easy, so it stood to reason."

"It doesn't make you, uhm, uncomfortable?"

She tilted her head in puzzlement. "No, why should it? I'd love to have a talent like that, or any minder talent at all."

"Not everyone would," he said carefully. "Some people think it's cheating, or worse."

Andra snorted. "Then they're civilians or flameouts." She paused a moment, then handed him the gun and the flechette. "There's no cheating in war. You use what you have—talent, experience, brains, oculars— whatever it takes to survive. To win." She pointed toward the target. "Use your talent and take your shot."

He loaded the gun and stepped up to the line. He raised the gun to sight, then lowered it. "To be honest, my talent's never been good for flechettes or needlers."

"Well, then," she said smugly, "I know who'll be buying the first round of beers."

He knew she was using his competitiveness to challenge him, but it was still effective.

The gun's grip was too small for two of his big hands, so he turned sideways for a one-handed stance and extended his arm. He felt for the target with his talent, but it wasn't working. He frowned and tried again, but it was like trying to grab mist. Finally, he gave up and just used the gun's scope and his experience to make the shot. It hit the outer ring of the target, so at least he didn't embarrass himself by missing altogether.

She wordlessly handed him another flechette, which he loaded.

He turned sideways again. She came up behind him and put her hands on his shoulders to knead his tense trapezius muscles a few times. "You're not making it look easy."

He nodded and took a deep breath and let it out slowly as he willed himself to relax. She stepped back, and he raised his arm and shot without overthinking it.

It was better, almost touching the line between the center and second ring. His next two shots hit close to dead center.

Andra took the gun when he offered it back to her. "So I'm guessing here, because you have the sexy minder talent and I don't, but maybe you're used to dealing with long-distance targets and close-to-supersonic speeds with your talent, and have to teach yourself about close-range and slow."

"Could be," he conceded. He was more struck by the revelation that she found minder talents sexy. Large segments of civilization were prejudiced against minders, sometimes virulently so, even against minders with negligible or one-trick talents like his. He'd avoided experimenting with his talent because he didn't want to be hated, but it hadn't changed anything.

She was just loading another flechette when a tinny synth voice informed all patrons that the range would be closing in fifteen minutes. They'd arrived late because the tour of the labs had taken longer than he'd thought. While the three-story Materials Science building only had one large lab on its top floor, the five-story Chemistry building had multiple labs of various sizes on four out of five floors. He hadn't imagined they'd have so many of them, and that didn't even count the separate three-story Math building's labs, which they hadn't visited. He'd hate to be in the lab manager's boots, keeping fourteen labs stocked, functional, and clean. Not to mention, dealing with scheduling conflicts, like the one Andra and Romila had engineered to their advantage.

"I say we call it a tie," said Andra. "Besides, I need to get home and submit something for work."

They packed up their gear and loaded it in the flitter, then strapped themselves in for the flight to her apartment building. The sunset was paradise-perfect as Jerzi released control of the flitter to the traffic system. He let the beauty of it infuse his mind for a long moment.

Andra cleared her throat. "Look, it might be none of my business, but, well, Pico has some nova-class math skills, and she's hiding them. I only noticed them because she slips up once in a while."

He sighed heavily. "I know. She pretends she doesn't speak Marathi, too." He quirked a corner of his mouth. "She's mad at her mother."

"Oh," said Andra. Understanding dawned on her face. "Ohhhh," she said again. "Dhorya is still a top-level accountant?"

He nodded. "The hell of it is, I doubt she'd care, even if she knew."

"Okay, I'll bite." She crossed her arms. "Why?"

He debated what to tell her. It wasn't only his secret to tell, but then again, Pico had revealed some of it already. "You probably guessed Pico is a teke, from the bit with the umbrella the other day." Andra nodded, and he continued. "Dhorya's family, the Sankirnas, think minders are, at best, a genetic defect, and at worst, an amoral abomination. Some in their oldest generation still openly advocate for purification. When I finally figured out my talent was real and not just good hand-eye coordination, I told Dhorya about it, not knowing what she'd been raised to believe. She said she loved me and didn't care, but I never brought it up again."

He adjusted the angle of the holomap, to give his hand something to do. "I think she really wanted to believe she was different from the rest of the Sankirnas, that it really didn't matter, but then Pico started showing signs of talent. She flatlined in age-twelve testing, though, so Dhorya convinced herself she'd been imagining things. Then... well, to make a long story short, when Pico was sixteen, something happened at space camp and she discovered she was a pretty good microteke."

Andra looked thoughtful, then nodded. "I get it. It was one thing for Dhorya to marry a minder, but another thing to produce one, because that meant her DNA might be defective, too."

Trust Andra to cut right to the heart of things. "Yeah. Took me a long time to figure it out. Dhorya never looked at Pico the same way again. Or me, for that matter. Pico didn't understand why her mother withdrew and could hate her for something she was. Pico denied her talent, even deliberately failed the seventeen-year testing, but it didn't bring back Dhorya's love, and all I could do was protect Pico the best I could. When Dhorya finally left, she made it abundantly clear she wanted nothing to do with either of us ever again. The Sankirna Trust is paying for Pico's education on the condition that she never use the Sankirna name, and never go to school anywhere on Vaylamoinen."

He looked to the darkening sky without seeing it, awash in memories. "Pico can't afford to turn down the money, but she doesn't want to be her mother's daughter anymore."

"That's really rough. Poor kid." She shook her head. "I spent a lot of years proving to my family that I was tough enough to be a gunnin, then smart enough to be a professor in a top university, but the only thing they notice is that I don't have children."

He couldn't help but laugh. "They did know Da'vin was a woman, didn't they?"

"*Si, claro.* It was no problem. They contracted with a sperm donor on my behalf." Her smile had a feral quality to it. "He wanted to come on the wedding trip. Da'vin sent him a holo of her dressed like a blood-splattered pirate-clan warrior, beheading a training dummy with her family's samurai sword. She told him she was looking forward to seeing *his* sword. He canceled the contract and moved to another planet."

It was a good thing the flitter was flying itself, because Jerzi laughed so hard he had to wipe away tears. "That's priceless. I wish I'd seen it."

"I'll show it to you sometime." There was a wistful quality to her smile. "It's a good legacy, better than a memory diamond, any day."

The flitter banked right, and they were soon setting down on her apartment building's flitter pad.

He intended to thank her for the afternoon and say goodnight, so he was surprised by the words that came out of his mouth. "Want to hunt down a beer later this evening?"

His wristcomp signaled. Ordinarily, he'd ignore it, but he checked in case it was Pico. He hadn't set up a distinctive signal for her local ping ref yet. He blinked in surprise when he saw the incoming ID. He apologized to Andra with a look and answered the ping via the earwire he'd almost forgotten he was wearing.

"Luka Foxe, what in the three moons of Albion Prime are you doing on Nila Marbela?"

CHAPTER 7

THE CHILDCARE PLAYROOM was more chaotic than usual when Pico arrived to meet Valenia. Even though it was a few minutes after six in the evening, when the center was supposed to close, half a dozen children, from ages five to twelve, were still there. Some days, it seemed the whole city was running late.

"Did the toy closet explode?" Pico nudged a small stuffed spaceship with the toe of her soft boot. Toys covered the floor and every available flat surface.

"No, a blended family gifted the center with a flitter-load of extra stuff. Méimuī didn't come in today, because the construction dust bothers her, even though it's the workers' day off. Since it was just me, I asked the afternoon kids to help me evaluate what we should keep."

Pico laughed. "Did they let you recycle *anything*?"

Valenia rolled her eyes. "Only if it was totally unfixable. Come on, help me clear a path."

Pico hung her bag on a hook by the door and started in. "What's your system?" One of Valenia's many gifts was organization. Pico had a few gifts of her own, but that wasn't one of them.

"By age-appropriateness and complexity." She pointed to six containers and two cabinets that she'd labeled with large, colorful signs. Artistic talent was another of Valenia's gifts.

As they picked up the toys, parents straggled in to collect their charges. For reasons known only to the Optimal Polytechnic administration, they'd placed the childcare center's windowless suite of rooms in the new Math building, citing convenience, though whose, she wasn't sure. Since it wasn't interconnected like the rest of the buildings on the island floater, and its airpad was temporarily closed to non-construction traffic, parents had to make a special trip to get there, sometimes in the rain.

On the other hand, Pico conceded, math students didn't often blow up things in their labs, like the chemistry students, or build combat robots, like the materials science students, so maybe the placement was a good choice. Since it was close to the public transport station, at least it made it easy for Pico to meet Valenia at the end of her shift so they could go home together to the flat they shared.

At twenty after six, only one child was left, a sunny-natured, six-year-old named Lyssi. Valenia enlisted her willing help in finding all the soft toys and putting them in the appropriate basket. Her harried mother came sweeping through ten minutes later, apologized for being late, and dragged her reluctant child out the door.

Pico wasn't impressed. "What's her malfunction?"

Valenia shrugged. "Breakup, I think. Lyssi likes it here better than at home right now."

"Poor kid." Pico remembered her own parents' split, though she tried not to. "Poor mother, too."

They spent another fifteen minutes before Valenia declared she was done for the evening, and the morning shift could finish what she'd started. "Not that they'll do it, mind you," she grumbled. "Three people, and they can barely get the kids cleaned up and fed lunch."

Valenia often complained about the parents and the paid staff, but she put up with them because she adored children, and they adored her right back, even the older ones who didn't think they should have to be in childcare when they weren't in school.

She secured the desk and wall comps as Pico fished in her bag. "I brought the sparkly wrist lights for us to try."

Because it was winter, the days were shorter, so it was already almost dark outside. It was a tricky balance, trying to keep Valenia from panicking in the dark, and being annoyed when her friends were obvious about accommodating her phobia. Pico was one of the few who knew there was a very good reason why the dark terrified her friend.

"The lights my sister sent? That'll be fun." She held out her wrists, and Pico snapped on the lights. On Valenia, they would no doubt look as if she'd chosen them specifically to complement her custom-designed tunic, pants, and accessories. With her tall, willowy figure and beautiful mocha skin, she could wear a recycle bag and look elegant.

Pico slung her bag over her shoulder and snapped the lights on her own wrists, then had to adjust them smaller so they wouldn't fall off. The story of her life.

"Okay, out with it. What's bothering you?" demanded Valenia. She turned off the lights and secured the door after it irised shut. Its light went out, signaling the center was closed. The wide and tall hallway was lit, so other people must still be in the wing.

Pico waved Valenia forward toward the main exit, but Valenia stood still with her hands on her hips and stared at Pico expectantly.

Pico sighed. She should have known Valenia would notice, when no one else would have. She really didn't want to talk about it, but Valenia would nag her all evening otherwise. "Sojaire's in town."

"*Here* in town?"

Pico gave her a wry smile. "Unless there's some other city named Tremplin on some other planet named Nila Marbela."

Valenia started walking, and Pico joined her.

"He didn't come to see you, did he?" Valenia's tone was half sympathy and half outrage.

"Of course not. He's traveling with his bosses." Pico sternly suppressed another sigh. She'd spent far too many of them on Sojaire Celeyron, and all it had done was waste perfectly good oxygen. "We're all invited to dinner with them at Dominar Carlotta's."

"Really? When?" Her eyes shone with excitement.

Pico waved a dismissive hand. "Tonight at eight."

"What!?" Valenia squawked. "Why didn't you say something when you came in?" She sped up, almost half running. "Move those short little legs, girl."

Pico kept her sedate pace. "I'm not going."

Valenia circled back to grab hold of Pico's arm and pull her along. "Yes, you are, if only to say you've been to the restaurant in the sky, and you can't go wearing that. You look like a sampan sailor from the history vids."

"I'm not going." She pulled out of Valenia's grip and stood her ground. "My main reason for coming here, well, my second-to-main reason, was so I could get far away from Sojaire. My main reason was to go to school with my friend Valenia, who understands why her friend Pico doesn't want to be in the same room as the boy who barely notices her most of the time." She crossed her arms and stared determinedly at her good-hearted but sometimes oblivious friend.

Valenia blinked, then wrapped Pico in a brief hug. "I'm sorry."

Mollified, Pico nodded, and they started walking again.

The hallway let out into the building's large, round atrium. They angled left toward the main doors. The crates and stacks of panels leaning against one wall reminded her that the north wing's third floor was finally getting finished. Rumor had it some wealthy family was getting naming rights for it.

"I wonder if the 'interesting times' curse will come visit while he's here." Valenia held up fingers to count. "There was space camp, of course, and that time in the finance center with the theft crew, the riot at the open market, and that warped woman who went berserk in Sojaire's clinic when you were visiting. Oh, and that gunfight in the park where your dad's company picnic was being held."

Pico snorted. "That old 'May you live in interesting times' curse is nonsense. Etonver is the weapons capital of the Concordance. Gunfights and riots happen every day. If you count getting lost in a finance center as interesting, you need to get out more. Besides, we weren't there by the time the crew arrived. Our autocab just got stuck in the traffic lockdown, like half of the city." Pico adjusted the bag so the strap slid across her body. "I've been with Sojaire lots of times when nothing happened."

"That's because he still thinks of you as a child."

Valenia's interpretation of "nothing happened" wasn't what Pico had been thinking of, but it was the crux of the matter. She'd had a crush on Sojaire ever since she'd first met him at space camp three years ago. They'd saved each other's lives, and discovered things about each other that no one else knew, but ever since, he'd treated her like a younger sister or a buddy, with no idea how she'd felt. She'd had a dalliance or two with boys her age in school, but they never lasted because they weren't Sojaire. Whenever she'd run into him, whether by luck or her design, her heart hoped, and got crushed each time.

The last straw had been when she'd told him she was going off-planet for her advanced education. He'd wished her well and hadn't even asked what she was going to study. Not that she'd known at the time, but she'd hoped he'd care enough to ask. To be fair, he'd never given her any indication that he might be interested in her, so she really only had herself to blame for letting herself get hurt again and again.

Being seven interstellar transit days away on a new planet, practically on her own, and making all new friends had helped dull the pain to an occasional ache. But now, out of five-hundred-plus settled planets in the galaxy he could have gone to, here he was, and she could feel hope stupidly blossoming in her again. It just wasn't fair.

Valenia stopped just before the exit and turned to face Pico. "I'll make you a deal. Let me dress you tonight like a classy, *adult* woman, who doesn't wear elephant-wide pants and ninja split-toed boots on a tropical planet. If Sojaire still treats you like the kid next door, he'll be dead to us both forever."

Pico wavered. The Tamheurre family was in the fashion business, and Valenia had an extensive, high-quality wardrobe. It would be idiocy to turn her down. If nothing else, a night on the town dressed like a supernova star would be better than moping in her bedroom.

"Okay," said Pico, "on one condition. The shoes come from my closet. Yours are downright dangerous, especially those spring-blade heels."

Valenia nodded. "I can work around that." She grinned. "Dominar Carlotta's will be a lot better than leftovers."

The main entrance door irised open, and a tall, slender purple-haired woman came floating in on an almost-silent glide board. They were forbidden in all of O-Poly's buildings, but after hours, students were rarely caught at it. The woman saluted them as she banked toward the left and vanished into the north wing.

Valenia turned to face the dark, took one sharp breath, then stepped outside. Pico stayed next to her, trying not to be obvious about keeping an eye on her. The campus was well lit all night, but it still left plenty of shadows. Their wrist lights created soft pools of light that moved with each swing of their arms.

"Do you have anything in your closet for my dad?"

Valenia gave her an incredulous look. "Why? Does he like wearing women's clothing?"

Pico burst out laughing at the thought, then covered her mouth because it was so loud. "He prefers it on women. His ping said he's bringing Professor De Luna, and I think he likes her."

"*Likes* her, likes her?" Valenia frowned. "Professor De Luna? She's got to be in her fifties or sixties, the way she dresses."

Pico sighed. Valenia couldn't help that her primary view of the universe always started with clothes, since it was her family's business, but it skewed her judgment about people. Pico knew Professor De Luna was in her late thirties.

"Yes, *likes* her, and the only nice clothes he brought with him got thrashed in the evacuation." Tremplin wasn't the place to buy business attire, unless one was very fond of jungle prints. "I want him to make a good impression on her. He hasn't been out with anyone since my mo… since forever."

Valenia shuddered delicately. "I couldn't imagine helping my father get ready for a date."

They arrived at the public transport dock, where a few other students were already waiting.

"That's because your mother would murder him in his sleep. Besides, he wouldn't need any help. He has stylists on call, plus your uncle's interplanetary chain of body parlors."

Pico stepped up to the transport call box and entered the coordinates for their apartment complex into the queue. "Promise me you won't mention the 'D' word to my dad, or he'll find an excuse not to go. It's not a date. It's just an evening with friends."

CHAPTER 8

ANDRA SHOULDN'T HAVE agreed to go that night, even though it was just a simple dinner with friends. Well, maybe not simple.

Dominar Carlotta's First Flight was one of the gems of the galactic tourist trade, and with good reason. The restaurant's airborne oval platform permanently traced lazy circles over the city of Tremplin at an altitude of five thousand meters, and offered spectacular views of the city lights and luminescent ocean reefs from every seat, day or night. Andra had no idea how Jerzi's friends from Etonver had managed to book seating for seven during premium dining hours, but she supposed all it had taken was money.

On the shuttle trip up to the platform lobby, the agreed rendezvous point, Jerzi had vaguely mentioned his friend Luka had recently come into an inheritance. She'd only half-listened because she'd been waffling between kicking herself for agreeing to an expensive dinner with strangers and enjoying the scenery, mostly of Jerzi in a red sunset-patterned knit shirt that clung to him like water. She was amused to note that she wasn't the only passenger admiring that particular view. Jerzi affably chatted with anyone and everyone, but stayed with her.

She'd been on the verge of turning him down for a beer after their range session, but when he'd unexpectedly invited her to meet his friends, she'd caught a vulnerable look on his face that weakened her resolve to get out of his orbit. He needed someone in his corner for once, considering how Dhorya Sankirna had ripped his family apart. Andra could go back to keeping a professional distance from the Adams clan after Jerzi left.

She liked Jerzi's friends. It was a pleasant change to be with people who didn't treat her like a barely tamed predator or an unstable thermobaric charge just waiting to blow. For all that the Optimal Polytechnic regents lionized her for her military background, the rest of the academic Materials Science faculty viewed it with varying amounts of disdain or alarm. She liked the new career she'd made for herself, but her personal life paid the price. Jerzi's easy company reminded her what it was like not to feel lonely.

Her seat at the clear, meltglass table, flash-formed into a heptagon for their party, gave her a good view of Luka Foxe and Mairwen Morganthur, and of their assistant, Sojaire Celeyron. Pico sat to Andra's right and Jerzi to her left, with Valenia in between Pico and Sojaire. The restaurant's acoustic design included tech that made it easy to hear their table conversation, and yet kept the chatter from the rest of the patrons to little more than white noise.

Andra pointed upward. "I've never seen sonic walls in a commercial setting. They're not cheap." She poured herself more wine from the bottle on their table. It was a smooth, complex-flavored red that was probably half a month's salary for a professor. Wines were rare on Nila Marbela, owing to unsuitable ecosystems, and transit-stable wines from other planets cost small fortunes.

Luka's eyes gleamed. "I'd like to see the tech behind them." He smiled genially. "I'm a fan."

"Focused wave dampeners," said Andra. "The university's physics engineers have some big ones in their lab." She pointed up to the ceiling again, which was lit with thousands of pinpoint colored lights that periodically morphed into popular nebula patterns. "These would have to be smaller and movable to match the changing table configurations, so they're probably synced arrays on a hex-grid."

Out of the corner of her eye, Andra saw Sojaire doing something on his wristcomp and Valenia looking around and fidgeting, and realized she'd probably been boring half the table. "Sorry." She held up her hands in apology. "Once a professor, always a professor."

Jerzi laughed. "You've always loved knowing how things work. Saved the unit more than once, back in the day."

Andra snorted. "No fault of mine that none of you lopars learned to read."

Jerzi and Luka laughed, and quiet Mairwen smiled a little. Valenia asked Pico what a "lopar" was. While Pico explained it meant someone who was obliviously, confidently reckless, Sojaire pretended to read his wristcomp. Andra wasn't fooled; he'd been wholly tuned to Pico the entire evening.

Andra gathered that all three of them had known each other in Etonver, and may have met at the space camp Jerzi had mentioned earlier. Sojaire had obviously never seen the version of Pico that looked exquisite in a designer dress that graced her small but lithe form, with a subtle cloud of twinkling fairy lights in her dark hair, and flawless makeup and body art with a fantasy theme. Taller, poised Valenia was similarly dressed to impress in flowing orange resilk, but might as well have been invisible as far as Sojaire was concerned. Andra almost felt sorry for the young man. He was well-mannered and handsome, without an ounce of arrogance, but he might have been taking his friend for granted. If Pico noticed Sojaire was off balance, she didn't let on.

Andra turned back to Luka. "I'd like to hear more about your company."

As Luka described his specialty in forensic crime scene investigation and his partner's focus on security assessments for commercial businesses, Andra watched them together. Luka was the same height as Jerzi, but much slimmer, with disarrayed dark hair, and the loose blue-green shirt he wore matched his eyes. He was handsome, in an exotic kind of way, with Nordic features but golden skin tone, and no beard. He seemed comfortable in the upscale surroundings, and joked with Jerzi and Pico, but she had the feeling he was registering everything he saw. She'd caught him focusing on her just as they were being seated, and she'd bet he could describe her elegant but conservative tunic set, hair, and jewelry in perfect detail. Da'vin used to get that look when she was on a reconnaissance mission, so Andra always thought of it as "recon eyes."

His partner, Mairwen, was an enigma. She was slender in a solid gray, long-sleeved tunic and darker long pants, which made her stand out in a tropical city famous for being clothing-optional. She was a centimeter or two shorter than Andra and had few feminine curves, but looked toned. She wore her pale blonde hair short with an asymmetrical spike cut, and no visible makeup or body art. The only jewelry she wore was a small but elegant percomp on the back of her hand that matched the one Luka wore. Andra was experienced at picking up subtle body language cues, but Mairwen was preternaturally still. She hadn't said much, though she'd become more relaxed, for lack of a better word, as the evening progressed. Luka was clearly in love with her, but Andra hadn't been sure the sentiment was returned until she saw Mairwen thread her long fingers through his when he was answering Jerzi's question about what brought him to Tremplin. He kissed their joined hands, and she gave him a soft, loving smile that transformed her face.

"We're following a lead," Luka said. "Someone has been the author of some very messy crime scenes, and the trail led us here." He gave Jerzi a quick smile. "To be honest, I hadn't remembered you or Pico were here until Sojaire reminded me."

Abruptly, Pico stood up and grabbed a surprised Valenia's hand and hauled her up out of her seat. "Freshers," she announced brightly, then pushed Valenia toward the aisle. Pico gave Jerzi a beseeching look, then turned to lead her roommate away.

Andra looked to Jerzi for enlightenment, as did everyone else left at the table.

Jerzi caught Luka's gaze. "Valenia is sensitive. Pico's afraid you're going to talk details about the 'messy crimes scenes,' and she doesn't want Valenia to hear."

"I wouldn't... Oh, she was a victim, wasn't she?" His eyes darted to Valenia's empty chair. "Or witnessed it. When she was younger."

Andra didn't know how he came up with that, but it was apparently right, because Jerzi looked relieved. "Both. She copes well, most of the time, but Pico is protective of her."

Luka nodded. "Understandable. I don't usually talk shop at dinner." Mairwen raised an eyebrow, and Sojaire had a sudden coughing fit and hid his face in his napkin. Luka laughed. "Okay, I do. I'll try to find less objectionable topics."

Jerzi grinned. "You may as well get it out of your system before Valenia comes back."

"Mutilation murders, victim and technique commonalities, a dozen planets, at least three years so far." He spoke hurriedly. "They have symmetry with another pattern of murders made to look like accidents or common crimes. Our client is the wealthy family of one of the mutilation-murder victims."

"Contract wet-work crew?" asked Jerzi.

Andra shook her head. "No crew I know has the funds to be multi-planetary." When Luka looked her way, she waved a finger between herself and Jerzi. "Our Forward Intelligence unit saw a lot of them over the years. Jack crews stay in their ships or bases and prey on interstellar traffic. They don't go after planet-based targets unless it's a really big payoff. Ground-based crews—theft, wetwork, enforcement, whatever—can control a big territory, and maybe a space station, but interstellar transit and real-time comms? That takes heavy investments, like energy firms. Or pirate clan, though they never go dirtside if they can help it."

"Pharmas, maybe or blackmarketers," said Jerzi. "Or just enterprising independent contractors with an interstellar ship."

Luka shook his head. "I don't know yet. I'm meeting with a law enforcement colleague tomorrow." Andra remembered Jerzi had said something about Luka being High Court certified, and having worked thousands of cases across the Central Galactic Concordance. It stood to reason he had contacts on a lot of planets.

Valenia and Pico returned the same time the main courses arrived. Andra hid a smile when she noticed that Pico's eyes went automatically to Sojaire first. She'd been much better than Sojaire at pretending indifference, but little things gave her away. Andra had seated herself next to Jerzi to stop herself from watching him all night, but she wasn't sure she was hiding her constant awareness any better than Pico was.

She took a small bite of the lamb dish she'd ordered, then dug in with pleasure, relieved to find the restaurant lived up to its culinary reputation. Jerzi and Luka got into a spirited discussion about spices and sampled from each other's plates and Mairwen's. Andra happened to catch Mairwen's eye, and she gave the quiet woman a crooked smile and tilted her head toward the bickering men. Mairwen twitched a corner of her mouth in what Andra hoped was shared amusement.

Andra was finished before anyone else, although Jerzi wasn't far behind. She'd grown up with greedy siblings and teasing cousins who would steal right off the plate of anyone who dallied, and she hadn't outgrown the habit of bolting her food. Jerzi had probably learned to eat fast in the military, where leisurely meals and blissful sleep were guaranteed to be interrupted.

Jerzi took a sip of fizzy water and pushed his plate forward a bit. "Luka, remind me again about the *hvalreki* that lets you afford to play generous host in famous flying restaurants."

"The man who said he killed my fath…" He trailed off and glanced at Valenia, who was giggling as she whispered something to a smiling Pico. "I inherited a half-dozen cybernetics patents last year, and some of them were worth licensing. We got a signing bonus for the first one a couple of weeks ago."

"What's a *hvalreki*?" asked Andra.

"'Lucky find,' in Icelandic," said Jerzi. "I learned it recently from Mairwen." He smirked and touched his finger to the tip of his nose, and surprisingly, the corner of her mouth quirked up. Andra hadn't been sure the woman responded to teasing. Or maybe it was a shared secret.

She would like to hear the whole story someday, but it was highly unlikely, since they were all leaving soon, and she wasn't. She loved teaching and working in a well-equipped lab, but the rest of academic life wasn't all that she'd hoped. She missed the happy camaraderie she saw between Jerzi and his friends. She sighed to herself and decided she'd better lay off the alcohol for the rest of the evening. It was making her melancholy, and she had enough of that to last a lifetime.

"Would you have some free time tomorrow?" asked Jerzi, looking at Mairwen.

"Yes," said Mairwen. "I make Luka's colleagues nervous."

Jerzi smiled as Luka patted her hand. "No, *ljósið mitt*, it's just they can't read you."

Mairwen shrugged, supremely unconcerned. Jerzi laughed, then asked, "How would you like to do a free security assessment for the Chemistry building on the Optimal Polytechnic campus?"

Andra shook her head. "That's not necessary—"

Jerzi overrode her. "Yes, it is. I barely know the basics. She's good." He explained to Mairwen about the accidents, and the odd mix of vulnerabilities and systems he'd seen on their tour that afternoon. "So will you do it?"

"Yes," Mairwen said, but she wasn't looking at him. She seemed distracted by something in the aisle behind Sojaire.

Andra didn't know how Mairwen felt about the request, but could see that Jerzi wasn't going to give up. She had to admit it wouldn't hurt to have an objective expert opinion to take to O-Poly's administration, if her own suspicions bore fruit. Andra tapped the table with her finger. "I might be able to convince one of the regents to give you full access, if I tell her you're donating your services."

Sojaire spoke up. "I can send you a credentials list and a quick proposal, if that would help."

"It would. Jerzi or Pico has my ping ref." She'd think of something to tell Regent Quan. She knew Vestering and Lavong, the labs manager, would block it if she gave them the chance.

Jerzi leaned back in his chair and stretched his elbows up and wide. She had a wild impulse to run her hands over the broad expanse of well-defined muscle that was his chest. After her last casual relationship ended a year ago, she'd realized she had nothing in common with the O-Poly faculty. With Jerzi, she had a lot in common, but he would be leaving soon. She made herself shift her gaze before he noticed her interest. Her hormones had always had bad timing.

A flash of movement beyond Luka's shoulders caught her eye. At the next table over, an older, red-faced Chinese man was gesticulating angrily at his two dinner companions. She couldn't hear anything but low buzzing because of the sonic wall, but he was obviously shouting. A younger Chinese woman at the table was shrinking away from him, wincing. Andra could only see the back of a long-haired blond man as he partially stood and put his fists on the table and leaned forward to yell at the older man.

Andra took a breath to warn her table companions, but Mairwen was already standing clear of her chair and facing the trouble. A flat, slender stiletto had somehow appeared in her hand.

"Luka," said Mairwen. He was already moving up and away, closer to Jerzi, when the older man stood and knocked over the table so he could launch himself at the blond man.

Andra glanced to her right. Sojaire and Pico were already standing, crowding closer to Valenia and lifting her to her feet. Andra stood at the same time as Jerzi. He was hemmed in by one of the restaurant's irregular walls, so she eased right, closer to Pico, to give him room to maneuver if need be.

The altercation suddenly escalated when she saw a bright blue beamer pulse shoot up into the ceiling. It must have hit one of the sonic wall arrays, because sounds of the Chinese woman screaming assaulted their ears, as well as the alarmed exclamations from the nearby table's occupants when the fighting men rolled and kicked their way, growling insults in Mandarin.

Andra could feel Jerzi practically vibrating beside her. A glance at his face said he was wanting to be in two places at once. She nudged him toward Luka. "Go," she said. "I'll protect Pico." He tossed her a relieved smile as he slid past Luka to stand closer to Mairwen. Andra edged in toward Pico, who was splitting her attention between the altercation and her friends. Valenia was watching the fight with horrified fascination. Sojaire gripped the edge of the table tightly, his gaze downward but not focused on anything. The meltglass table wouldn't protect anyone against a beamer.

Two young restaurant servers stepped up, but they clearly didn't know what to do about the fighting men. Once again, Andra was wishing for her shockstick. It would give the idiots something to think about besides pounding each other. Maybe she needed to start carrying one, at least as long as Jerzi was in town.

"Stop them!" screamed the Chinese woman in heavily accented English. She grabbed the arm of one of the servers and tried to push her forward. "He has beamer—he kill him!"

Both the servers backed up fast. "The police are on their way," said the male server, who looked barely seventeen.

Only because Andra was watching did she see Mairwen execute an exquisitely timed, perfect snap kick that knocked the beamer up and out of the younger man's upraised hand just as he was aiming down while straddling his opponent. Unfortunately, it left the older man free to stab a steak knife into the younger man's shoulder.

The younger man roared in agony and rage as he pulled the knife from his shoulder. He gripped the knife overhead with both hands and arched back, murderous intent on his snarling face. Jerzi intervened and lifted him up, then slammed him into the soft floor. The impact knocked the knife loose and sent it skittering a meter away.

Mairwen was kneeling on the chest of the older man, apparently showing him her deadly knife… knives, because now she had two of them. The second one was pointed toward the Chinese woman, who was now cursing a blue streak in street Mandarin, screaming something about her father.

One of the restaurant bartenders entered the fray and surprised the Chinese woman by pulling her wrists back and tying them with a zip strip. She tried to kick him, but all she managed to do was break a thin-strapped high heel. She fell to her knees, sobbing noisily.

Andra stole a snapshot glance at Pico and Valenia. They seemed fine, so she sidled closer to Luka and spoke quietly. "Tell Mairwen the police here tend to confiscate all weapons and sort them out later." As if she'd heard, Mairwen slid one of her knives into its wrist sheath.

Luka nodded, but his attention was on the blond man. "Let him up, Jerzi. He needs a medic."

Luka's words snapped Sojaire out of whatever had kept him frozen, because he left Valenia's side to approach the bartender. "I'm a licensed first-response medic on Rekoria. Do you have a basic kit?" Most bars did, and this one was no exception. The bartender ordered one of the gawking servers to get it, and sent the other after the beamer before someone decided to pick up a free, untraceable souvenir.

Mairwen caught the bartender's eye. "Zip tie?" He fished one-handed in his front tunic pouch and tossed her one. She caught it deftly and rolled the Chinese man over and had him restrained before he knew what was happening. She made her other knife disappear as she kept the man on his side by the simple expedient of kneeling on him again. Andra made a mental note to never, ever spar with Mairwen.

While Sojaire treated the blond man's stab wound, the restaurant manager moved the rest of the nearby patrons to other newly configured tables, away from the commotion, smoothing things over with free drinks and future vouchers.

The police arrived a few minutes later to efficiently take everybody's statements, and to collect the bloody steak knife and the beamer. Andra was sardonically amused to note that by the time they got around to questioning Pico and Valenia, they were only going through the motions, and missed the fact that Valenia was clearly a filer, with a filer's perfect memory. She'd accurately described Mairwen's knives, but no one else had mentioned them.

When Sojaire was acting as a medic, he'd been calm and competent, making Andra think he might be a few years older than Pico and Valenia, rather than the same age as she'd originally thought. After the excitement had died down and peace had been restored, the restaurant manager thanked them quietly for handling the situation, and told them their meals and drinks were on the house.

"What was the argument about?" asked Pico. "All I got was that the old man was the woman's father."

"The old guy called the blond guy a 'stinking minder,' and something about stealing business secrets," said Jerzi. "The blond guy called the old guy a 'brown dwarf star.'"

Pico looked confused.

"It's an insult," explained Andra. "Sort of like 'failure to launch' in English, but always blaming someone else for it." Andra had a cousin or two that the term described perfectly.

"See, I told you," said Valenia meaningfully to Pico. "Interesting times." She tilted her head back toward Sojaire, who was back to fiddling with his wristcomp and pretending not to notice Pico.

Pico rolled her eyes. "Oh, please. This is a university town. Fights like that happen every night." She took a delicate bite of her on-the-house citrus sorbet.

Jerzi glanced at her in alarm, then looked relieved when he must have realized she was exaggerating.

"Power down, Commander Crush," Andra said quietly. "She's fine. The campus is safe."

Jerzi smiled ruefully and murmured, "Am I that obvious?"

"Only to people who know you." She teased him with a momentary smart-ass smile. "Of course, that's only half the galaxy, because you're such a shy and retiring fellow."

Jerzi tilted his head in acknowledgment. "I like people."

"And they like you, gunnin," she said, acknowledging to herself that she liked him, too, far more than was good for her. She doubted she could keep her heart if she got involved with him, and she couldn't take another loss. For her own peace of mind, he needed to get right back on whatever interstellar transport brought him and not look back.

CHAPTER 9

* Planet: Nila Marbela * GDAT 3241.146 *

NIGHT HAD FALLEN on another day in paradise, and there Andra was, walking with Pico toward the Math building. As soon as she left Pico with Valenia in the childcare center, she'd have a whole hour to herself before seeing Jerzi again. Somewhere, the universe was laughing at her for her late-night decision to keep her distance from the Adams clan.

Since Sojaire had gone to the trouble of sending the proposal after last evening's eventful but excellent dinner, she'd quickly forwarded it to Regent Quan, with a tactful note suggesting that a professional security assessment of the Chemistry building might ease the minds of the sponsors and commercial partners who'd had to be evacuated after the lab accident. She knew the budget was tight, so she'd asked a friend from the military for a favor, and the assessment would be free.

Quan unexpectedly responded within the hour, instead of the couple of days later Andra had guessed it would take. Optimal Polytechnic would be delighted to accept such a generous offer, and had taken the liberty of arranging access first thing the next morning. Andra was to accompany the Foxe Investigations representative for the assessment, even if it meant canceling her classes.

She supposed it could have been worse, if she'd had to drag Vestering along, too. Reading between the tea leaves, as her great-great-aunt used to say, Andra guessed the regents were trying to get in front of the news stories that had finally started trending planet-wide. It was a major miracle the university public relations staff had managed to keep it off the net for four whole days, considering how many people had been affected. The university hated negative publicity and enforced strict message control.

Mairwen looked all business in a nicely tailored navy jacket and pants, and not nearly as dangerous as Andra suspected she could be. Jerzi, in all black, stayed in the background and hardly said a word. Andra felt his presence constantly, like a subtle magnet, but she was surprised how often others barely noticed him. It must be a skill he'd learned in the personal security business.

Andra learned a lot just watching what Mairwen made note of and what she ignored. She was more talkative than she'd been at dinner, but mostly because she was asking questions. Andra tried to answer with as much objectivity as possible, so as not to prejudice the assessment with her own suspicions. She couldn't say the same of Chief Laboratory Manager Lavong, who'd attached himself to their group like a limpet.

She mostly knew him from two-plus years of biweekly faculty meetings. He was probably middle-aged, nearing a hundred, and big and portly, sweaty, and given to bombast. He was an ally and backer of Vestering's unofficial campaign to become a regent. He knew the labs intimately and had a comprehensive knowledge of the facility, equipment, and procedures. He took any criticism of them personally, so when Andra brought up the accidents in a recent faculty meeting, he'd blustered defensively and essentially told her to mind her own business, or she'd be sorry.

During the tour, he'd slid between obsequious, defensive, and truculent, and was transparent in his agenda to convince Mairwen that everything was in perfect order. Jerzi's solid, watchful presence had apparently suppressed Lavong's habit of bullying anyone he perceived as weaker, though Andra would have paid good money and bought a jumbo bag of candied salt nuts for anyone who wanted to watch him try it with Mairwen.

She hadn't realized the new interior lab on the fifth floor made the thirteenth lab in the Chem building, or that the second-floor lab had been repaired so quickly because of outside funds. The university often collaborated with commercial companies for research programs and joint ventures, and the companies sometimes rented the labs for short-term projects. A contract research company had been using the damaged lab for critical experiments and needed the lab restored quickly, so they'd offered the O-Poly a grant to make it happen. Lavong was unhelpfully vague about the nature of the projects, citing nondisclosure agreements, and suggested Mairwen ask the public relations office if it was important. To Andra's admittedly inexpert eyes, the newly replaced lab equipment looked more state-of-the-art than usual. It would be interesting to learn how often the accidents had impacted the commercial companies. Maybe it was a sneaky way to get them to ante up for keeping the labs modernized.

At the end of the assessment, after they left the Chemistry building and walked through the Materials Science building to its airpad, Mairwen invited Andra to the hotel that evening at eight for a preview of her findings. Jerzi had insisted on arranging a pickup time so Andra wouldn't have to depend on public transport, making her regret mentioning that she didn't have transportation of her own. He, of all people, should know better than to treat her like a helpless princess, even if his heart was in the right place.

"Dad said you kicked his ass at the shooting range yesterday," said Pico. She shifted the cross-slung bag off her hip and pulled down the plaid kilt where it had ridden up. Today, she looked like an ancient Scottish guard, complete with white socks, billowy-sleeved blouse, and beret. Pico had the most original taste in clothes of anyone Andra had ever met.

"It was a tie." Andra smiled. "That's my story, and I'm sticking to it."

Pico grinned. "Good. He needs a challenge."

Andra wasn't touching that one, just as she hadn't touched the other hints Pico had been throwing about Jerzi for the last ten minutes, under the guise of idle chatter as she'd helped Andra straighten the classroom before leaving. It was nice that Pico was giving her tacit encouragement to get close to Jerzi, but it was a bad idea. However much she might want to spark with now-single, nova-hot Jerzi, an interstellar-distance relationship was on the top-ten list of things she *didn't* want to have, right under the Cruzdon plague.

"I thought Valenia didn't work at the childcare center every day," said Andra.

Pico made a sour face. "She's not supposed to, but the manager takes advantage of Valenia's love for children. I should have slipped out of class early to meet her."

The very full Practical Applications class often ran late, this time by thirty minutes because they'd been reviewing the POGS Day projects. Andra had brought in a professor from engineering specifically to do the post-mortem on Ms. Dortief's malfunctioning combat robot and Mr. Ravlenko's ambitious attempt at a catalytic resonator for a super-radiant emitter. As Ms. Grien had guessed, the phase gate had failed because Ravlenko was a lopar who couldn't be bothered to check his math. The professor had been surprisingly good with the students, and seemed to enjoy the cross-discipline energy of the class. Andra wondered if he'd be interested in co-teaching and expanding the curriculum if the university added a second section. As an added bonus, the collaboration would twist

Vestering's knickers extra high and tight.

The pathway lighting made it easy to follow the artfully meandering walkway across the floater. Andra was glad she'd had the foresight to wear comfortable shoes and a vest with extra pockets that morning, so she didn't need to carry a bag.

"If you don't mind my asking," Andra said, "did I hear Valenia say you met Sojaire at space camp?" She felt only a twinge of guilt using Sojaire to forestall Pico from further attempts to extol her father's considerable virtues. Andra would bet good money that Pico had more than a passing interest in the young man.

"Yes, he was one of the staff. He was going for his B-level medical certificate at the time, and he was hired as a temporary replacement for the camp's regular medic." She was silent for a long moment. "Then they tried to kill him."

Andra raised her eyebrows. "Sad what some employers will do to get out of paying a contract fee."

Pico smiled lopsidedly. "He found out something he shouldn't have, so the directors tried to space him like it was an accident. I saw him trapped in the sabotaged airlock. I got him out, and they chased us into the station's hydroponics section."

"What did he find?"

Pico re-slung her bag to ride against her other hip. "Dad says you're okay with… that you like minders." Her voice was suddenly quiet as she peered up at Andra warily.

Andra blinked at the sudden shift in topic. "Yes. They're just people." She made a face. "Except the CPS Minder Corps, who are mostly *pendejos arrogantes*." No one in her Forward Intelligence unit could stand them. She'd even had a couple of their Academy-trained students in a class once, and neither she nor they had enjoyed the experience.

Pico snorted. "Probably cousins of the arrogant assholes who work in the CPS testing centers. The space camp directors got a bounty from the CPS Testing Center on Etonver for every minder kid they discovered, so they put us in dangerous situations so we'd be forced to use our talents. A kid nearly died. Sojaire figured out what was going on and was going to report it. When we ran into the hydro section, they came after us with beamers. I was scared and mad, and I didn't want them to hurt Sojaire again. Somehow, I flatlined all the tech within about a hundred meters."

"Impressive." Andra knew that heavy tekes, who could handle big things like chairs or desks, got all the attention, but she'd always thought the microteke ability to work with small and microscopic things would be much more useful.

Pico shrugged one shoulder. "Anyway, the police assumed it was caused by an unlucky shot from a plasma beamer, and I let them. Dad always said it was better not to have the CPS know who you are."

"I agree with him." For all that the CPS offered a safe haven for minders whose very existence scared the ignorant, the agency also had a habit of enhancing minder talents with chems that had harsh side effects. Everyone she knew had a family member or friend who was disabled or died early because of them, though the CPS always found something else to blame it on.

"Anyway, ever since, Valenia thinks Sojaire and I together are catalysts for extraordinary events." Pico frowned and fell silent.

Ordinarily, Andra would have scoffed, but she'd been thinking the same thing about Jerzi and herself, what with lab explosions, rogue robots, and restaurant stabbings. It was statistical nonsense, of course, but it had made her feel better that morning to slip a collapsible, powerful shockstick in a hidden pocket of her vest. Still, if "interesting" things had to happen, she'd rather have Jerzi by her side over anyone on the planet.

The Math building's large round doorway irised open in front of them, and they entered the bright atrium. The acoustics in the atrium made it possible to hear anyone speaking in it, so it was often used for impromptu speeches. It was the newest building on the floater, and she'd heard that the Physics Department was still bitter about losing it to the Math Department, who'd turned out to have deeper-pocket sponsors that year. It had a smaller footprint than either the Chem or Mat Sci buildings, had only three stories, and had short, angled wings instead of curving donut walkways. Whoever had designed the campus had a serious love affair with all things circular. Andra only noticed it again when she saw it through the eyes of others, such as Mairwen and Jerzi on that morning's tour.

Andra had never been to the childcare center, so she assumed the three children sitting in the south hall indicated its presence.

"What the hell?" muttered Pico. She picked up her pace. As they got closer, Andra saw the door under the center's sign was closed and dark.

Pico stopped next to two dark-haired children, a boy and a girl. They were both sitting against the wall, and the boy was hugging his knees, looking down. "Miguel, what are you doing out here?"

The boy, who was maybe eleven, didn't look up. "*Esperando a para nuestros padres. Ya se tardaron.*" Andra could barely hear him. She didn't think Pico understood much Spanish beyond swear words, so she translated. "Waiting for their parents. They're late."

A little redheaded girl sitting on a separate bench piped up. "When the man came, Ms. Val told us to wait out here." Her Old British accent made her sound impossibly cute.

Pico waved her hand over the wallcomp, then knocked on the irised door. "What man, Lyssi? One of the parents?"

Lyssi shook her head back and forth vigorously, her springy curls bouncing. "I don't know."

Andra heard heels tapping behind them and turned to see an overdressed woman in brilliant green and yellow approaching. She looked like an annoyed parrot. "Lyssi, come here, immediately." The little girl's face fell as she stood and brushed her hands off on her loose pants and picked up a small backpack. The woman rounded on Pico. "I know the center closes at six, but you can't just leave children in the hall. Forty minutes isn't that late. I pay good money for a secure facility. I'm reporting you."

"I don't…" began Pico, but the woman interrupted.

"It's too late for excuses." The woman grabbed Lyssi's hand and leaned into Pico to hiss, "I'll have your contract for this. See if I don't!" She held tightly onto the miserable little girl's hand as she hauled her back down the hall.

Pico muttered what Andra assumed was a vile insult in Polish as she activated her wristcomp. "I pinged Valenia at six when I saw class was going to run over, but she didn't answer. I figured she was just busy. The center takes advantage of her."

On a hunch, Andra squatted down next to the boy, Miguel. "*¿Se fue Valenia con el hombre?*"

He nodded, confirming her guess that Valenia had gone with the man.

"*¿Hace cuanto?*" If it was only a few minutes ago, maybe they could catch them.

Miguel looked up at the clock display on the wall. "*Hace treinta minutos.*" Thirty minutes ago was the center's closing time. Maybe the man had been one of the administrators?

Pico was pale and tense as she furiously worked her percomp. "She *never* leaves without telling me who she's with. And she wouldn't go with a stranger in the dark, not even a security guard, if we had any."

Andra gently elicited more details from Miguel. He, his sister, and a number of other kids had been playing as usual when a pale-skinned man came in and talked to Valenia in a language Miguel didn't know. A few minutes before closing time, she'd shooed all the remaining kids out the door and locked it, then went with the man toward the atrium. Miguel thought she didn't want to go with him and that she was scared. The boy was clearly worried, and his sister clung to his hand like he was a life raft.

Maybe Luka Foxe's serial killer case had given her an overactive imagination, but dread was spreading like ice in Andra's stomach. She pulled Pico away from the children and spoke quietly. "I don't like this. If you stay here with the kids and to wait for Valenia, I'll take a quick look around the building."

She reached into her vest pocket for her shockstick and started to take off down the hall, then turned back. "Ping your dad and tell him we're going to be late."

CHAPTER 10

JERZI WATCHED ANDRA with his peripheral vision as they rode the Math building's lift down to the first floor. She was strong and resilient, but no one would come away from what she'd seen without cost.

"Damn it," she said softly. "I really, really wanted to be wrong. As wrong as I was when Da'vin died."

It was the first non-professional words he'd heard from her since he got there. He crossed his arms and crammed his hands under his armpits to keep from pulling her in and holding her tight. Nothing in her body language said she wanted comfort right then.

He'd just arrived at Pico's apartment when he'd gotten Pico's ping about the delay. She'd asked him to stay in case Valenia came home, and he had, until the ping from Andra that Valenia had been hurt, and his daughter needed him. He'd cursed the Tremplin traffic system for the ten minutes it took to get queued and in the air, and the twenty minutes' flying time to the university.

Working his way through a plethora of university security, Tremplin police, and emergency responders, he'd found Pico on the third floor of the Math building, seated in a single chair in the hallway outside an office. He knew her shuttered expression, the one that said she was blaming herself for whatever had happened to Valenia. He'd seen it often enough when she thought she was the reason their family was falling apart.

Pico the child would have thrown herself into his arms, but adult Pico simply took hold of his proffered hand when he dragged another chair out of the open office and sat next to her.

"Professor De Luna tried to talk me out of coming up here, but Val was asking for me."

"What happened?" he asked.

"Val said a man came to the childcare suite, asking questions like he wanted to bring his kid there. He spoke French, but with a Slavic accent, like when I speak French. He made Val nervous. She tried to hit the security panic button, but he stopped her. He said he'd hurt the children unless she went with him. He took her to the north wing lifts and stunned her with something. She passed out. When she awoke, she was in the construction area." Pico pointed down the hall toward the unfinished area. "She recognized it because she'd had to chase down a kid here last week. The area was already bloody when she woke, but it wasn't hers. At least then. He cut her up all over, and told her not to leave until midnight, or he'd come back and kill the kids. Professor De Luna found her."

"Have they already transported Valenia to the medical center?"

Pico nodded. "I need to be there. She'll need someone who knows to leave the lights on."

"Do you want me to take you?" He didn't want her out of his sight, but it wasn't up to him.

She was pale, but her voice was steady. "The inspector said she'd take me. She wants more details from Valenia."

He nodded. "I'll be wherever you need me to be." He squeezed her hand. "I know you won't believe me right now, but this isn't your fault."

"My head believes it," she said quietly. "My heart doesn't. I should have been there. We couldn't have missed him by more than fifteen minutes." Her lips thinned in anger. "It's not fair that it should have happened to Valenia. Not after what she's already been through."

"No, it isn't fair, but she's alive, and she has you looking out for her."

A tall, powerfully built woman in a flexin-armored police vest and arm braces approached them. "Ms. Adams? The inspector is ready to leave, if you are."

Pico stood and slipped her bag over her shoulder. She turned to him. "Could you check if Professor De Luna has a way home?"

"Yes, of course. Ping me with updates."

After Pico had left, he used a technique he'd learned from Luka and politely but persistently kept asking for Andra until he'd found the right person who could take him to the office they'd left her in. Her relaxed body language and neutral expression would have fooled most people, but he knew she was on edge and thoroughly annoyed.

"Are the police being *burros malditos*?" he asked, knowing he was mangling the pronunciation for 'damned asses.' She made Spanish sound expressive and fluid; he sounded like a tourist.

"The police are fine. I've had multiple pings from the regent, the university's PR whip, and Vestering, all variations on 'keep your mouth shut.'"

Jerzi was surprised Andra wasn't telling the callers to launch themselves ass first into the nearest black hole. No gunnin liked political games, Andra least of all, when he'd known her. Academic life must have made her more patient.

He'd offered her a ride home, and she'd accepted without argument, which told him how upset she was underneath her professional façade.

The lift doors opened and let them into the harsh light of the atrium. By tacit agreement, they didn't speak again until after they'd walked to the Materials Science building, retrieved his flitter from the rooftop stacker, and cocooned by the cozy darkness of the flitter, headed toward her apartment building. Only the map display and the flitter's console provided light.

"Pico kept saying 'not again' about Valenia," said Andra.

Jerzi sighed. "I don't know all the details, but when Valenia was eleven, she and her older sister were kidnapped for ransom. They were kept in a pitch-black cellar for days, and molested. The sister said she wouldn't fight it if they left Valenia alone. When the police swooped in, the kidnappers slit both their throats, but Valenia lived. Her body is perfectly healed, but it took a lot longer for her mind."

"Was she a filer by then?"

He kept forgetting how comfortable Andra was talking about minder talents. "Yes, that was part of the problem. One of the family matriarchs didn't trust telepaths or sifters, and her parents had to fight her in court. Once Valenia finally got treatment, it took years to track down all the memory traces that had taken root, and to train her brain not to react to them. She'll probably always be afraid of the dark."

"What is it with warped fucks and kids?" asked Andra. "You'd think, as a species, we'd grow out of it."

His wristcomp signaled a ping, which he answered when he saw it was Mairwen. He hadn't remembered until that moment that Andra was supposed to visit Mairwen that evening for a debrief on the security assessment report.

He routed the audio-only call to the flitter's speakers, then apologized to Mairwen for standing her up and explained why.

"*We know,*" said Mairwen. "*Luka's colleague asked him to consult. He agreed when he heard the name of the victim. We're at the scene now.*"

"That's… surprising," he said. "We must have just missed you."

"Luka wants to know if Andra knows of any other incidents in the building today."

Jerzi looked to Andra, who was frowning with indecision. "Yes," she said finally, "but you didn't hear this from me."

"Agreed."

"There was a fatal accident this afternoon at the loading dock behind the Math building. A body was found in the water near a boat. The Math airpad and the dock are temporarily reserved for construction use only, but some people ignore the signs. Something my boss said makes me think the victim was a rich sponsor for the Chemistry department, and maybe the money came from controversial sources."

During the pause while Mairwen relayed the information, Jerzi asked, "How often do accidents happen?"

"It's rare, as rare as assault. Two incidents on the same day has the university in full spin mode. That's why they were ordering me to keep quiet." She tossed him a wry smile. "Optimal Polytechnic has killer message control."

"Hah," he said.

"Luka says thank you."

Jerzi thought of something. "I don't know if it will help," he told Mairwen, "but Valenia said blood was already there. Tell Luka she's a filer and remembers everything."

"Yes." The call cut off.

"She's not, er, talkative," said Andra.

Jerzi chuckled. "No, she's not good in social settings. I don't think she hates people; she just doesn't know what to do with them."

The flitter console told him they were nearing Andra's apartment building. He could probably fly there blind, as often as he'd been there since arriving in Tremplin.

He set the flitter down. She thanked him and started to get out.

A sudden pang of loss hit him hard. "Are you going to be okay?" He touched her arm, because he couldn't stop himself.

"I'll be fine, Jerzi. I'm just really rotten company right now, and you deserve better." Her face was hidden in shadow, so he couldn't tell what she was thinking. "Go be with your daughter."

She patted his hand twice, then got out of the flitter and walked away without a backward glance.

He input the coordinates for the medical center and focused on things that didn't hurt, like how proud he was of his daughter, and the beautiful city lights reflecting off the water as his flitter rose into the dark.

Chapter II

"You're Mr. Foxe, yes?"

Luka looked up from the large, borrowed police display to see a gold-haired Asian woman standing in the doorway of his tiny borrowed office. Her one-piece, sleeveless Tremplin police uniform was crisp and fresh. Unlike his clothes, which stank from being worn for twenty-three hours and counting. He'd become more conscious of odors since sharing his life with a woman who had extraordinary senses.

"Captain Majeed said to tell you the briefing is starting."

"Thank you." He stood up and stretched, realizing he'd been so immersed in his data hypercube that he'd been sitting in the same position for more than two hours. He'd make it up to his back later. After he got some sleep. After he ate something. After the meeting.

He sent the report, then took the cup half full of cold coffee and dropped it in the recycler in the station's kitchen area. His stomach rebelled when he contemplated getting another cup. He'd lost his tolerance for the acid-wash that police departments the galaxy over called coffee. Kaffa was easier on his stomach, but had less caffeine and was too sweet.

Luckily, District Captain Rana Majeed, his contact on Nila Marbela from his former life as a civilian forensic reconstruction specialist for the military, would be presenting the data in person to the Tremplin Police Magistrate, Commander Farrow, and his assistant. All Luka had to do was stay awake long enough to answer questions. He was unaccustomed to all-nighters, and his eyes felt gritty.

Farrow, a round, bald man in an expensively tailored version of the island-style Tremplin police uniform, grunted when Luka sat, which apparently passed for a greeting. Luka couldn't bring himself to do any better.

Majeed knew how to make her boss listen when she told him a serial killer and a contract killer, who were likely the same, single person, had been plying his or her trade in Tremplin. Two accidental deaths in twenty-four hours that fit the pattern Luka had been pulling together from previous records. She showed Farrow the data commonalities that were too strong for coincidence. As the icing on the cake, Majeed's precinct forecaster-slash-finder had agreed with Luka's hastily assembled profile.

Luka would bet considerable funds that the killer took advantage of the lack of communication between planetary and interstellar police departments. He'd only seen the pattern because his intuition said the killer was highly experienced, so he'd crafted data search routines to dive through crime records throughout the Concordance. One of the privileges that made it worthwhile to keep up his High Court certification in forensic reconstruction.

It was last night's crime scene that had Luka's intuition sparking like a live fusion wire. The injuries on the young woman stirred uneasy ghosts from past crime scenes. It meant delving back into his blood-drenched memories of other reconstructions he'd done for a comparison. His hidden minder talent for being able to reconstruct scenarios in his head without needing forensic test and measurement equipment ensured he remembered each and every detail. But each time he activated that talent, it drained his body heat, to where he felt like he was in a cold box, even when everyone else in the unfinished construction area had been sweating. It was a small price to pay, considering his talent used to be so out of control, and the images in his memory so overwhelmingly horrific, he'd go into catatonic shock. Then he'd met Mairwen, a woman with extraordinary control, who'd helped him find a way to keep his dangerous talents leashed until needed.

His interview with the victim, Valenia Tamheurre, had convinced him the attack was the lucky intersection between whoever had left a trail of mutilated bodies across the Concordance, and the series of "accidents" and "natural deaths" that had befallen interesting people on the same planets. The murders were ritualized, with the environments chosen as carefully as the victims to satisfy the killer's warped, pathological need for death theater. The "accidents" had been harder to trace, but they, too, had repeat elements, and the victims were what Luka had come to think of as key players, such as an ambitious politician, a whistleblower, the president of a monopoly, a crusading journalist, or a blackmailing joyhouse worker.

Tamheurre had been fragile but lucid, and her filer's memory superb, providing more than enough detail to give him cover for what his secret talent had already told him. The man who had attacked Valenia was short and slender, about Mairwen's height, with pale skin and short blond hair, and a mild manner, at least at first. Valenia thought he might be a shielder, a minder who could block his thoughts from any telepath, and lock down and fully contain both telepaths and telekinetics if he wanted. He'd made a comment that his "magic" didn't work on everyone. She'd been terrified that he knew about her filer talent, and that he'd kill her because of it, but he hadn't.

Pico had already arranged for a sifter who specialized in victim trauma to help Valenia through the interview, and a therapy telepath would start working with her first thing in the morning. Luka had always thought of Pico as Jerzi's amiable child until he'd seen her at dinner, and realized she'd grown up. He respected how she'd taken charge of the care for her roommate. Jerzi was the solid, trustworthy friend he'd always been, though quieter than usual. He'd retreated into what Luka thought of as mental sniper mode, probably as a way of handling what had happened.

"This is all fascinating," said Farrow peevishly, dragging Luka back to the present, "but we can't do anything about an accident that technically happened in the water. You'll have to talk to Division Colonel Bittman." Farrow's expression was the picture of regret, but his relaxed body language belied it.

Luka had already encountered the jurisdictional problems in Tremplin. He'd spent most of yesterday with Majeed, looking for "accidents," and they'd come up with a second "misadventure" death of a local pharma representative in Tremplin, on the mainland. Luka had convinced her the death was strikingly similar to at least two other accidents on other planets.

Optimal Polytechnic had its own security force that also didn't play well with others; only the horrific nature of the assault on Pico's roommate had convinced them to let the Tremplin police take over that case, which fell in Majeed's bailiwick. The university was very unhappy that Majeed had banned construction work for three full days, as a precaution to preserve the crime scene. Luka hadn't known about the fatal accident in the water near the loading dock behind the Math building until Jerzi's friend Andra De Luna had been willing to share what O-Poly wouldn't.

The Central Galactic Concordance Command's Water Division had purview over any ocean waters on Nila Marbela. Because the rich sponsor's body had been found in the water, Majeed had needed to spend hours working her unofficial contacts to get the military's investigation results sent to her. Fortunately, water-related "accidents" were a tried-and-true technique of the contract killer, and Luka was able to provide five similar examples with the same unexplained ligature marks, tiny upper-spine burn marks, head injuries, water craft placement, and broad-daylight timing.

Just as Luka had been about to call Sojaire for a flight back to their hotel, the pattern that had been teasing him, driving him crazy in fact, snapped into place. The killer had made Valenia bleed to disguise the fact that the construction area had been used in an earlier crime, the "accidental" death of the man with high placement in a notorious theft crew family. Whether it was arrogance or expedience, it was the first mistake by the killer that Luka could find in the three years of data he'd pulled together.

Majeed cleared her throat and displayed the document she'd spent half the night getting. "We spoke to Colonel Bittman an hour ago, sir, and we have her full cooperation. She's assigned an inspector."

Luka hid a smile at Farrow's startled frown. He was, according to Majeed, a champion at avoiding responsibility, and Majeed had just made it impossible for him to use jurisdictional squabbling as an excuse. Bittman brought her own set of problems, in that she was bucking for promotion to High Command on Concordance Prime, and based everything she did on whether or not it would look good on her record, but Luka had convinced Majeed they needed the resources of the military to help close in on possible suspects. The military could immediately access all interstellar travel records, including in-system space stations and spaceports, which would be key to finding their killer.

If the pattern he'd been reconstructing held true, the killer had arrived in Tremplin no more than three days ago, and the "accident" victims would turn out to be connected in some way, such as a hidden alliance or a business dispute. In the secret part of his pattern, the part he'd never committed to any record and had only whispered to Mairwen, the multiple "accidents" often turned out to benefit the interests of the Citizen Protection Service. Mairwen had escaped from a dark program of theirs, and Luka had made it his business in the last four years to very quietly study the CPS, in case they ever discovered she was alive. He knew they had covert units that believed themselves exempt from planetary law. Only the CGC military had the resources to go up against the CPS, if it became necessary.

Farrow made a few more token objections, but Majeed had outmaneuvered him and he knew it. He ended the meeting when his assistant reminded him of his next appointment.

Luka followed Majeed to her office. "Just before the briefing, I sent you some search parameters for finding our target." A yawn ambushed him.

"Get out of here, Foxe," Majeed said with amusement. "You're no good to me flatlined."

"Yes, sir," he said, smiling as he sketched a casual salute. "You're wasted as a district captain. You could run the whole agency if you wanted."

Majeed laughed and shook her head. "Not for all the trust funds on the planet. I like my quiet little fiefdom here in paradise, where I get to go home at night." She yawned. "Well, most nights. I'll be on your heels out the door, as soon as I send your data to the analysts. I'll ping you if something flares."

Luka could have asked for transport to his hotel, but he'd asked for enough favors for one day, so he pinged Sojaire instead with a quick message.

He half dozed in the tiny borrowed office until his percomp pinged. When he went up to the airpad to watch their rented flitter touch down, he was surprised to see Mairwen piloting. He couldn't help but smile at her as he got in. He didn't think he'd ever get over the pleasure of seeing her again when they'd been apart, even when it was only hours. It had been astounding luck that brought them together and kept them alive long enough to enjoy it.

"Sojaire?" he asked, as he strapped himself in.

"Studying." The traffic system and the flitter took over flying, but she kept her hands on the controls. The love of his life considered most technology to be unreliable. "How is your case?"

"Sparking. Majeed is good. We might have a list of candidates by the end of the day."

"And if the target is in *school*?" It was their code for people who worked for the CPS.

"Then we'll transit out." He was too exhausted to be more tactful about it.

She was silent for a long moment. "I'm happy that you love me, but you can't protect me from the universe."

"I know." It was what kept him up some nights, especially when they were apart. "But sacrificing you won't stop the *students* or their *teachers*."

She let go of the flitter controls and reached to take his hand in hers. "We humans deserve justice. We need it." She caressed his hand with her thumb. "Use your brilliant mind and think of a way to get it."

CHAPTER 12

SOME DAYS, THE ghosts tried his patience like dull needles in his joints, but today, Taliferros Radomir could ignore them. He'd replenished his strength yesterday with just a taste from a mid-level energy source, and it had worked better than he'd imagined.

There were no energy sources in the hotel bar, only ghosts. They were worthless, except perhaps the skinny, barefoot, dark-skinned male in navy hunched over his percomp, because no one else in the bar gave him a second glance. Taliferros, safe in the shadowed corner booth, experimentally curved his shoulders as hung his head and angled his pelvis to round his back. It was an art form, hiding in plain sight among the talentless ghosts, one he practiced daily. When he revealed his true glory, they tended to react badly, or at least remember him. He often wished for a twister or a cleaner talent, able to change or erase the memories of the inconvenient ghosts who'd noticed him. It was, however, gratifying to use his high-level shielder talent to block holier-than-thou minders—energy sources—and make their bodies betray them, so he would gratefully accept what the exacting gods of his father had given him.

It was time. Taliferros had rigorously trained himself to track seconds, minutes, and hours, but he'd cultivated a habit of checking a clock, because that's what the ghosts did. He carried his empty glass to the recycler, under the guise of being courteous, but it was also good practice not to leave biometric traces around. He regularly had his fingerprints altered, but good habits stood the test of time.

He smiled at the vacation-clothed female ghost with two children and held the lift door for her. The older child eyed him distrustfully, crowding into a corner to get as far away as possible. It embarrassed the female ghost, and she gave him an apologetic smile. He shrugged, as was expected of him. The mother ghost was a null, or close enough, and the toddler was too young to tell, but he suspected the older child, a girl, was a budding energy source, and had brushed up against the black hole of his powerful shield. Perhaps it would teach the stupid child not to poke her talent where it didn't belong.

Taliferros collected his small bag from his room and presented himself in the executive suite Dixon Davidro had designated as his office. Dixon's things were untidily spread out everywhere, as usual. Renner, standing in the corner, crossed his arms and glared.

Dixon looked up from the display he'd been reading and waved him toward a chair, then noticed his bag. "Oh, didn't Lamis tell you, Mr. Radomir? We're staying for a few more days." He smiled and tilted his head toward the wide expanse of view windows that overlooked one of the harbors. "We've been ordered to cool our jets in this fine city while we wait for our special project to arrive." That explained Dixon's choice of eye-wateringly bright orange short pants and net shirt, and the waxy look of new body art on his arms.

Taliferros carefully set his bag on the floor to cover his sick feeling of claustrophobia. "Then I'm afraid we might have a problem, sir." At Dixon's puzzled look, Taliferros continued. "You asked for speedy action. An independent investigation firm has made the connection between the two deaths, and has convinced the multiple local law enforcement agencies to work together. If we were leaving as planned, they wouldn't have time to organize, but if we stay…" He trailed off and let Dixon imagine the rest.

"How do you know all this?" Dixon's tone was skeptical, bordering on suspicious. His face, however, was wooden. He was probably still recovering from the morning trip to the body shop, judging from the new pink-to-black hair and deep cherry-red mustache.

Taliferros considered rolling his eyes to show exasperation, but went with clasping his hands behind his back, to display confidence and pride. "You contracted with me because I'm a professional, sir. It's my job to know who's tracking m… us."

Dixon didn't need to know that Taliferros had become aware of Foxe Investigations two planets ago. Before he'd been unlucky enough to be caught by the Citizen Protection Service and assigned to Dixon, Taliferros had spent fifteen years developing a finely honed awareness of when he was being hunted. Unfortunately, yesterday's "boat accident" victim had awakened from being stunned earlier than planned. He'd cut himself trying to escape and bled all over the dusty floor. In hindsight, it had been unwise to improvise by capturing a sacrificial lamb to disguise his staging area, but he'd relied on Dixon moving his entourage when he said he would. Even if the dimwitted police eventually figured out there were two blood types there, by then, he would have been long gone, as usual. Besides, the girl wasn't his type, and the life-force play had been enlightening, so neither Dixon nor Renner would ever know about her. She'd awakened early, too, though, so perhaps his homemade stunner needed repair.

"Hmm," said Dixon, looking thoughtful, or perhaps bilious. It was hard to tell. "What do you recommend?"

He paused, as if he hadn't led Dixon to ask that exact question. "Hire a local specialist to keep the investigators busy. They are the fulcrum."

Dixon was silent a long moment, and Taliferros disciplined himself to stay perfectly relaxed, as if he didn't care. "Very well, but no more deaths." Dixon emphasized the last three words and gave Taliferros a steely look. "They're not common enough in Tremplin, or on the planet in general, to go unremarked. No more newstrends. If you're feeling constricted, we will make suitable arrangements for a reward outing at our next stop."

"Thank you, sir." Taliferros displayed a slight tinge of boredom. "Shall I make the arrangements, or would you like Mr. Renner to do it?" It was a gamble, suggesting an alternative, but Dixon wasn't usually interested in details. Taliferros planned to take care of Foxe Investigations one way or the other, but it would be a bonus if the CPS paid for it.

They were interrupted by the entrance of Georgie, Dixon's idiot-savant forecaster, who skipped in and plopped himself bonelessly at Dixon's feet. Dixon absently petted the 60-year-old man's shock of dark orange hair as if he were a spaniel. The suite door opened again to reveal a thoroughly irritated Lamis bel Doro, Dixon's official CPS assistant, a filer with a perfect memory and the intelligence of a curtain weight. Taliferros would have drained her long ago, except for Dixon's multiple ways to exact painful, protracted retribution.

"I don't want to take a shower," announced Georgie. "It's wet."

Lamis put her hands on her wide hips and declared hotly, "I am not a farkin' nursemaid, I'm a class delta-four administrator. He stinks. Either he gets clean, or I transit out."

Georgie whimpered dramatically and latched onto Dixon's hairless, pattern-etched leg. Dixon winced, probably because the new body art was still tender.

Replay one thousand and one of the Lamis-and-Georgie show. Taliferros almost felt a pang of sympathy for Renner, who had to listen to them day in and day out. He glanced at him, only to be caught by Renner's pointed glare that said he suspected Taliferros was lying about something. Taiferros's stringent, pious parents had burned the fear out of him, but he could feel unease, and disliked pain. All of Dixon's contractors, or his "pets," as he liked to call them, subverted his will, but Renner was rarely caught at it, and would gladly throw Taliferros out the next airlock if he had the chance.

Taliferros comforted himself with the certainty that neither Dixon nor Renner had any idea he'd discovered a new way to siphon life force when *he* needed it, not when Dixon chose to provide it with what he called "reward outings." The ignorant CPS thought of Taliferros as a garden-variety serial killer, when he was so much more. His new technique was akin to snacking instead of eating a full meal, but as long as the victim lived, there would be few newstrends, and fewer opportunities to get caught.

If only he could find as satisfactory a solution for the control-drug problem, and the Renner problem.

He had to give Dixon credit for maintaining perfect security on the drug cocktail that bound Taliferros to the CPS. His present condition, of needing the drugs more often, was the result of a lapse in judgment on his part. He'd been starving and had mistakenly assumed softhearted Neirra, Dixon's pet healer, would be defenseless once he'd used his shielder talent to contain her talents. He'd learned two valuable lessons. One, that a top-level talent could break free of his shield, when sufficiently motivated by pain and rage; and two, that some healers were vicious, vindictive snakes who could destroy his health as easily as improve it. For some mysterious reason, she'd told Renner about the attack, but not Dixon, and equally mysteriously, Renner hadn't told Dixon, either. Taliferros had been very glad to see the last of the unpredictable Neirra when Dixon had let her retire. But it did give him hope that another healer could completely cure his debilitating addiction, assuming he could find one he could trust.

The Renner problem continued to vex. He was dangerous in more ways than one; the most important being that he was completely immune to shielders or telepaths. The gods of his father knew how hard Taliferros had tried to contain Renner, to the point of nearly blowing out his eardrums. His secret life-force talent was no more effective; it was like trying to drink from a plasma charge.

Another reluctant Dixon contractor, a sifter with the ability to detect any talent, had said Renner was a "unique," meaning he fit into no known category cataloged by the Citizen Protection Service Testing Centers. Taliferros had been extremely careful to maintain full shields around the sifter at all times, lest his own unique talent be exposed and reported to Dixon for exploitation. Renner could easily be killed by any number of "accidents," but it would have to be absolutely perfect, and a method he'd never used before, or Dixon would have Taliferros killed immediately and with extreme prejudice. The method also couldn't damage or kill Dixon, or Taliferros would die from drug withdrawal within three days.

"Pinging Mr. Radomir."

Taliferros wrenched his attention back to the hotel room and Dixon's sing-song, sarcastic comment. Taliferros displayed sheepish remorse. "I'm sorry, I didn't mean to be rude."

Georgie was now practically in Dixon's lap, and Lamis was stalking out the door.

"I said, go hire a specialist to take care of your problem." He sighed. "It looks like I'm going to be occupied for a while."

"Yes, sir," said Taliferros. He picked up his bag and headed back to his room. Both Foxe principals were troublesome, but going after both at once would be too splashy. He'd just have to tell the hired help to choose whichever was the more vulnerable.

In the interim, he planned to select a series of body shops to change his hair, eyes, and skin color again. Perhaps a hint of burn scars on his neck and face, because they made people flinch and look away. Good habits always stood the test of time.

CHAPTER 13

"WELL, WHAT DO you think?" Pico twirled before Valenia, who was seated in the grav chair they'd used to bring her back from physical therapy. Valenia wore an elegant, loose-weave, drapey tunic and pants that hid the faintly visible scars from her assailant's wire-form cutter. She'd refused to be seen in standard patient gowns, so Pico had brought her a selection of clothes from home.

"It's very, er, white, and, uhm, full." Valenia shook her head. "I give up. What are you supposed to be?"

Pico pretended to frown. "Considering your family business, you are shockingly ignorant of costume history." She pointed to the design on the front of her apron. "I'm Florence Nightingale." She pulled out the full skirts and curtsied, which was harder than it looked when wearing a corset. She was glad she hadn't bothered to make the bird-like hat that went with it, because it would have never stayed on her head.

"Who? And why did she wear a red plus sign? Did she invent math or something?"

Pico grinned. Valenia played the bunny-head better than anyone she knew. She had a sharp mind for business and wanted to build hotels, hence her study focus on the hospitality industry. "She was a rehab medic."

"She was a nurse, actually. The patient-care kind, not the breastfeeding kind."

Pico jumped at the sound of Sojaire Celeyron's voice, then kicked herself inside for showing any reaction at all. Damn him. She summoned a smile and turned casually. "Hey. We almost gave up on you."

He shrugged a shoulder. "I fell asleep studying, and woke up late. I've got another medic cert test in a few weeks. Sorry."

He probably really was sorry. He wasn't selfish, just supremely oblivious of people's feelings. Or maybe just hers. "Forgiven."

"Guess who pinged me while I was in with the physical terrorists," said Valenia.

"Chadd Sovereign," Pico replied promptly. "He wants you to be the mother of lucky child number eleven, as soon as he's done with this season of *First Pirates of Andromeda*."

"The therapists aren't supposed to hurt you," said Sojaire. "Didn't they bring in a healer?"

Valenia waved a hand. "Of course they did, I just detest boring exercise. I wouldn't have that man's baby if my life depended on it. He's too hairy."

Out of the corner of her eye, she saw Sojaire relax, though she could tell he was still professionally evaluating Valenia's condition.

"Dorf. That's what your uncle's body shops are for." She crossed her arms. "I give. Who pinged?"

"The director of the childcare center. After some butt-covering legalese about 'get better soon, but we're not liable,' he asked if I knew anyone else who could fill my volunteer slot until they can get someone else in." Valenia looked straight at Pico. "I said I'd ask around."

Pico held up her hands to ward off the request. "Can't, I have class." She quirked a smile at her friend. "Besides, Lyssi's mother said she'd 'have my contract terminated,' remember?"

"You don't have class tomorrow afternoon, and it'd just be from two to six. Those kids need some consistency in their lives right now. Lyssi especially. Miguel and Celia, too."

Only Valenia would be in a critical trauma rehab center and worrying about someone else's kids. No wonder they loved her. "What's the matter with what's-her-name, the *paid* employee, Meow-meow, or whatever? The kids know her a hell of a lot better than me."

"Méimuī," said Valenia. "She termed her contract. She used what happened to me to get out without taking a penalty. She claimed the center has insufficient security."

"And that's why Pico should say no," said Sojaire firmly. "It's not safe."

Pico turned toward the bed and clenched her jaw to keep herself from telling Sojaire to space himself without an exosuit. Who asked him to come seven transit days from Etonver and treat her like a frelling space camper? She took a deep breath and let it out slowly, counting her heartbeats as she did, and unclenched her fists.

"Sojaire?" said Valenia sweetly. "I mean this in the nicest possible way, but go sit on a flux engine and spin."

Pico would love Valenia forever for that. She looked over her shoulder to steal a glance at Sojaire's face, expecting him to look confused, or condescending. Instead, he looked apologetic. "I'm sorry, Pico. I didn't mean to be rude."

Pico turned to gape at him for a second, then closed her mouth. "Who are you, kind stranger, and what have you done with Sojaire? About your height, same thick blond hair and blue eyes? Fibonacci design on his chest? Triple-pierced left ear?"

Sojaire half-smiled. "I'm the illegal clone from a secret First Wave lab."

"I loved that show," said Valenia wistfully. "My sisters and I held a little memorial service when it ended."

Pico grabbed the control for Valenia's chair. "We're making a break for it. Wanna come?" She half hoped he'd turn her down. He was the most dangerous to her sanity when he was engaging with her.

"Yes. Am I underdressed?" He looked down at his loose-wrapped blue shirt and casual green kilt-shorts combo that revealed more of his well-shaped legs than usual. He wiggled his toes in his snug blue sandals.

"You're always underdressed," said Valenia, "but we like you anyway." She pointed toward the door. "Go be the lookout."

He walked out the door casually, as if sightseeing, then nodded to them. "Clear." The gleam in his eye said that for once, he was enjoying breaking the rules.

Pico gave Valenia the chair's control unit and told her to turn left in the hall. During Valenia's therapy sessions, Pico had scouted the medical center, partly out of boredom, and partly out of habit instilled by her dad, who'd trained her to always know more than one way out of a building. "Left at the intersection," she said, "then take a right at the hallway."

She purposely took them through the less-traveled hallways, so as not to be caught by someone who'd ruin their fun. Valenia's grav chair was silent, and the cushioned floors absorbed the sounds of her and Sojaire's footsteps. The happy look on Val's face when she saw the indoor garden, complete with holos of birds and butterflies, made it totally worth the effort.

"If *mademoiselle* will deign to ground *la chaise*…" intoned Pico in a French accent that made Valenia wince. She turned to root around under a large hydroponic stand for the bag and container she'd hidden there earlier. A poke in her tender underarm made her vow never to wear a full corset again, not even to distract her best friend. Not to mention, wearing a long skirt and petticoat in the overly humid room was making her thighs sweat. "Voila!"

Valenia was appropriately impressed when Pico served her a bowl and handed her a spoon. "Where did you get honest-to-stars real pomegranate ice cream in Tremplin?" At least, that's what it sounded like, since her mouth was full of bright red, icy goodness.

"Chef's secret," Pico replied, as she handed the other bowl and spoon to Sojaire. Dairy-based food products were hard to come by in a city where the nearest milk-producing animal was on another continent.

"What about you?" Sojaire asked. He pointed to the empty bag.

"Bowls and spoons," she said, dipping two fingers into the carton and scooping out a big glop, "are for lightweights."

Thirty minutes later, Pico helped arrange the blanket over Valenia's hips, so she could grab it more easily if she got cold later. The trip to the garden had worn her out. Modern medics and healers could work miracles, but their procedures were hard on the patient's stamina for a few days.

"I'll do the kid-minding for you. Just this once."

"Thank you." Tears welled and escaped from Valenia's eyes, but they both ignored it. "They need your strength."

Pico adjusted the color range of the all-weather light she'd brought in and stuck to the wall above Valenia's bed. Blue was still plenty of light, but didn't interfere with sleep patterns. Sojaire stood near the foot of the bed, next to the cot Pico had made the hospital bring in for her. His expression said he was in professional medic mode again.

Valenia touched Pico's hand. "Hey. Don't let Mairwen Morganthur near the children. She'll scare them."

"She's not scary," said Pico. A little odd, yes, but she suspected Mairwen was a hell of a lot less of an emotional train wreck than Pico was right then.

"She has knives," said Valenia groggily.

"They're letter openers," said Sojaire, confusing Pico, until she realized he was trying to ease Valenia's worries.

Valenia snorted. "She has three of them. I saw a sheath on her back, too."

Pico smiled impishly. "Maybe she gets a lot of letters. Need anything else?"

Valenia rolled onto her side and closed her eyes. "I'm fine. Better show Sojaire how to get out, or he'll get lost and we'll never see him again."

"Hey," protested Sojaire. Valenia smiled.

"I'll be back soon." Pico caught Sojaire's eye and tilted her head toward the door.

On their way out, she checked the wallcomp to make sure the must-read notice about leaving the light on was still active. She'd already spoken to the staff about it, but it never hurt to be sure.

Sojaire stood in the hall and waited for her to pick the direction. Valenia had been right to worry about him. He was a fine medic, but the boy could get lost in a three-room apartment. *Man*, she amended. A sexy, mercurial, funny, infuriating man who would likely shred her heart again and not even notice. Still, she appreciated that he'd come to see Valenia, who needed understanding friends right then.

"Thanks for not treating Val like a victim," Pico said. "The medics here mean well, but…"

Sojaire shrugged a shoulder. "I know. How is she, really?"

"Good, considering. In a way, I think she's less traumatized than the therapist who had to hear all the details." She tapped her temple to indicate the telepath who'd done the initial evaluation. "Val had to live through the aftermath alone last time. This time, she'll get the help she needs immediately."

"How soon does her family get here?"

Pico pointed left, toward the wide bank of lifts. "Her parents will be here tomorrow, late. I think others are en route." She hoped to hell that Valenia's bigoted, sententious great-grandmother wasn't one of them. Pico stabbed at the wallcomp to tell the lift their destination. If that poisonous *suka* tried to meddle again, maybe Mairwen could be persuaded to go with Pico on a late-night visit and bring all her knives.

The lift doors opened, and she and Sojaire stepped inside. The doors closed quietly and the lift began to rise.

Sojaire was gazing at his feet. "I don't think I ever got a chance to say it, but sorry about your mother leaving."

"Thanks. It totally tanked." She was glad that with him, she didn't have to pretend that it had been anything other than awful. At least her mom had just abandoned her, instead of desperately trying to control her life by sabotaging her career. "Sorry about what your father did. Have you had to file any more injunctions since I left?"

Sojaire shook his head. "No, the weeks of top-trend bad publicity for his lies took care of that. It all but tanked his 'gentleman jack' image. If he wasn't the team's high-scoring star player, they'd have termed him. As it was, their lawyer threatened to sell his contract to a frontier league if he ever said another word about me, ever, public or private." He shoved his hands in his pockets, then tilted his head up to look at her. "But if I hadn't lost that internship, I wouldn't have asked Luka for a job, and I wouldn't be here."

It was the "here" part that was eroding her defenses. That, and his treating her like someone he cared about. She wished she'd worn her homemade mech-suit chest plate, to protect her heart. "You still like it, then?"

He nodded. "Yeah, I do. Luka and Mairwen are great." He smiled almost sheepishly. "Not at all what I'd expected to be doing with my medical certificate."

"Do they know about your, uhm, gift, or do they think you're just a medic?" His healer talent had helped save both their lives in the space camp escape. She hadn't understood why he'd kept it hidden until her own mother had taught her what most of the galaxy thought of minders. They'd made a solemn pact after that to keep each other's secrets.

"They know. That's why Luka hired me. Mairwen doesn't like medics, and won't step foot in a medical center. She trusts me because he does." His voice held a touch of satisfaction, or perhaps gratefulness. No surprise there. His hateful, vengeful father would have used the knowledge to get his son's license yanked, like he'd tried to before by paying a family to claim his son's malpractice had killed their grandmother. Sojaire was no more suited to being a professional pelotón player than she was to being a two-meter-tall, mech-suited Jumper.

She didn't know how to handle Sojaire right then. He'd been less guarded and more open in the last hour than he'd been since, well, ever. She loved the light banter, but had always dreamed of more, and never gotten it until now. She drew a deep breath and let it out slowly, and told herself it didn't mean anything. She distracted herself by calculating the T'Schuh anti-diagonal hypercubic progression in her head. She always knew what to expect from numbers.

The lift vibrated a little as it went from going up to going sideways. Tremplin's main medical center was big enough to need a capsule system to get people around.

Sojaire cleared his throat. "How's your dad coping? I don't get to talk to him very often. I know he got promoted recently."

Pico sighed inside. She couldn't fault him for ignoring her this time.

"Good, I think. Took him a while." She let out an audible sigh. "I had to have the talk with him about sex."

Sojaire quirked a smile. "You mean, that you know he's having it?"

"No, that he's *not* having it." She smoothed the front of her apron. "He needs affection."

"Still in love with you mother?"

"No, she killed that dead. He just thinks he tanks at relationships." She smiled a little. "Might be hope for him yet, though, with Professor De Luna." He'd changed his shirt three times before the fancy dinner the other night, and worn his nicest jewelry.

"She seemed nice." He frowned. "But what does she think about, uh, secrets?"

Pico closed her eyes a moment. Did he really think she was that careless with her dad's happiness? "She says she doesn't care, and I believe her. She knows about dad and me, and it hasn't changed how she treats either of us." The lift paused, then started up again. "I asked Mairwen what older women like in a man, so I could give my dad some hints about Professor De Luna."

Sojaire laughed. "And what did she say?"

"That she'd have to think about it." She remembered the serious look on Mairwen's face. "I don't think she was putting me off. I think she's really thinking about it."

The lift doors opened, and they stepped out onto the rooftop airpad. Fortunately, the stacker kiosk was only a few steps away, so he couldn't get lost finding it. She watched while he entered the code and paid the fee. The stacker slots began rotating like a giant articulated chain. Newer stackers had robot arms and adjustable slots.

A gentle breeze animated his side-parted long hair and pressed his shirt tight against his sleek chest, which had filled out with muscular definition since last she'd seen him. He was shorter than average, but the perfect height for her. She stepped backward toward the lift. She'd always felt a visceral attraction to him, like a pulsar in her throat and chest, and tonight was no different. Actually, it was worse, because he'd been so companionable. *Absolute zero, hard vacuum, null chance*, she told her hopeful hormones. She turned to the lift tube's wallcomp and entered Valenia's room coordinates. Luckily, the capsule was still there, and the lift doors opened.

"Pico, wait. Would you have dinner with me tomorrow evening?" His words were rushed.

She turned, smoothing her expression as she did so. She eyed him cautiously, but saw only sincerity on his face. It was the invitation she'd been fantasizing about for three years, where they'd acknowledge their special connection and talk about the future.

Then she remembered two nights ago, at Dominar Carlotta's, where he'd said all of ten words to her and spent the rest of the dinner glued to his percomp. Tonight's illegal clone version of Sojaire had made her hope, but just like in the show, the clone would get kidnapped by the evil jack crew, sold to the sex slavers on the frontier planet, rescued by the dashing pirate-clan captain who loved him, and betrayed to the secret lab researcher who wanted him back for more evil experiments. Which would leave her with the baseline Sojaire, the one who either forgot she was in the room or treated her like a child.

"Sorry, but I'll be worthless after kid wrangling." She smiled and shrugged, to show she didn't care. "Another time, perhaps." Like, say, in her next lifetime, the one where she couldn't be hurt by him again.

He shrugged a shoulder. "Yeah, sure. Another time." He turned away to watch the stacker deliver his small rental flitter.

She decided it was her stupid, ever-hopeful heart that made her imagine the look of loss on his face. She stepped into the lift and didn't turn around until the capsule was past the first drop.

Since looking back hurt too much, she decided to look forward. She'd be glad to recycle her beautiful but uncomfortable Florence Nightingale costume when she went home tomorrow morning. She thought the kids would like her favorite pirate clan outfit. Luckily, she had a rich roommate with a home autotailor and enough spin thread to travel to the six moons and back. Otherwise, she'd have to make them all by hand, which would seriously cut into her time for making more rockets like the one she'd be launching the day after tomorrow. Now *that* was going to be stellar.

Chapter 14

* Planet: Nila Marbela * GDAT 3241.148 *

"DON'T MAKE ME pull rank on you, gunnin," Andra said, giving Jerzi a mock glare. "My invitation, my restaurant choice, my treat."

Jerzi glared right back. "No go, Lightning. You pay yours, I'll pay mine." The corners of his mouth started to drift upward. "And when Mairwen gets here, we'll tell her she's buying because she's late."

Andra laughed. "*You* can tell her that. Me, I like breathing too much."

Jerzi chuckled as they each used their percomps to transmit cashflow account information in the table's terminal. "Nah, she'd just become selectively deaf."

At two thirty in the afternoon, the quiet Blue Clouds in Sky restaurant, away from the student and tourist haunts, was almost deserted, which is why Andra had chosen it. That, and the multi-ethnic cuisine that was both good and reasonably priced. Jerzi and Mairwen deserved better than the questionable choices near the university. Students would eat anything, and tourists would pay anything.

Jerzi had recommended they order their meals, rather than wait, as there was a good chance Mairwen wouldn't have anything except water.

"Eats like the proverbial bird, does she?" She poured them both some fruit-infused water from the iced pitcher on the table.

"Most of the time," he agreed. "But every once in a while, I've seen her pack it away like a Jumper after a battle." There was a good reason why tourist buffets in Tremplin often made visiting active-duty Jumpers, the elite shock force of the Citizen Protection Service, pay double.

As this was her only day off, she decided to treat herself to her favorite spread of appetizers, rather than a meal. She'd known them as *tapas* growing up, but her well-traveled family had happily pilfered from a variety of other ethnic cuisines, so Blue Clouds' eclectic menu was comfort food. Jerzi ordered a salad with strips of pickled sweetfish and a rice-wine dressing. He said he'd had a big breakfast before his morning workout and short run. He looked relaxed in his grey cargo shorts and loose-weave red shirt.

Andra had lasted a whole day before giving in to fate regarding further entanglement with the Adams clan. She wanted the briefing from Mairwen on the security assessment, and it felt wrong excluding Jerzi. Besides, she felt bad about the awkward way they'd parted the other night. She'd been mad at all of humanity at the time, and his solicitousness had made her feel vulnerable She'd had to walk away to stop herself from asking him for comfort. It would have led to sex, probably hot sex, and then he'd leave the planet with a part of her heart.

"How is Valenia?" she asked. "For that matter, how is Pico holding up?"

"Valenia's wounds are healed. She'll need body shop work to remove all traces, but the cuts were more painful and bloody than anything else." He selected a small, dark roll from the breadbasket, then dipped it in the garlic-infused olive oil. "She's getting top-level mind therapy, because she can afford it, and because Pico made it happen. She thinks she ought to have been there to protect Val, so being her unofficial patient advocate lets her feel like she's making up for it. She even agreed to take Val's childcare center shift this afternoon."

"That's true dedication. Can't say I'm impressed by the center's management, though. From what Pico has said, they rely far too much on volunteer labor."

Jerzi nodded. "She's only taking the one afternoon shift so Val will stop worrying about the kids. After that, the center is on its own."

They were interrupted by simultaneous pings on their percomps. The message was the same to both of them, from Mairwen, who was stuck in a traffic holding pattern because part of the Tremplin traffic system was malfunctioning. She would ping again to set up a new meeting time once she was free.

The decision to stay or leave was made moot by the arrival of their food. In between bites of *pincho moruno*, spicy beef on a stick, Andra decided to tell Jerzi what she'd been up to. She had no one else she'd rather talk to about her unofficial investigation into the sabotage—or not—of the Chem building's labs.

"When I got home after we found Valenia, I was too keyed up to sleep, and something Luka said the other night at dinner about murders made to look like accidents got me curious. That man who died in the accident behind the Math building that I was ordered to keep quiet about? His family has enough historical newstrends to fill a hypercube with allegations of shady business, mostly theft crews and blackmarket cloning of licensed pharma drugs."

She pushed a small dish of spicy sausage slices toward him. "You'll like these. Hot as the fires of stellar creation, but good."

He smiled and speared one with his fork. "Thought I'd have to distract you to steal one."

"Yeah? Good luck with that." She brandished her fork in her left hand as she popped a stuffed olive in her mouth with her right. "Anyway, I got to wondering if Optimal Polytechnic gets funding from pharmas. They do, and lots of it, but it's all grants and gifts to the Human Medicine department. It's the university's second biggest department, outside of Marine Science. Human Med has an entire building of organic labs, part of the mainland campus and two islands, and a dedicated skyskimmer. We—Physical Chemistry and Materials Science—get a small, crowded floater and public transport tokens."

"How un-inclusive of the pharmas. Is the local blackmarketer family more civic-minded?"

She shook her head. "Not that you'd notice, at least not officially."

He put one of his sweetfish strips on one of her empty small plates. "Trade you for a *sarma*." He pointed to one of the bulgur-and-walnut stuffed grape leaf rolls. She pushed the dish toward him.

She speared the sweetfish strip. "During her assessment, Mairwen asked about funding. Lavong implied that lab funding and purchasing are handled by O-Poly administration, and he has little control. That's not what he says during staff meetings, though, so yesterday morning before class, I stopped in at some of the labs to ask the supervisors and monitors about it. They say he knows the budget exactly and makes them report expenses down to the fourth decimal." She ate the pickled sweetfish and stabbed a marinated mushroom. "Both could be true, of course, just spins for different audiences. Romila's good at finding out that sort of thing, because she's a low-level finder, but I don't want to involve her if it might get her hurt."

He nodded. "I don't know her at all, but I don't think she's very, uhm, stealthy."

Andra laughed out loud. "Nope, not subtle at all." She saw he'd polished off the spicy sausages while she was talking, so she started in on the cubed lamb in persimmon sauce, before he got to that, too. She'd always liked that he had an adventurous palate.

"So this morning, I read a tiny trend about this local pharma rep who died by 'misadventure,' whatever the hell that means, the night before the blackmarketer had his accident behind the Math building. Care to guess which pharma company's sales have been cratering lately because of a flood of clones?"

"*Two* accidents?" The sarcasm in those two words could have cut a steak.

"Exactly. That's what I hoped to talk to Mairwen about."

He swallowed the last of his water. "Uncovering patterns like that is more in Luka's star lane, I think." He held up the water pitcher. She shook her head and selected another olive. They were too salty today, but still good.

She suddenly felt guilty for talking business while he was trying to enjoy a meal. "So, have you done any of the touristy things? Dive the Great Reef? See the galaxy-famous Offering of the Naked Nubile Youths to the Volcano ceremony? Overpaid for souvenirs?"

He shook his head. "No. I probably should do something normal, or my boss will tease me endlessly." He snorted in good humor. "She says I need to live a little. *Laissez les bons temps rouler.*"

"'Let the good times roll' is a better life philosophy than most. You like working for her?"

"Best boss ever, present company excepted."

"I wasn't your boss, gunnin. Higher rank, yes, but never your superior." She didn't want him thinking of her as an officer, even though they both technically were by the time they each left the service. Their Forward Intelligence unit worked because they'd been equals, more or less, who regularly pulled off miracles for the colonel, so she'd have clout when High Command wanted her to deploy the unit for something stupid or suicidal. Mostly, it had worked like a charm, except the one devastating time it hadn't.

He raised his hands in surrender. "Okay, you tanked as a boss."

She smiled. "*Burro.*" She surveyed the remains of her food and decided it wasn't worth taking home. She put her napkin on the table with his. "Ready?"

She was amused to see he'd been stacking the dishes and flatware to make it easier for the server to clear. "How long did you work in restaurants?"

He smiled as they stood and headed for the exit. "I started about eight or nine, as soon as I was big enough to carry plates. It's easy to get off-the-net jobs in food service." Central Galactic Concordance law said kids under fourteen weren't allowed to take jobs, even if their parents signed the contract waiver, but anonymous cashflow jobs could be found almost anywhere.

Andra nodded to the manager as they left the restaurant's lanai and turned right. The walkways were narrower in this part of town, intended for residents, rather than gaggles of tourists. She congratulated herself on wearing good walking shoes, casual shorts, and a sleeveless, side-buttoned knit top, because winter in Tremplin was still warm, and they'd had to park Jerzi's flitter several hillocks away in a small, almost empty flitter stacker. Most of its customers were probably away during the day.

Tremplin didn't have blocks, it had winding paths around a mix of short and tall structures designed to harmonize with the jungle-like growth. Even stackers were designed to blend in. The current fad was for tree houses, which made Andra grateful to live in her tall but more conventionally designed apartment building, with convenient lifts, stairs, and airpads. If she wanted to climb rope ladders every day, she'd do it at the gym.

The winter weather in Tremplin was only about fifteen degrees cooler than the summer, and more humid. She was glad she'd opted for comfort and worn her hair in a high bun, or her neck would be soaked with sweat after a few meters.

She glanced at the time on her percomp. "I'd hoped to have heard from Mairwen by now."

Jerzi shrugged. "Traffic does what it wants."

They walked and chatted easily on the way to the public flitter stacker. She kept wanting to apologize to him for hurting his feelings the other night, because she was pretty sure she had. She couldn't explain it, though, without taking their relationship somewhere it couldn't go, considering he was leaving in four days. She'd just have to enjoy the time they had.

The path widened as it approached the stacker. On one of the long benches near it, 21.64 meters up ahead, according to her oculars, three men and a woman had draped themselves across it like hyenas on a savanna. Their clothes were dark and tight, and they were all wearing heavy boots. One man wore a brown-stained flowered tourist shirt like a trophy. A beefy, dark man with a slanted red mohawk and a man who was painfully thin pretended to be dozing, but the thin man's teeth clacked, a symptom of too much performance chem. None looked their way.

"Shit," she said under her breath, at the same time she heard the same word in Polish from Jerzi. "They're a long way from The Solitario." Tremplin's bad part of town was tens of kilometers to the north.

The woman, with pale skin and flat, micro-short dark hair, stood and made a show of arching back in a stretch. Her breasts nearly overflowed the shiny black vest's neckline. She had some muscle definition, but she looked like she hadn't eaten well recently.

"Run?" asked Jerzi as they both slowed, but still continued walking. "That'd work in Etonver, but here?"

She considered the narrow path behind them. "That's what they want. They're probably on adreeno. Local favorite." It was a popular chem for athletic thrill-seekers because it temporarily sped up reaction times, like a ramper could do with minder talent. Used properly, it could be an effective short-term advantage. Muggers and hyena packs liked it for that reason. Long-term abuse caused tunnel vision and sapped muscle strength.

"So they'll flatline, if we last long enough, and they don't have weapons. Great." He took a deep breath and blew it out slowly. "I don't suppose you brought your shockstick along?"

"Sadly, no. Made a funny lump in my sexy bra." If they made it through this, she was never going out without one again, lumps or no lumps. "Let's do this."

Andra began walking faster, and Jerzi followed suit. May as well bottle them up against the bench if they could.

"Skinny lopar with the jittery jaw and the woman are mine," she said to Jerzi.

Suddenly, Jerzi sped up and got in front of her to blitz the tallest man in the tourist shirt. Goddamn it, Jerzi was *protecting* her, like she was a farkin' civilian. She gritted her teeth and moved in fast to salvage the element of surprise. She veered to the right to take the woman first, and her focus narrowed.

The woman pivoted and made fists but kept them by her side and snarled. It probably frightened the tourists. Andra extended her arms and put up her open hands, one leading the other. "Easy, now. *Cálmese.*"

The woman's eyes betrayed her intention to launch. She was scary-fast with a roundhouse punch at Andra's jaw as she cocked her other fist for a lower follow-up, hinting at some training. Andra barely managed to fold her own arms around her head and face to block, but it gave her time to get close enough to trap the woman's arm under one of her own long enough to swing her around to derail the skinny man's attempt at an overhead punch.

Andra grabbed the woman's head in a front-controlled headlock and raised a fast knee into the woman's solar plexus, but the woman was surprisingly limber and evaded most of the impact. Andra swung her again to keep her off balance and blocking the skinny man, and tried again with a front kick into the woman's ribs. It connected. She switched legs and got another two solid kicks in.

"*Pórni!*" the woman growled. She engaged with a flurry of hits to Andra's sides and shoulders, and got in a heavy-booted kick to her bare shin, but while adreeno provided temporary speed, it did nothing for building strength or skill. The woman snarled in rage and tried to turn her head to bite Andra's arm. A quick elbow smash to the woman's collarbone distracted her, and she stumbled to one knee. Andra brought her own knee up and the woman's jaw down to meet it, and the woman was down.

The skinny man nearly tripped over his fallen pack mate, but righted himself quickly. He had height, reach, and blinding speed, and managed a whistling punch that scraped her ear painfully before she connected with a punch to his jaw, and a second to his solar plexus. She took advantage of his involuntary hunch forward to get his head and neck under control. Three fast front kicks into his ribs, and he was on his knees. Andra punched his jaw hard with the heel of her hand, whipping his head sideways, and he toppled like a tree. She gave a swift kick to his jaw again to make sure he was out.

Andra looked to Jerzi just in time to see him smash the mohawk-haired man with an elliptical punch to the temple. His tourist-shirted pal was curled on the ground, rolling and moaning. Mohawk man got in a couple of rapid-fire shotgun punches at Jerzi's abdomen, but he might as well have been hitting a wall for all that Jerzi noticed. A flash of movement from tourist-shirt man caught her eye, but even as she leapt toward him, she knew she'd be too late to stop him from firing the flechette gun. Jerzi roared in pain when the darts stitched a line up his calf and thigh, but amazingly, he stayed upright and head-butted mohawk man's face and flung him onto tourist-shirt man.

Mohawk man fell to his knees as Andra waded in to stomp hard on the knee of tourist-shirt man. She used her forward momentum to kick mohawk man's head. He landed on his hands, then collapsed forward onto his cohort.

"Get off!" yelled tourist-shirt man, pushing at mohawk man's mostly inert form. Andra took the opportunity to kick tourist-shirt man in the gonads. His high-pitched scream was almost inhuman. After that, it was easy enough to take the flechette gun away from him. It had jammed, which explained why Jerzi only had four darts in him.

She shoved the gun into the back waistband of her shorts and checked the other assailants. The pale woman was on her hands and knees, shaking like a leaf, tears streaming down her face, trying to wake the skinny man. She cast a vitriolic glance at Andra that bespoke of vengeance. Andra ignored it, figuring the adreeno burnout would make her barely able to stand, much less pursue them.

Jerzi's left leg was bleeding profusely, mostly from the hole in the meaty part of his thigh where he'd pulled out one of the darts. "Leave them in, Jerzi. They're stopping the blood loss."

He gritted his teeth as he limped a few steps away from their attackers. "At least I didn't destroy another set of clothes." He looked down at his left running shoe, where dripping blood had darkened its red cushioned top. "Oh look, it matches."

"While the hyenas are still decommed, let's get your flitter out of hock and burn flux."

Jerzi started to slip the extracted flechette into his pocket, then hesitated.

"Here," she said, taking it from him and sticking it through her bun. She'd had far less pleasant things in her hair than blood. "Can you walk?"

"Limp, anyway." He started up the walkway, toward the stacker's kiosk. She followed behind a little, turning a couple of times to make sure the hyenas were still staying down.

Once he stopped at the control unit, she caught up to him. He looked a little paler than normal, but good. "That woman called me a 'trollop' in Greek. Who uses that word any more?"

"Maybe they're an ancient literature study group gone bad." He hissed when he moved badly and had to put more weight on his left leg. "I think the red-haired guy is crew."

"Why do you say that?"

"Body art hidden under cheap skin spray, better street skills. When the chemmer with the gun started to pull it the first time, the red-haired guy said 'shoot the woman.'"

"Is that why you suddenly sped up and got in front of me?"

"Yeah." His swollen right eye was red and already starting to bruise. His beard probably hid another on his jaw. "You were already focused on the other two. I didn't think you'd seen it."

She frowned. "I hadn't." She shook her head at her sloppiness. "I thought you were being a knight in shining armor again. Sorry."

Jerzi was sweaty and a little winded, probably from breathing through the pain. He fished his percomp out of his pocket and paid to release the flitter.

"You need more than a wound pack and a pain patch, *compadre*. I'm flying. Closest minor care, or a real medical center?"

He looked down at his leg and sighed. "Medical center. I can feel one of them grating against my bone." He tilted his chin toward her. "You need diagnostics, too."

"What, this?" She wiped at the blood that was trickling down her neck from her torn ear and wiped her hand on her already bloody top, careful to avoid her inexplicably bruised ribs and keep the weight off her badly bruised right shin. "I've had worse than this in faculty curriculum committee meetings. Academia is a cutthroat business."

CHAPTER 15

MAIRWEN STOOD IN the doorway of the childcare center, watching the six children who were playing, but occasionally casting wary eyes toward the stranger in the room. Her. She opened her senses to get a baseline of the sounds in the suite and beyond, though the suite's heavy door and impressive acoustic insulation blocked most outside noises. Pico's rushed instructions to play games with her charges had assumed Mairwen knew some to play. She was reasonably certain that knife target practice would not be suitable. For one thing, her knives were too big for their small hands.

Mairwen had been just arriving at the hotel in their small rented flitter when she'd received a ping from Andra De Luna about the attack that had sent Jerzi to a medical center for treatment. It disconcerted Mairwen to know that her friend was hurt, and that had she been there instead of stuck in traffic, she might have prevented his injury. When she'd pinged Luka at the police station with the news, he said he'd already found out from Pico, who was stuck at the childcare center and very worried about her father. The simple solution was for Mairwen, who was much closer to the school than Luka and Sojaire were, to take Pico to the medical center.

When she'd arrived, however, Pico turned out to be the only adult on the premises, and wouldn't leave the children. Pico was so distressed that Mairwen had impulsively offered to lend the flitter to Pico. The young woman had accepted with alacrity and left after a flurry of instructions, temporary access codes, and a quick tour of the suite. Which left Mairwen with a roomful of fidgety children and at least ninety minutes until their parents started coming for them.

When she'd pinged Luka to let him know where she was and why, he'd pinged back to say he'd have the police drop him and Sojaire at the big medical center to retrieve their flitter, and would come to her rescue as soon as possible. His word choice had amused her at the time, but as she looked around the room at the children who were depending on her, she conceded she might need rescuing.

She'd never seen so many stuffed animals, child-sized comps, and reconfigurable play centers in one room. She carefully threaded her way through the obstacle course of toys to get close enough to delineate the unique scent of each child in her care, to help her remember their names. Pico had told her to watch the younger children especially, but Mairwen couldn't guess how old any of them were, so she asked them their names and ages as she introduced herself to each. Miguel, a reserved brown-skinned boy, was eleven, and his shy sister Celia was five. Lyssi, with the energetic red curls and outgoing nature, was six. The others were Davalia, age seven, Parekh, age four, and Isiro, age five.

She went back to stand by the front door and consider her options. While she could simply stand guard the whole time, Pico had been adamant about the children needing engaged supervision and directed activities.

The child called Lyssi approached her, hesitantly stopping a meter away. "Is this your first day?" Her English and intonation had a hint of Old Britain to it.

"Yes," said Mairwen. First and only day, if the universe loved her.

"That's all right. Would you like to play with me?"

The little girl's hopeful trust was puzzling. Mairwen had seen adults interact with children, but never thought to pay attention to their techniques, since she'd never have any of her own. "Yes." She glanced at the other children, and inspiration struck. "Since I'm new, perhaps all of you could teach me to play a game."

It worked. The ensuing argument among the children consumed six minutes as they worked out which game to play, four minutes in clearing a suitable space on the floor and finding markers with which to draw on the floor, and another three minutes and thirty seconds teaching her the rules. Miguel and his sister had only watched at first, but Celia got brave enough to let go of his hand to help draw diamond shapes on the floor. Miguel sat on a chair in the corner and folded himself into a hunched posture with arms on knees in front of his chest.

The game involved stepping or hopping into the numbered diamonds and a simple math progression to determine which direction to go and which diamonds to avoid. She had the children go first, then give her instructions as she stepped. When she asked them for another game, they taught her a rhyme, so each child could invent movements to go with the words while jumping over a rope held and wiggled by the others.

As the other children relaxed around her and laughed at her deliberate mistakes, Miguel did as well, though he stayed in his chair. He wasn't injured, that she could tell, but perhaps didn't care to play with younger children. When Isiro tripped over the rope and began to cry, however, Miguel was there to pick the boy up and dry his tears, and she realized Miguel saw himself as a protector. She gave him a respectful nod of thanks, as one guardian to another.

Several games later, she and the younger children were sitting in a circle and trying to tell a story one word at a time. The story had become quite convoluted and nonsensical when an older man came through the door of the center. Mairwen stood quickly and watched him. He couldn't have opened the door if he wasn't authorized, so she didn't move forward to confront him, but she kept a close eye on both him and the children. She didn't miss the initial tension in Miguel, Celia, and Lyssi. Isiro jumped up and ran to the smiling man, chattering rapidly in Japanese and addressing him as "Grandfather." The man gave her a brief bow of thanks, then used his biometric to open the door to leave, carrying Isiro on his back. The arrival of Parekh's father caused a repeat of the rise in tension in the children, and the story game fell apart when they all had to help find the little boy's shoes, socks, shorts, and shirt, apparently a common occurrence with him.

Mairwen may have known next to nothing about children, but fear was easy to recognize. She wasn't as smart as Luka, who would have figured it out much sooner, but it was a logical supposition that the tense children had seen the man take their caregiver, Valenia, and he had frightened them. She also suspected Miguel was a developing minder talent in one of the telepath categories who was having trouble controlling his talent. Since she'd moved in with Luka with his unique minder talents, and worked every day with Sojaire, who had more conventional talents, she had become more familiar with their subtle habits and challenges.

She couldn't change the past for the children, any more than she could change her own horrific existence before she'd escaped the secret program that had created her and her kind, but she could, perhaps, help them deal with what they'd experienced, and give them a tool for the future.

She asked Celia, Lyssi, and Davalia to take their chairs and sit in a circle near Miguel. She dropped to her knees and sat back on her heels.

"I want to teach you a game, but first, we need to talk about what happened with Valenia and the man who came for her. What did the man do that scared you?"

For a long moment, they looked at each other, or her, round-eyed with uneasiness. Celia stuck her thumb in her mouth. Miguel frowned.

Lyssi spoke first. "He pinched Ms. Val's arm and hurt her." She rubbed the back of her arm above her elbow.

"He was nice at first," said Davalia in a small voice, "but when Ms. Val wasn't looking, he looked like a lion that wanted to eat us."

Mairwen turned to Miguel, who was back to folding in on himself. "He was like a black hole."

She nodded. "It's smart to be scared of bad people. But you don't have to let it stop you from doing something about it."

The girls looked puzzled, but Miguel frowned. "Like what? We couldn't have fought him. We're just kids." His Spanish accent softened his consonants, but his disdain was sharp.

"Yes," she agreed. "But you have advantages that adults don't have. You're small, and you know this suite very well."

"So what?" said Miguel. His tone was a blend of anger and despair.

"I will show you in the game," said Mairwen. She rose to her feet and led the children to the front door.

"What's this game called?" asked Lyssi, who liked naming things.

Mairwen gave them all a tight, feral smile. "The Hunter and the Fox."

Four minutes before six, the childcare center's door chimed and the wallcomp blinked for attention. Mairwen cocked a questioning eye toward Miguel, who had frozen in the act of stacking a chair. Because it was so close to the end of the day, she'd convinced the children to help restore order to some of the chaos in the childcare suite. Lyssi had become enamored of the cargo loops on Mairwen's pants. Celia and Davalia were sorting through the dishes in one of the playhouses, by means of pretending to be serving each other what she assumed were invented food items, because the girls were nearly incapacitated with giggling.

"Someone without a code wants in," Miguel said, his expression losing animation. "That's what the man did."

"Yes," she said. It would have been the only way to get to Valenia. How and when he'd targeted her were unanswered questions.

She keyed the wallcomp to show who was at the door, and was unsurprised to see the faces of Luka and Sojaire, who had pinged her ten minutes ago that they'd landed. The traffic system glitches she'd experienced must have cleared up for them to be able to arrive just before the center's closing time.

"They're the partners I told you about," she told the children, making sure Miguel saw she was pleased to see them. As far as she knew, no conventional minder could read or affect her, so she wanted to reassure the boy that they were safe.

She entered her temporary access code, then stepped back when the door irised open. The children all looked up to watch the men enter. Luka turned straight to her, a smile playing on his handsome face. Sojaire moved to the side, and the door irised shut again.

"Pleasant afternoon?" he asked. A hint of concern laced his tone.

"Yes." She kept her face straight and serious. "I only used the ropes once."

Lyssi, who had deliberately gotten her hand stuck in the cargo loop on Mairwen's left pant leg, shook her head vigorously, making her red curls bounce wildly. "No, twice." She looked up at Luka earnestly. "Once with me and once with Isiro. He cried."

Luka tried to cover his alarm, until he realized he was being teased. "Oh, the usual, then." He grinned. Mairwen twitched a smile in response. It was rare when her teasing left him nonplussed.

She helped Lyssi extract her hand, then introduced her and the other children to both Luka and Sojaire. She then enlisted the men into doing as the children directed them for moving the heavier play houses to a more even spacing.

As soon as she got the chance, she spoke quietly to Sojaire. "Miguel needs help. He was here when Valenia was taken. I think he's an empath." Sojaire would know what to do. Unlike her, he was a natural at nurturing, when he wasn't distracted or second-guessing himself.

Davalia's older sister arrived almost exactly at six, as expected. The little girl waved goodbye as her sister led her out the door.

To give Sojaire time with Miguel, Mairwen asked Lyssi and Celia to show Luka the real kitchen, not the one in their make-believe spaceship, to see if it was ready to be left for the night. She used her percomp to review the list of instructions Pico had pinged her after taking off in the flitter. Mairwen was reluctant to move away from a clear view of the suite's only outside entrance, so she sent Luka and the girls to the nap room, freshers, and tiny office to check that they, too, were squared away for the evening.

She was about to resort to asking the children to teach Luka the story game when the front door irised open to reveal Miguel and Celia's parents, two smiling Hispanic men. The little girl ran to her taller father, who smiled and scooped her up into his arms for wet, smacking kisses, to the girl's giggling delight. Miguel said goodbye to Sojaire, then made a point to catch Mairwen's eye. "*Seremos zorros.*" He retrieved his shoulder bag and Celia's sweater from a hook by the door, and the family left.

Lyssi tugged on Mairwen's pant leg. "Will you carry me?" She held up her arms.

The request made no sense. The room was only twenty-five meters at its longest, and the girl had traversed it countless times. "To where?"

Lyssi pointed to the hooks by the door, only a couple of meters away, then held up her hands expectantly.

Mairwen looked to Luka for help. The exasperating man laughed and nodded. "I'll explain later."

Mairwen lifted Lyssi up and felt arms and legs wrap around her neck and waist. Lyssi smelled of dust, the lingering scent of her favorite coconut cookies, and the unique scent that was Lyssi. Mairwen carried her the seven steps to the hooks, then let her down. Lyssi lifted her small, translucent backpack from its hook and slid her arms into its padded web. "Mum said she'd be on time tonight." She sat on a stool under the now empty hooks and looked expectantly at the door.

The phrase "on time," Mairwen had quickly learned once she'd established a life in the real world, was a relative term. To her and her fellow death trackers, it meant seconds, or if she was in full tracker mode, milliseconds. To the rest of the galaxy, it could mean anywhere from a few minutes to an hour or more, depending on the speaker and circumstances. To Lyssi's mother, it apparently meant twenty minutes after closing time.

The woman swept into the door, barely waiting for the iris to open before stepping in and standing on the threshold so it couldn't close again. She looked at Mairwen, Luka, and Sojaire, then smiled in evident satisfaction. "I see the manager acted on my recommendation." She held out her hand to her daughter. Lyssi obediently moved to her mother's side and slipped her hand into her mother's.

Mairwen ignored it as a non-sequitur comment. That seemed to irritate the woman, but after one supercilious sniff, she turned and marched out smartly, forcing Lyssi to half run to keep up.

The door irised closed, and Mairwen relaxed for the first time in ninety-seven minutes.

Luka tilted his head toward the door. "Peculiar woman."

"Hmph," said Sojaire, crossing his arms. "She thinks she got Pico's contract termed, and that we're the new staff."

Luka gave Mairwen an evil smile. "Want to volunteer again? We could…"

"No," she said flatly.

Luka laughed, undoubtedly feeling he'd avenged himself for her earlier teasing. "Anything else we need to do here?"

She reviewed the checklist from Pico one more time. "No."

She entered her temporary access code to open the door. Once they were in the hall, she waited until the iris closed and the light over the door's threshold went dark before turning to leave. She was grateful to be able to hear the sounds of the building, and to smell more than just the childcare suite, which had only the one door to offer new scents.

The hallway was easily wide enough to walk three abreast, with Luka to her right and Sojaire to her left. It was brightly lit, as was the atrium. It was a stark contrast to the evening shadows once they left the building and headed toward the Materials Science building and the flitter stacker.

Murmurs of watery waves provided a subtle accompaniment to everything else she could hear. She tried not to imagine how vast the dark, deep water was beyond their artificial island, but she caught herself edging toward Luka as they walked.

Sojaire was focused on his wristcomp. "Luka, you still haven't answered that encrypted ping from Ms. Zheer."

When she looked to Luka for an explanation, he frowned. "She asked me to meet a man named Lièrén Sòng, listen to what he has to say, and 'evaluate' him. Her word."

"When?"

"Tomorrow, here in Tremplin. He's the CPS diplomatic liaison assigned to a frontier planet called Abasarran." He shook his head. "Setting aside for a moment the question of how she knew we'd be on Nila Marbela, or why he's so far from home, it's not like her to want anything to do with the CPS."

Mairwen tamped down an instinctive frisson of fear. "The External Relations Division is where the CPS sends misfits."

"Or embarrassments," he agreed. "Sojaire's research on him turned up a scandal on a covert operations group out of Concordance Prime from a couple of years ago. It was a top newstrend until he vanished."

"He's from the wealthy Sòng family," said Sojaire. "The CPS probably didn't want to tangle with them."

With her, the CPS had done exactly what it wanted, when it wanted, but perhaps her unknown family hadn't had the same clout. She was glad the decision on whether or not to meet Sòng was Luka's. Her judgment was irreparably compromised when it came to his safety and her freedom. "If you're going, do you want me there?"

"No," he said firmly. "Hell, I don't want to be there, either, but I will. I trust Zheer. I owe her." He slid his fingers through his hair. "Sojaire is having a hard time finding a secure, easy access, anonymous meeting space with multiple exits."

They were all hampered by their unfamiliarity with the city. She only knew one location that fit the bill. "What about the construction area in the Math building?"

"What? Oh, you mean for the meeting." He slowed to look over his shoulder at the building behind them. "Thanks to Majeed, it's still sealed, and I still have access." His head tilted a little. "It's a bit macabre, but it has no cameras yet. The killer has already vetted it, and we know *he's* security-minded. It'll do." He faced forward again and brushed her hand with his. "Have I told you lately how much I value your unconventional ideas?"

She brushed her fingers against his. "Yes." He smiled, and she returned it.

"On an entirely different subject," said Luka, "Jerzi thinks the attack on them this afternoon was targeted at Andra De Luna. Could be her questions about the lab sabotage disturbed a sleeping wolverine or two."

"I don't know the politics, but the security setup is unusual."

"How so?" he asked.

"The university relies heavily on security for show for the floater—visible security systems, security programming in the building AI, automated access control points—but it's thin and brittle, and remotely monitored. The Chemistry building has new, more robust systems and security staff who pretend to be students or low-paid workers. The manager pretends ignorance."

Luka was amused. "You're going to say 'pretends' in your report?"

She crooked a smile at him. "I'll provide examples. They can choose their own word."

The stacker was close to the shore, where the waves crashed more loudly. She needed to distract herself. "Why did Lyssi want to be carried?"

"She just wanted a hug, *ástin mín*." Luka slipped his hand into hers. The warmth of his hand and the familiar scent of him soothed her.

Why would a child seek physical affection from a stranger? Had she been alone with Luka, she might have asked him, but Sojaire knew little about her unusual background, and she preferred to keep it that way because she liked him. He knew about her extraordinary senses, and that her physiology was different, but she'd never told him how or why. The less he knew, the better chance he had of being left alone, if the ultra-secret CPS "paracommando pathfinder" program ever discovered she had lived through the fiery death it had taken her years to plan and stage.

Luka, her wonderfully brilliant partner and caring lover of four years, knew more, but even he was ignorant of all she'd done for the CPS. Strictly speaking, she was no longer entirely human. She'd been one of the handful of "students" who survived highly illegal alteration of her DNA, erasure of all childhood memories, and the CPS's sadistic but brutally effective training program. She knew many ways to kill people without mercy, but had to work out by trial and error how to do normal things. She was lucky Luka was so patient with her.

He squeezed her fingers briefly. "I've never seen the Brigadier side of you, ordering those kids around. How did you make them behave—show them your knives?"

"I considered it," she said. Luka snorted in amusement, evidently believing she was joking. "I asked them to teach me to play their games."

"Why did Miguel say 'we will be foxes'?" asked Sojaire.

"I taught *them* a game. Were you able to talk to him?"

"Yeah," said Sojaire. "You were right about his talent. He said Val hid how terrified she was from the other kids, until the man got impatient and made her close the center and leave. He said the man was 'a black hole,' which is what strong shielders feel like to empaths. It's corroboration of what Val said."

She heard Luka's breath catch, and his hand in hers stiffened. He said nothing until they were in their rented flitter, their seats crowded together in the cramped passenger section. Sojaire was at the controls, waiting for the traffic system's countdown. Out of self-preservation, she and Sojaire took turns flying or driving, because while Luka knew how, he lost patience quickly and tended to ignore traffic rules. If he was distracted by a case, he was a menace.

Luka broke the silence. "Unless the case breaks tonight, I'm ready to leave Nila Marbela after the meeting with Sòng. The pattern is usually a clusters of kills, then moving on." She guessed that another lead pointing to the Citizen Protection Service, however obliquely, had made him unhappy. Strong shielders were rare outside the judicial system and the CPS.

Sojaire's shoulders tightened, but he kept his focus forward. "The locals say no one matching his description has gone through any spaceport or the space station. Shouldn't we try to catch him before he can hurt another girl like Valenia?" Sojaire didn't often try to tell Luka what to do, so Mairwen guessed he was upset because the victim had been a friend. Mairwen sympathized.

Luka frowned and looked away from her toward the city lights as the flitter locked into the traffic system and ascended. She knew him well enough to know he was irritated with planetary politics and the slow pace of the case, and was worried about her being noticed by the CPS. At the same time, he was driven by his strong sense of justice, especially since the latest victim wasn't an anonymous stranger.

He already knew her opinion, so she left him to his thoughts. She considered the security assessment report she'd be sending the university that evening, and wondered if there was some way to phrase her recommendations so they'd do something meaningful, instead of adding a few sensors here and there and calling it done. She'd performed hundreds of assessments for organizations large and small, and she could count on one hand the number that had acted on all her recommendations.

"I'll give it a couple more days," said Luka finally. "He didn't kill Valenia when he could have, and that's new. He might make a mistake because of it."

Sojaire's shoulders visibly relaxed. "Thank you." He blew out the breath he'd been holding and looked back at Luka. "Pico blames herself for not protecting Val. She'll feel better if the mistake you discovered gets the warped bastard caught."

Underneath his good humor and compassion, Sojaire was usually in firm control of his emotions. His rare use of a swear word suggested he was having a hard time with that at the moment. Perhaps he could talk to Luka later about what was bothering him. She wished she was better about being a friend, but she had so little experience.

She thought she might enjoy being friends with Andra De Luna, who also found humor in small things, and Mairwen liked brilliant minds. Too bad their lives were on distant planets.

Maybe it was her constant uneasiness about deep water, or just a wish for different star lanes than the ones on her chart, but a longing for comfort welled, and suddenly, she understood a little girl's request to be carried when she could easily have walked.

Too bad she was an adult woman with adult responsibilities. For all that she'd dreamed of it and sacrificed to win it, life in the real world was sometimes full of frustration.

CHAPTER 16

JERZI STOOD WITH his fists on his hips in the middle of Andra's high-rise apartment. It was small, but open and airy, with gentle blue seashell curves to its architecture. One wall was privacy windows that probably had a nice view of the city. "I'm fine."

Andra's eyes narrowed. "Says *el burro terco* with six wound packs, a temporary bone regenerator on his thigh, and a subcutaneous flush port for his formerly broken ribs." She pulled out a chair at her kitchen table and patted it. "Sit."

The medical center had wanted him to spend the night there, and he'd wanted to spend it anywhere but. He had no idea how she'd bullied him into going to her apartment.

"Don't make me use my shockstick, Commander Crush." He had a hazy memory of her threatening to flatline him and carry him out in one of the center's antigrav chairs. "They only let you go because I said someone would be with you." She glared and pointed. "Sit!"

Jerzi held firm a moment more, then sighed and gave in. He limped to the chair, then hid a wince as he angled his hips so as not to jostle the leg with the regen unit. The movement made his sore ribs ache. He missed the excellent minder healers they'd had in the military. "You're the only one who calls me stubborn."

"R-i-i-ight," she said, drawing out the vowel. She pulled a cold beer from her cold box, then opened a cabinet and rooted around for a mug. She set both in front of him. "Hungry yet?"

He made a noncommittal sound, even though his stomach felt hollow. Accelerated healing treatments and regeneration units made most people ravenous, once the pain patches wore off. For reasons he didn't care to examine too closely, he was reluctant to owe her any more favors than he already did. "Go shower."

Her messy hair, wound-sealed ear, blood-stained top, and dirt-streaked shorts reminded him of wilder days from when they were both young and immortal. And fluxed red hot with hormones, but he definitely wasn't going there.

She started toeing open the clasps on her shoes. "Not saying you're a liar, my friend, but your stomach's been growling loud enough to scare the whales at sea." She kicked her shoes onto the mat near her front door. Her bright floral gun bag slumped nearby. "But I'm tired of smelling like blood and wound seal, so I'm taking advantage of your stubbornness." She patted his shoulder once as she passed by. "Anything in the cold box is fair game. Don't pass out while I'm gone."

With that, she vanished into the fresher and closed the door.

The medics warned him to stay away from chems and alterants, but they didn't mention beer, so he considered it a gray area. He took a sip and savored it. Tremplin wines might not be paradise, but its beers were good, and Andra had good taste.

His leg, where one of the flechettes had scraped his thigh bone, hurt more than he'd expected, once he'd hobbled to the flitter. He was glad Andra had been there to fly him to the medical center and home, but she'd taken advantage of his painkiller-addled state to take him to her apartment instead of Pico's. Andra's home had no clean clothes except the stray jacket he'd left in the flitter, but it did have an actual spare bed in a private room, instead of the flimsy cot crowded into the corner of Pico's shared living space.

While in the not-so-gentle hands of the medics and doing his best to distract himself from what they were doing to him, he'd decided that the red-haired attacker, who'd had combat training, might have hired the chemmers to target Andra. Otherwise, it made no sense to ignore the looming threat Jerzi had presented in favor of shooting Andra. Flechettes could kill, but they were better at disabling. Most crews—and mercenaries—had access to far more lethal weapons, although if he were working with adreeno abusers, he'd be worried they'd accidentally shoot themselves or him. If they were after Andra, as he suspected, it was for a decommission, not a kill. Andra had been skeptical of his theory, but had nonetheless complied with his request to ping the idea to Luka.

His gnawing hunger made him restless. He levered himself up and limped to the cold box to see what it offered. It wasn't as empty as he'd feared, but the motley collection of recyclable containers suggested she ate out a lot. He did the same, far too often, now that he lived alone. It was more fun cooking for others than for just himself.

As he heated a thick fish stew, he tried to keep his leg from freezing up by limping to the view windows. With a little fiddling with the nearby wallcomp, he made them translucent instead of opaque, and was rewarded with a panoramic view of the twinkling city lights that led to one of the smaller harbors. He used the wallcomp to dim the interior lights, making the room less of a fishbowl to passing flitters, thought the traffic system usually kept them well above the roofline. He was amused to see several spots where bugs had smashed into the windows, despite the altitude. Over-achieving little buggers.

He chuckled at his own feeble joke as he walked back when his food was ready, trying not to limp this time because it made his ribs ache. He scrounged around for a spoon, then took the bowl back to stand by the windows so he could enjoy the view—and occasional tiny thumps of more suicidal bugs. His stomach almost cramped with the first few spoonfuls, but settled down once it realized more food was coming. The stew was satisfying, and just spicy enough to be interesting.

Andra's voice startled him. "You found something. Good." He turned to see her tying the belt of a short, iridescent purple kimono. Her dark hair was slicked back with water, but was already frizzing up. "Fresher is all yours, if you want. Solardry is in the far corner." She made a beeline for the cold box.

"Nice view," he said, pointing a thumb over his shoulder at the windows, but knowing he also meant the sight of her toned and well-shaped body, barely concealed by the thin fabric. A subtle shadow on her ribs and hip gave a tantalizing hint of serpentine skin art, which was new. Everyone in their Forward Intelligence unit had seen each other naked often, but maybe because it was in her elegant apartment instead of the communal military showers, it felt different. He resolutely turned to face the windows. "Terrace looks comfortable. Except for the bugs."

"Moths only migrate in the spring." In the window's reflection, he saw her pry open the lid of a bowl and sniff.

"Well, some critters are giving their all against your windows tonight." She put the bowl in the hot box and keyed it. "What do they look like?" He shrugged. "Black splats."

"How helpful." She crossed the room toward the windows. He pointed toward the area he'd first seen them.

She focused on the glass, then blinked rapidly twice, which he knew was her activating her oculars for closeup work.

She suddenly stumbled back, swearing in a torrent of Spanish. She blinked again as she grabbed his arm and pulled him back.

"We have to get out of here. Now." She shoved him toward the apartment's front door and ran to grab her shoes.

His adrenalin spiked as he strode to the entry wallcomp. If Andra said they needed to go, then they did. Luckily, she'd already given him temporary access via his palm print, so he slapped it against the reader. The door opened. He put his empty food container on a nearby decorative table.

"Grab my gun bag," she ordered. Instead of joining him at the door, however, she ran to a low kitchen cabinet and began pulling out pots and pans. She fished back behind them to pull out a well-worn black backpack.

"Shit! I need my percomp." She darted glances to her bedroom door and the windows.

The forgotten hot box signaled that her food was ready. She left her backpack on the floor and opened the hot box to remove the bowl of soup she'd heated. Inexplicably, she fast-walked it to the windows and splashed it on the area with the greatest concentration of insect strikes. She dropped the bowl and ran to the bedroom.

He picked up the backpack, which was much heavier than it looked, and slung it over his shoulder, hissing when it put pressure on his sore ribs. He slung her gun bag over his other shoulder just as she appeared with a wad of clothes in her arms.

"Flitter!" She raced out the door ahead of him and turned left.

He followed at a half-run, ignoring the pain of his thigh and ribs, wondering what had her so spooked. If anyone else on the floor heard them pounding down the well-lit, green water-colored hallway, they didn't open their doors to see what the commotion was.

As if she'd heard him, she said, "Those weren't bugs, they're an airborne explosive array."

She was leading them to the back of the building, away from her apartment. As she ran, she was fumbling in the pocket of the shorts she'd been wearing before her shower. "Individual nodes slip through almost any security perimeter. Once they achieve coherence threshold, they link and detonate whatever explosives the nodes are carrying." She wrestled her percomp out and slapped it onto her wrist. She activated it just as they got to a stairway door. She slammed her palm on the reader to open it and pointed. "Up!"

He was heartily glad her apartment was on the top floor. He could probably handle one flight of stairs without completely exhausting his reserves. Andra hadn't even had the chance to eat since getting the same accelerated healing treatments he had. As she yelled into the percomp, arguing with the building security office, he cast furtive glances at her, knowing his worry would irritate her.

"Yes, goddam it, I'm sure!" She slowed to taking one stair at a time instead of two.

"*We can't possibly evacuate the residents,*" the man's voice said. "*People would panic.*"

Andra swore a vicious oath in Spanish. "Then trigger the building's tornado warning system, and get people away from the windows." She was breathing heavily. He wanted to help her, but the best he could do was keep up.

At the top of the stairs, she slapped her hand on the reader. The door opened quietly. As he stepped through, he heard a rising, multi-pitch alarm sound from the wall speakers, followed by a calm but authoritative synth voice.

"*Tornado threat imminent. Move away from terraces and windows and move to the center of the building. This is not a drill.*" The alarm and announcement kept repeating.

They ran to the flitter stacker so she could key the request for his flitter. He rested his hand on the wall and bent forward, gasping for air.

Just as the stacker disgorged his flitter, a deep, loud explosion shook the walls and floor so hard that he nearly fell to his knees. He staggered forward to catch Andra as she slid sideways. Multiple alarms began wailing immediately as the shaking stopped.

He opened the flitter and keyed open all its doors so he could toss the backpack and bag into the back.

"Launch now, or we'll never get clearance," she said urgently. She climbed into the flitter's passenger seat as he requested entry to the traffic system, then shut the doors and webbed himself into the seat. He lifted off manually, away from the side of the building where Andra's apartment was. Or depressingly more likely, where Andra's apartment *used* to be.

He didn't relax until the traffic system took control of the flitter and they rose into the dark sky.

"Where did you tell it to take us?" she asked. Her voice sounded thready, and he risked a peek at her. Her eyes were closed and she looked completely spent. He doubted he looked any better. Or smelled it, either, since sweat was still pouring off him.

"Nearest police station. Traffic systems usually prioritize those requests."

She nodded. "Smart."

Now that he wasn't running for his life, his body took the opportunity to report its extreme unhappiness with him, starting with his thigh, ribs, and newly aggrieved shoulders. "What in the name of the cosmos do you keep in that backpack? It has to weigh at least forty kilos."

A smart-ass smile ghosted across her face. "My sex toy collection."

* * * * *

Andra didn't want to know what time it was. She already knew it was past eleven, and the night wasn't over.

She and Jerzi had done well to present themselves at the police precinct station. It kept them off the top of the suspect list. Jerzi had done one better and gotten Luka to ping his police contact, Captain Majeed, whose ensuing interest in the case kept the questioning, if not genial, then at least not overtly antagonistic. They'd even let her change out of her silk kimono into the knit pants and shirt she'd grabbed from her laundry basket. She regretted not grabbing underwear and a bra, but it couldn't be helped.

Owing to a colorful family, she'd long ago learned it was best to be polite and not burden the police with too many details or to volunteer information. She let them assume it was her military experience that enabled her to identify the airborne explosive array. And more importantly, to assume that the muggers would have targeted anyone walking by and that the explosives array went to the wrong address, rather than both targeted at her, as Jerzi suspected. She was grateful he'd followed her lead, because it wouldn't have been his first instinct. He was an inherently honest man who liked being helpful.

She was distracted by the realization that she was temporarily homeless. The preliminary damage assessment by the police's remote cameras suggested it would take a week or two for her apartment to be made habitable, assuming the building owner's insurance paid quickly. Some of her personal belongings might be salvageable, but she wouldn't be able to check for a few days. Fortunately, most of the physical things she valued were in her bags in the flitter. Or sitting next to her in the police interview room, trying to find a comfortable way to sit in deliberately uncomfortable chairs.

She was conflicted about Jerzi's presence. If she'd been on her own, she'd likely be in the medical center with flechette injuries from the adreeno freak, or from explosion injuries. From what she'd seen in the police forensic images, the blast pattern had been predominantly outward, more messy than lethal, but she'd still have been hurt.

Because Jerzi had been there when she was threatened, his protective instincts would be rising. If she was honest with herself, she felt protective of him, too. He'd been hurt because of her. If someone really was after her, they probably viewed him as collateral damage at best, or a lever against her. If they stayed together, they could protect each other.

But each additional hour spent in his presence was a threat to the status quo between them. For the first time since Da'vin died, she'd found herself wanting a real relationship again. She'd had more than a few recreational hot-connects and visits to joyhouses in the last five years, because she'd been sad, not dead, but none of them had resonated with her emotionally or had her thinking about the future like Jerzi did.

She tilted her chair back against the wall and sighed. It was just like her to spark with a potential lover who lived half a galaxy away. Not to mention, who would be gone in a few days. Not to mention, who had never treated her as anything but a buddy, but that might be because he thought she only loved women. Bisexuals like her sometimes had to make it clear that it wasn't the gender that attracted her, it was the person. Jerzi was just plain hot.

The return of Kenin, the sour detective who'd left them cooling their jets for the past thirty minutes, saved her from further brooding. She righted her chair.

Kenin looked squarely at her. "We're going to let you go for the evening, but we may need you to come in for further questions." The man tried to sound authoritative, but his thin, breathy voice and stooped posture weren't up to the task. No sense pointing out they'd stayed in the spirit of cooperation and could have left at any time.

"I can be available when I'm not teaching." She stood, and Jerzi did the same. "Do we need clearance to get our flitter from your stacker?" She pointed up to indicate the rooftop airpad.

"No, it's public. Just enter the code." He escorted them to the lift, but that was apparently the end of his courtesy.

She and Jerzi rode up in tired silence to the roof. The stacker was open-air, and there was no one else around, but she waited until their flitter was delivered and they were safely webbed in to speak.

"Pico's?"

"Yes, please." He sounded like a man trying not to sound exhausted. "You could stay there, too. Pico's at the medical center with Valenia."

She entered the destination in the flitter's console and signaled the traffic system. Almost immediately, the traffic system gave them a countdown warning. Either they'd gotten lucky, or leaving the police building had the same priority as arriving.

"Thank you, but no." She'd love more than anything to wrap herself around him for the night, but her conscience wouldn't let her." If I am at the top of someone's hit parade, as you believe, I'm not going to invite them to your daughter's doorstep."

She lifted the flitter and let it and the traffic system take control. She activated the percomp on her wrist and sent a quick query. She was glad she'd managed to save it.

He leaned his seat back flatter, apparently to accommodate his sore leg. She hoped Pico's apartment had more pain patches, or he was in for an uncomfortable night. "Where will you go?"

"Secure hostel. I just pinged a general query for available rooms."

"Try Luka's hotel. It's probably a fortress, if Mairwen had anything to say about it."

"I can believe that." She added the hotel name to the query list.

Now that she could almost relax, she decided her ear was the most annoying of her injuries. The medics had put it back together, but they'd paid no attention to aesthetics. She'd need an afternoon at a body shop so it matched her other ear again.

"I have to ask," he said, "why did you throw soup against the windows?"

"To give us time to get out. The array can't detonate until enough of the nodes are stationary. The nodes are designed to move if the environment changes significantly. The heat from the soup convinced enough of them to move that it delayed the coherence threshold."

Jerzi chuckled. "Whoever deployed them must have been surprised."

"Probably not. They're not a precision weapon. They're more useful as a distraction."

"So the bigger question is, who would want to hurt you?" She didn't have to look at him to know he was frowning. "The police might buy that the array went to the wrong address, but I don't. Luka doesn't."

She blew out a breath in frustration. "That's just it. The only enemies I have are Vestering, who thinks I want his *maldito* job, and maybe Lavong, who thinks I'm trying to get him in trouble for the lab accidents. Academics don't send hyenas or pincushion bombs, they slant peer-review results, or write scathing letters to journals, or start a rumor that you're trading grades for hot-connects in the storeroom. Violence implies your ideas are too weak to stand on their own. Why do you think I downplay my military background?"

"If not them, then maybe people they're associated with? Like the boat-accident man with theft crew ties. Hyena gangs and stealth weapons would be in any crew's playbook."

"Hah! We'd have to look at half the university's big-donor list. Nothing like a little upstanding charity to mask the odor of suspicion, or to distract enterprising journalists."

The flitter banked southward, over a small bay, then dropped to a lower altitude. The console chimed a gentle notice that they were ten minutes out from Pico's apartment building. Andra checked her percomp for the results of her query, then booked a hostel near the university, which put her near restaurants and an autotailor or two so she'd have something to wear to class the next day besides exercise clothes. She also ordered an autocab to pick her up from the apartment building's airpad. Even though it cost double, it was worth it not to have to haul her evacuation backpack and gun bag to the nearest cab kiosk.

"I know you're worried about me, and it's nice to know you care, but I can't stop my life because I *might* be a target." She acknowledged release from the traffic system and set the flitter down softly on the stacker's landing zone, so as not to jolt poor Jerzi's injured body more than necessary.

Once they got out and he'd let the stacker take his flitter, he stood with her while she waited for the autocab. It wasn't worth arguing with him that she'd be fine. "Would you like a mega pain patch or two? I have some in my backpack."

He started to say something, then frowned. "The gunnin in me wants to tell you 'no, I can tough it out,' but the truth is, my thigh is killing me, and who knows what Pico's got." He snorted. "And Valenia's room terrifies me."

Andra smiled as she opened the first-aid pocket in her backpack.

"Frilly?"

"You have no idea. I think she owns every body and fashion appliance known to humankind."

She handed him the patches, then resealed the pocket. "Do anything that requires brains beforehand. They pack a punch." She stood side by side with him and looked up at the starry night sky. "I'm sorry you got hurt because of me, but I'm not sorry you were there to have my back. Thank you." His solid presence relaxed something inside her.

He was silent for a long moment. "It's what I'm good at." He seemed to be conflicted about that.

"It's not the only thing you're good at," she said. "You're a brilliant sniper. You're a great cook. And you're the best father I've ever seen."

"Thank you for that, but I'll never be father of the year on anyone's planet. I spent more time away from her and her mother than not, even after I left the service. I transited in and out of their lives, and missed practically every milestone she had. Dhorya got stuck with the day-to-day work of raising her. Hell, we were practically children ourselves."

"It's good that you recognize your mistakes, but give yourself some credit. Pico's a smart young woman. She wouldn't love you so much if you didn't deserve it."

A warm gust of wind stirred up a thin cloud of dust.

"No wonder Pico says you're a great teacher." He put his hands in his pockets and gave her a crooked smile. "You're good at knowing exactly what people need."

She was tempted to just accept the praise, but she didn't want him to think she was a miracle worker. "I try different things and see what takes. I think most teachers do." She edged closer to him and nudged his shoulder with hers. "Finding people you mesh with, like compatible neural nets, is special. You and me, we've always been... *simpatizamos mucho.* Very sympathetic. It was like that with Da'vin, too. You have it with Pico."

He nodded. "We think alike. When Dhorya left, it's probably what saved us."

"You miss her, don't you?"

"Yeah, I do. She's the best daughter anyone could have."

"I meant Dhorya."

"Oh," he said. He looked at her, and then away. "Yes, and no. I miss the younger woman she used to be, when we were both happy. I miss being part of a family. Not her nasty family, but the one we made with Pico." He took a deep breath and let it out slowly. "I don't miss the angry, bigoted, hateful woman she became. I can't forgive how she ripped Pico's heart out."

"And yours, Jerzi." She nudged his shoulder again, as a sorry substitute for hugging him like she wanted, like he needed. "She ripped your heart out, too."

"And mine." His voice was quiet, but not despairing. "It took a long time to stop bleeding for her."

Tears threatened, and she looked up to the canopy of a million stars. "Losing someone is never simple. It's always messy." She was glad her voice sounded steady.

An autocab descended from the heights at the same time as her percomp notified her of its arrival. It saved her from the temptation of telling him how much she wanted him right then, because it was a bell that couldn't be unrung. Still, it was beyond her willpower to resist the chance to stay in his orbit another day.

"You should come by the central commons area at the university tomorrow. According to the schedule Vestering approved, we're having a domestic *lunch*." She winked and pointed to the sky while making a rocket sound effect.

He loaded her heavy backpack into the cab's storage net, then gave her a wide smile. "Wouldn't miss it for the world."

CHAPTER 17

JERZI SQUINTED IN the noonday sun as he walked the center part of the path across the campus commons and wished he'd brought his sniper's cap with its fold-out visor. He'd look like a dorf, to use Pico's current favorite word, but it'd be easier on his eyes. Winter in paradise was still hot enough to make him glad he'd worn a red sleeveless knit shirt with his cargo pants and boots. His favorite gold-and-ruby earrings made him more dressed up than most.

The original plan had been to launch from the Materials Science building's loading dock, but it appeared the event had locally trended, because fifty or sixty students had found various reasons to be in the area. Vestering's corner office had a clear view of the loading dock, so Andra told everyone to head to the Math building's loading dock instead, across the floater and well away from disapproving eyes. As a bonus, the dock wouldn't be busy until construction resumed. The university had explained it as "permit issues"; they still hadn't admitted the third-floor construction area had been a crime scene.

From what Andra had said, it was a light day for classes, which was why she chose it for the launch. There were still several hundred people on the floater, and more seemed to be joining the launch party. The cluster of buildings and people made the one by one-and-a-half kilometer floater seem small. He could see why Andra thought it was overbuilt.

Up ahead, a flash of color caught his eye. Andra's short gold and white jacket over green pants with gold detail stripes stood out in a sea of more casually-clothed students as they walked along. He liked the suit because it was tailored tight enough to highlight her beautifully muscular figure. He told himself that just looking was fine; it was touching that would cause trouble.

Jerzi's left thigh felt surprisingly good after the morning's visit to a different medical center that had a minder healer on staff. Bone regenerators were all right, but he'd take a good healer any day.

The walk afforded him his first good look at the building exteriors on the floater from the ground level, this time without the rain. The designers had created a pleasing blend of engineered curves and tropical flora. The repeated architectural theme of roundness made a dramatic and exotic impression, though he suspected it was aggravating when trying to hang something on the wall. Still, the Math building's abundant glass reflected the equally abundant glass of the three-story Materials Science building and five-story Chemistry building behind him, which in turn reflected and multiplied the lush trees, vines, and big-leafed flowering plants. The multiple light and heavy flitters in the air over the taller building looked like big, lumbering hummingbirds. Some of the flitter paint jobs made his sparkling red Pazorbaal look dull by comparison.

Out of habit, he'd been keeping an eye on Pico as she walked with the launch team, even though he knew she'd call it hovering. She wore a sleeveless white-and-red jumpsuit. Her hair was now cherry red and silver, but pulled back in a clip to hang down her back. She'd added a dashing red-and-white checkered resilk scarf. It was an homage, she'd told him, to the first space exploration suits, except for the self-contained environment apparatus, lasers, and armor.

He'd been surprised to see Sojaire Celeyron had shown up for the launch, since he was supposed to be working. He'd even dressed in nice boots and a slant-hemmed tunic and pants for the occasion. Jerzi knew Pico had once had a teenage crush on him, right after space camp, but she'd stopped talking about feelings once their family began disintegrating. Looking at them together, he wondered if they might be seeing each other differently, now that they were young adults. He snorted to himself. The last thing she'd want from her father was advice on her love life, considering how badly his tanked.

Andra, who had been leading, dropped back to speak to Pico and the rest of the team, who were carrying the rocket parts. Jerzi had met them earlier, when he and Pico had arrived at Andra's office after stacking his flitter on the Materials Science building's airpad. In addition to Ms. Grien, of the watery-native body mods, the team included Ms. Dortief, of Doomreaper robot fame, and two others. Andra pointed toward the Math building's doors. The team, plus Sojaire, veered off and headed in that direction.

Andra looked around until she saw Jerzi, then waited for him to catch up. "I sent them through the building so they could get to the dock first and set up a perimeter. We'll take the rest of the horde around the long way."

"Good idea," he said. "Who are all these people?"

"Romila's Chemistry students, the Practical Applications class, and most of my classes." She shaded her eyes with her hand and blinked once as she focused on the Math building entrance. "I think we have Ms. Grien to thank for the impromptu audience. The PR business lost a shining star when she opted for the sciences."

"Speaking of Romila, I thought she'd be here." He'd heard one of the launch team express disappointment that Romila wasn't there to witness the success of his homemade rocket fuel.

"So did I." She frowned. "She's not answering pings. It's not like her."

He glanced at her, catching worry on her face before she smoothed it away. "You're afraid she might also be a target."

"I should have thought of her last night." Her voice was quiet, with a subtle thread of guilt.

He shook his head. "You and me both. I'm the one with the suspicions."

"She'd never forgive me if I sent the police to check on her, even if I could convince them to do it." She heaved a heavy sigh. "All we can do for now is wait."

The pathway curved to the left of the Math building, and was more shaded. Signs at the fork up ahead pointed left to the public transportation dock and right to the loading dock. The group veered to the right, completely ignoring the notice that the dock was closed to non-construction traffic. Like students everywhere, he supposed.

They rounded a sharper, southward curve, and the edge of the floater, the loading dock, and the sea beyond came into view. The spectators were spreading out up ahead, but so far staying behind the makeshift barrier of chairs and lengths of flexible fiber conduit that he suspected might have been lifted from the unattended construction supplies in the lobby.

Andra deftly separated her Materials Science students and set them to guarding the perimeter and the food. Jerzi and Sojaire hung back with the crowd until Andra found them and sent them forward to help the launch team if needed.

The dock turned out to be ideal, with not even a pontoon to get in the way. As the team set up the rocket, Jerzi took the opportunity to examine the setup. As he'd remembered, it was built from salvaged household items—a sink hose, a kaffa machine cone, and a child's toy—and ignited by a standard wirekey. The fuel was a mix of household and garden chemicals.

He stepped back again, closer to where most of the team and Andra were now standing. Truòng, a nimble and wiry man, was using a telescoping wand with a mirror at one end to help him attach a cable to the bottom of what looked like the naked control cube for a holoviewer. Dortief, a short, muscular woman, was hammering a stake into the self-healing surface of the dock. The attached tie line would prevent the stand from flying into the crowd.

Jerzi smiled at his daughter. "I'm looking forward to seeing this. How do you know you have the right energy ratio for the lift? Did you test it?"

Pico and Grien exchanged glances. Andra looked up to the sky and whistled nonchalantly, the picture of not hearing what was about to be said.

"Oh, no," said Grien with wide-eyed sincerity. "That would have been against the project rules. Adams did the math, and the team verified it. The launch will be the proof of concept."

Pico shook her head. "No math needed. I just looked stuff up." Pico sidled closer to him and lowered her voice confidentially. "Theoretically, the exhaust smells like burned green coffee."

"Oh, good... uh, I mean, a plausible working theory," he said.

Truòng and Dortief finished their tasks nearly simultaneously and rejoined the team, and Andra stepped closer. "We'll save the speeches for later. Ms. Adams, if you'll do the honors."

Pico looked to Truòng, and he nodded. "Three... two... one..." She pointed at Truòng. He pressed the button.

The wirekey on the rocket lit up. The chemical propellant hissed loudly, and after a momentary hesitation, the little rocket zoomed upward.

Some of the students cheered immediately, but most were still watching the rocket's trajectory. Though they'd launched at an angle toward the sea, the prevailing higher breeze had already straightened it. The rocket wobbled as a gust of wind blew it toward the Math building's south wing, then continued its upward trajectory.

Pico alternated between watching the rocket and a readout on her percomp. "The winds are killing us."

Andra swore quietly. Jerzi glanced at her, and saw she was tracking the rocket with her oculars. "The trim fin is about to... there it goes." The rocket started spinning and losing altitude, and another gust of wind knocked it sideways, directly toward the Math building's roof.

"Phien, destruct. Now!" ordered Pico. Trường didn't argue, he just pressed a third button on the controller. After a heart-stopping moment, the rocket exploded with a fiery orange bang. Several bigger pieces plummeted down into the water, but the rest blew farther along with the wind, depositing debris like confetti.

The spectators cheered, like it was a Founder's Day fireworks show.

"That's it," said Andra. "Better get to your classes before we all get in trouble."

The crowd laughed and began walking away. Andra had the team put the rocket stand and cables in the box of supplies they'd brought, then promised she'd personally take care of hauling it back to her office.

Pico ran over to Jerzi for a quick hug. "Sojaire is walking me to the Chemistry building because he wants to talk, but first, I promised Val I'd stop in to see the kids in the childcare center." She rolled her eyes and pointed toward Sojaire. "*Someone* told her that Mairwen taught them to play a game, and Val is worried they've been traumatized for life."

She picked up her bag and slung its strap across her body, then went to join Sojaire, who was waiting on the walkway that would take them around the Math building's south wing.

Jerzi picked up the box before Andra could, and looked innocently up at the clear blue sky when Andra raised an eyebrow and crossed her arms.

"*Burro terco,*" she muttered, but a smile hovered around her mouth.

In her Materials Science building office, a windowless, beige-colored room with odd angles and curves, she had him put the box on a shelf in her supply closet. On the floor, he noticed her backpack and floral gun bag as he stepped back. "Thank you for inviting me, by the way. I'm proud of my kid. Sorry, my adult, has-her-own-life-now kid."

"You're welcome, and you should be." She closed and biometric sealed the closet's door. "I've been meaning to ask about Ms. Tamheurre."

"She's better. They're letting her go tomorrow. Her parents came in, which meant Pico finally got a good night's rest in her own bed last night." He smiled. "So did I, thanks to that pain patch. That thing could knock a Jumper cold."

She waggled her eyebrows and grinned. "Who do you think I got them from?"

He laughed. Before he lost his courage, he said, "I'm going back to the range after lunch, and I saw your gun case in your closet. Care to come along?" Inside, he rolled his eyes. He probably sounded like a fifteen-year-old asking for a first date.

Fortunately, Andra only smiled ruefully. "I'd really love to, but I have ten minutes to eat and get to class, and I won't be done until six. My worldly goods are here because I'm switching hostels tonight. Hopefully, I've booked one *without* chemmed redball fans who have to be rounded up by the university's anti-riot squad."

"That must have tanked." He smiled sympathetically to cover his disappointment. "I hope your new one is better." He couldn't ask her out tomorrow without sounding desperate. He tried to tell himself it was for the best, since he was leaving the day after, and it would probably be years until their paths crossed again. It made his chest feel as hollow as when he'd said goodbye to Pico.

He gave her a sharp, proper salute, and she returned it.

"It's been a pleasure to see you again, Subcaptain Lightning." He wanted to smile, to show he was unaffected by the end of their time together, but he couldn't lie to her or himself. Instead, he memorized her strikingly pretty face and the solid strength in her stance. She was like no one else he knew.

"Same goes, Commander Crush." She nodded respectfully, and clasped her hands behind her back.

He turned and left her office, before he said anything stupid about wishes for a different path or the ache in his chest.

At the east end of the building, he took the stairs up to the airpad instead of the lift, then walked to the north kiosk and entered his code. Two students arrived moments later and entered their codes. The stacker was noisy, slow, and balky, and an older woman was ahead of him in line, so he crossed a few meters to the north edge of the building and looked out to sea.

The public transport stop to the west was temporarily idle. The windsocks at the sea gate entrance, where public ferries entered the control channel, were deflated, barely twitching. Hazy lumps of green on the horizon hinted at islands, but clear, blue-green water dominated. He could almost hear the calm water lapping against the floater's edge. He'd miss that gentle sound when he went back to landlocked Etonver.

He was startled by the sound of a whining flitter airfoil, and suddenly, a large flitter the color of an oil slick streaked fast overhead as it banked up north and east to turn hard around and bullet toward the east.

"Farkin' frybrain!" one of the students waiting in line yelled. Jerzi couldn't agree more. If he knew who had airspace jurisdiction, he'd ping a complaint. Stunts like that so near an airpad could be fatal.

While the stacker was sliding his flitter onto the airpad, his percomp pinged with a mysterious message from Mairwen. *"Bad air traffic coming."* She'd probably meant it for Luka, somewhere in Tremplin, and accidentally included him and Sojaire. Mairwen and technology weren't friends.

In his flitter, he selected the coordinates for a restaurant near the gun range. He could have waited on the airpad for the traffic system to connect, but out of courtesy for the next person in line, he lifted off and drifted slowly over the north edge of the building, away from the public transport stop with its multiple boarding docks for the large, fast water taxis that serviced the islands and floaters.

Just as the one-minute countdown began, an emergency hazard warning sounded and flashed on the flitter's control panel. Protocol said to land or get out of the way, but neither the control panel nor the viewscreen showed him what he was supposed to be avoiding. Maybe Mairwen's warning had meant the Tremplin traffic system was acting up again.

Or maybe she somehow knew about the five combat-modified flitters that rose in tight formation from behind the Chemistry building to the west. Their stylized red-to-gold color was wrong for the military, and their silhouettes said they carried dual wide-array beamers.

Growling every bad word he knew in any language, he killed the traffic system request and flew his eye-catching, bright red flitter as close as he dared to the edge of the Materials Science building, while considering his options. Leaving the floater was out of the question, since Pico was still there. Andra, too. If Mairwen's message was about the merc ships, she was likely on the floater, and there was a good chance Luka was, as well. That meant that everyone he cared about on the entire planet was in the same place as five mercenary gunships, which could only spell trouble.

He nudged his altitude higher, just in time to see a small blue flitter launch from the airpad toward the east. He took advantage of the free airpad to land his flitter, bouncing it a little in his haste. He didn't want it stuck in the stacker, so he eased east, off the airpad, onto a graveled area that separated the airpad from the rooftop foliage. He opened the doors and scrambled out. After a moment's hesitation, he put on his cap and multi-pocket vest, and grabbed his gun bag, then sealed the doors. If his suspicions turned out to be baseless, he could laugh at himself later.

He took the stairs two at a time down to the second floor, and fast-walked to Andra's office door. It was sealed and dark; she must have already left to grab a bite and get to her next class. He sent her a fast ping message and kicked himself for not having done so sooner. For good measure, he also pinged Mairwen, Pico, and Sojaire, using his hastily applied earwire to subvocalize quick messages about what he'd seen.

In the meantime, he needed a better view of the Chemistry building's roof. Thanks to two days' worth of tours through the buildings, he had memorized the reversed-J-shaped layout, so he headed up the central stairs to the big third-floor Materials Sciences lab in the southwest corner of the building. The lab's western windows were about fifty meters from the Chemistry building, and had a clear view of the front. He wouldn't be able to see the taller building's airpad, but he could see whatever was in the sky above it.

As he approached the lab entrance, he pulled his cap lower on his head and looked down, slouching his shoulders, like he was just another maintenance worker doing his job. He kept wanting to tap his earwire to make sure it was working. Someone should have responded to his pings by now.

He slid into the open doorway and turned left, which took him toward a bank of storage lockers. No one paid him any attention, because they were all clustered at the western windows, staring at the Chemistry building.

"What blew up?" said a dark-skinned woman with close-cropped hair. "Lavong can't blame us this time."

"Knowing *those* morons," said a blonde woman with a German accent, "it was another gas leak."

The young, bald, blue-skinned "native" man activated his wristcomp. "Wankers. My sister's in that building."

Jerzi eased a few steps into the room so he could see what they were looking at. Where the third-floor Chemistry lab windows should have been, empty, scorched frames gaped, and smoke wafted out. Because he'd seen them before, he recognized the scorch marks caused by a wide-array beamer.

Behind the smoke, he thought he saw shadows of human movement. If the university followed the procedure they'd described to Mairwen, they'd start evacuating the Chemistry building, and seal off the Materials Science building connecting doors and walkways.

The question was, did he want to be inside the Chemistry building, where Pico might be, or stay in the Materials Science building, where Andra might be? What the holy freakin' hell were the merc gunships doing on a university campus? And why wasn't anyone answering his *kurczę* pings?

CHAPTER 18

ANDRA WAS HALFWAY up the center stairs to the third floor, where her first afternoon class was, when she'd received a strange ping from Mairwen Morganthur. Andra couldn't imagine what "bad air traffic" meant, or why she was supposed to care.

After Jerzi had left, she'd made herself eat the sausage roll she'd brought, even though she'd felt like the bottom was falling out of her stomach. It was a stark reminder that she'd never wanted to again depend on someone else for happiness, and lose herself in grief when it was gone. Her reminders hadn't done any good.

The fact that she'd stopped to read the ping probably saved her life, or at least some pain. On the very next step she took, she heard the unmistakable sound of plasma rifle fire, and a scream that cut short, coming from the top of the stairs. She bounded back down the stairs and back down the hall until the curvature hid her from view. She listened intently, but didn't hear more weapon fire, just a man and woman arguing. She couldn't make out the words.

She activated her earwire and pinged an emergency priority message to building security. No one responded, but she assumed they were busy, what with people in the third-floor hallways with plasma rifles. Since security was handled remotely, during safety drills, the university expected faculty and staff to first keep themselves safe, and second, keep the students safe. This part of the second floor was mostly carved up into tiny offices for faculty, staff, and researchers, with numerous individual doors, all closed. The other side, past the stairs, had classrooms and larger lecture halls. She was as safe as anyone, for now, so they had to be her priority.

Listening hard, she walked stealthily toward the stairs, watching for movement. She launched and sprinted past them. At the first occupied classroom, she stopped, took a calming breath, and opened the door. She told the startled professor and students that she'd seen people with guns, and to seal their door and get out of view of the door and the exterior windows and stay that way, until building security told them differently.

She did it with each of the occupied classrooms she came to, delivering the same message with calm authority, to reduce the likelihood of panic. She was about to start doing the same in the Chemistry building when she heard the blast of an explosion. She scrambled back out of the donut walkway and saw shattered glass raining down from above, and a red-and-gold mercenary flitter firing a wide-array beamer above her, into the third-floor lab windows. The gunship rose out of sight soon after. The donuts were built to withstand powerful natural forces, but she doubted the designers had considered a military-style attack in their risk scenarios.

At the moment, all the action was centered on the third floor of both the Chemistry and Materials Sciences buildings, and she desperately needed information on what was happening. Da'vin had been the recon wizard, but Andra could get the job done. The only scenario she could come up with at the moment was a daylight theft, though of what, she hadn't a clue. Mercenaries were expensive and not particularly suited to punch-and-haul operations. Killing local comms, however, was definitely a mercenary trick, because they could rely on their own encrypted comms. Ground-based theft crews liked tech suppressors better, because they increased the success rate for the low-tech methods they preferred.

She carefully and quickly slid past the stairs again, then sprinted down the hall to her office, where she slapped the biometric reader. She closed and locked the door behind her fast, and opaqued its view window, then activated the deskcomp, but it couldn't find a net connection. To be thorough, she tried the wallcomp, which was fiber-connected to the building systems, but it wouldn't even tell her the time.

She opened her closet and pulled out her gun bag. It wouldn't be practical or wise to carry around her Hellrim combat rifle, because to civilians, a projectile gun and a plasma rifle were practically the same. The university security guards, when they finally arrived, would likely shoot her first and ask questions later.

Flechette guns, on the other hand, looked almost like toys, and she had two of them. She was glad she'd kept the no-name one she'd confiscated from the hyena pack, and that it had been easy to repair and reset the biometric trigger to her fingerprint. Her larger Lipara was simpler and better, but the second gun would do in a pinch. She wished she'd had time to practice with it with the heavier Lipara flechettes, but at least she had plenty of boxes, despite having led Jerzi to believe otherwise.

She eyed her backpack and considered its contents. Her new white-and-gold jacket was too bright, but it did have pockets, and all she had on under it was a sports bra, because the long-sleeved jacket was too hot to wear with anything else. The multi-pocket combat vest in her backpack all but screamed military. She couldn't carry seventy kilos on a spy mission, so she reluctantly left her backpack alone. The other fun toys in it weren't called for, at least yet.

She swapped out her darker dress boots for the red running shoes she kept in her office. They'd improve both her traction and her stealth. She stuffed flechette boxes in her pants pockets. Too bad the speed clip for the Lipara was still in her trashed apartment. She loaded both guns with flechettes, six in the smaller gun and eight in her Lipara, then stuffed them in her jacket pockets, rather than the waistband of her pants. It would be too embarrassing if she shot herself in the ass.

She grabbed a small mirror from her desk, then remembered the mirror on a stick the launch team had used, and fished it out of their supplies. She crouched at her door before clearing the view window and holding up the mirror. She didn't hear or see anything, so she cautiously hand-cranked the iris open enough to stick her mirror into the hall. It was deserted.

She pulled the mirror back and collapsed its wand before stuffing it in her upper chest pocket. She palmed open the door and sealed it behind her, then hugged the curving wall as best she could as she walked quietly toward the back stairs near the airpad lifts. Thankfully, most of the office doors she passed were closed and dark. For those that weren't, she gave them the same instructions she'd given the classrooms: Lock the door and hide.

The back stairway was the least bad option for getting to the third floor, since it was at the east end, farthest away from the Chemistry building. Stairway doors were always recognizable because they were some of the few ordinary, rectangular openings on the campus, owing to city fire-safety codes.

She climbed the stairs purposefully and quietly, listening intently. If she lived through this, maybe she'd get hearing implants to go along with her oculars. Professors in quiet universities in paradise shouldn't need such things, but mercenary units shouldn't be shooting up said universities, either.

She'd only just exited the door when she heard the lift doors chime. She ducked back into the stairwell and watched via her mirror through the door's view window, leaving the door slightly ajar so she could hear. Four mercs, in red-to-gold uniforms that made them look like a gun-toting dance troupe, stepped out, various weapons at the ready.

"*Zhànshì, bàogào zhuàngtài,*" a woman barked loudly in Mandarin, ordering someone to report. A thin, dark woman stepped into view and stood at attention.

"Still no comms, sir." She spoke English to a tall, bald man with enough gold earrings to start his own store. "No tech suppressor controls in his office." She tilted her head to indicate the executive suite. "One of the lab crew shot August Two before the connecting doors closed, and January Six is missing." Mercenary companies had picked up the military habit of call names, to reduce the enemy's ability to associate a name with a face. Interesting choice of words, "lab crew."

Unfortunately, the leader didn't conveniently mention mission objectives, but at least they took their team member with them when they marched smartly down the hall toward the west. Andra eased out the door slowly and glided to the far wall. On the far side of the elevators, someone had burned a jagged hole right through the ornate iris door that led to Department Leader Vestering's palatial office suite.

As much as she disliked the man, she had to see if he or his admins had been hurt or needed help. She used her mirror to check the hallway, then slipped fast through the large burn hole and into the suite's reception area.

She found Vestering in his corner, view-window office, unharmed but shaken. He had the start of a bruise on his jaw.

"You shouldn't be in here, De Luna." He seemed coherent enough, but his naturally resonant voice sounded thin, and he gripped the arms of his expensive executive chair like they were his only hold against zero gravity.

"Sir, you need to leave." She looked around his disarrayed office briefly. "Is anyone else here?

He shook his head. "No. They told me to stay."

"Who, the mercenaries? Red uniforms? They're busy. You need to leave now."

"They said they wouldn't hurt anyone if I gave them my codes and biometrics." He shuddered. "Thank the stars, Baerlin was at lunch, or they might have killed him when they shot the door."

"They'll only keep that promise if it's convenient. Let's get you out of here." She made it an order. Vestering abruptly stood. She ignored his obvious embarrassment over the fact he'd wet his pants. Even trained gunnin sometimes lost control of bodily functions when the primal brain took over.

She led him to the ruined door, checked the hallway, and had him into the stairway in a matter of seconds. She listened for a moment, then started down the steps and motioned for him to follow.

He balked. "My flitter is upstairs." He pointed up to indicate the airpad above them.

"So are the mercs. You need to be where they aren't."

He frowned, then nodded and followed. He tried to walk quietly, but his spring-heeled dress sandals weren't suited to stealth.

"Where is everybody?" she asked, keeping her voice low. "The halls are deserted."

"They made me order all our classes to the big Chem lecture hall for an emergency briefing, one wing at a time. I did the third floor, then the comms went down." He touched his bruised jaw and winced. "They got mad when I couldn't tell them anything about a tech suppressor."

At the first level, she had him stand against the wall inside the stairwell while she poked her mirror out the always-open doorway. The path looked clear all the way to the Math building's main entrance, which was only forty meters away.

"They called for reinforcements, before the comms died." Vestering said suddenly. "The big bald man ordered three more units to lock down the floater."

"Any clue why they're here?"

"No, but they asked if I knew where Lavong is. I told them to check his office or any of the labs."

"We're going to the Math building. It's standalone, so I'm hoping it's a secondary objective. Your best bet is the emergency evacuation boat under the loading dock. If you run into people you know personally, take them with you."

He frowned. "You aren't coming?"

"No. I'm more useful here. Let's go."

Vestering wanted to run, but she held him to a brisk walk. They'd lose time and attract attention if he fell. She kept her left hand on the flechette gun in her pocket and darted quick glances around the sky and empty commons. She all but shoved him through the Math building's doorway and pointed to the southern wing. "Get off the floater. Keep checking comms. The minute you can, call in the police and the military. Tell them the mercs probably have hostages in the Chem lecture hall."

He gave her one final, unhappy frown before turning and walking fast across the atrium. She had the feeling he'd be taking the boat by himself, but it couldn't be helped. His executive authority would bring a faster response.

She tried her percomp and earwire again, but wasn't surprised when nothing happened. Someone had locked down the floater comms against the mercenaries, and she'd bet her next ten beers that it wasn't university security.

On her way back to the Materials Science building, she heard a commotion at the public transport stop that was to her right, between the buildings. She wavered, then figured a quick look wouldn't hurt. She used the vegetation, which was fortunately overdue for cutting back, to cover her approach. She was puzzled as to why the dock was deserted except for one unattended people-mover boat, until she crept out a little more and saw the pair of large race boats blocking access to the sea gate, two hundred meters out. She used her oculars to confirm that the boats were well armed, and painted to look like sea monsters with teeth.

The source of the commotion was a couple of men who were dragging an unconscious or dead mercenary, trying to get her legs free of a tangler vine. The men were dressed like students, in casual shorts and transparent knit shirts, but they were older, with typical crew body art and jewelry.

"*Den échoume chróno gi 'aftó!*" the shorter one hissed. Andra's Greek was rusty, but she thought he said, "We don't have time for this."

The taller man shoved his companion toward the north along the path. "*Kratíste to rolói,*" he snarled, ordering the other man to keep watch.

The taller man's intention became obvious when he pulled out a phase knife and slit the woman's pants, while undoing the waistband of his own. Some rockbrains, usually men, were so fucking predictable.

Andra pulled out and aimed both her flechette guns, then shot the shorter man in the back of his neck and kidney and the taller man twice in the throat before either one knew what was happening. They crumpled in boneless heaps of dying flesh and pouring blood. The merc woman was on her own for now.

Andra reloaded her guns, then went back to the Materials Science building's east entrance. She watched a flitter leave the Chem building and cross overhead. The arc of the flight said it was landing on the Math building's airpad.

More than ever, she needed information. And a platoon or two of gunnin, while she was asking the universe for favors.

CHAPTER 19

SOME DAYS, LUKA could be patient, but not today. He'd arrived on the campus floater forty-five minutes ago, with Mairwen landing their flitter on the Materials Science airpad. They had compromised on her desire to be nearby when Luka met with the man called Lièrén Sòng, and Luka's desire for her to be safely far away. He would walk to the Math building, and she would keep watch from the top of the Materials Science building. Sojaire had already asked to go to Pico Adams's rocket demonstration for her class, so it was a thin but plausible cover story.

Though they'd agreed to meet at twelve-fifteen, Luka wanted Sòng to be early, so he could listen to what the man had to say, use his "essence" talent on him, because that's what Zheer had really been asking, then leave.

Precisely at the appointed time, the temporary construction door chimed. Luka verified the man standing outside looked like the image he'd been sent, then opened the door. He was relieved that the man seemed older and more relaxed in person; his official photo made him look like a priggish twenty-year-old.

Luka stepped back to allow the man to enter. He was shorter than Luka by six or eight centimeters and wore nondescript brown pants and a tan shirt. Once over the threshold, he bowed. "Thank you for agreeing to meet with me, Investigator Foxe." His Standard English was impeccable, but there was a Mandarin cadence to his speech.

"Please, call me Luka." He closed the door behind them, then waved toward the two borrowed office chairs and a crate for a table with cups of water. "It's the best I can do for amenities, I'm afraid."

Sòng looked around with interest as they walked. "I've not had the opportunity to visit many police investigation sites."

Once they were seated, each carefully, as if the chairs were untrustworthy, Luka's impatience got the best of him. "I'll be honest. I'm here primarily because someone I respect asked me to meet you."

Sòng nodded solemnly. "I appreciate your honesty, and your

forbearance. I asked people I respect to help arrange this, because I owe you a debt."

Luka raised an eyebrow. "Are you here in your capacity as the Citizen Protection Service diplomatic liaison to Abasarran, or as the Sòng Family Trust representative?"

Sòng smiled slightly. "My fame precedes me, as does yours." Luka took that to be an admission that he'd done research on Luka, too. He imagined the CPS had access to a lot of records. "The debt, however, is my own. My actions in the past caused you and many others harm, and I am doing my best to atone. In your case, the harm was nearly fatal, so my debt is considerable and must be personal."

Despite his best intentions to remain detached, Luka was intrigued. "The only time I was nearly killed was by that *helvítis raggeit* pedophile in the joyhouse kitchen. I know everyone who was in that kitchen, and you weren't there…" Intuition sparked bright and hot. "But you *were* when he escaped CPS custody in the first place. Or perhaps should have been?"

Sòng blinked, then smiled ruefully. "Your fame is deserved."

Not, Luka noted, a denial.

Luka usually went kilometers out of his way to avoid remembering the Collector case, where a pair of depraved pedophiles had converted an interstellar ship into a corrupt, grisly playroom, and stacked the bodies of dead children in the ship's subzero hold like winter cordwood. The case had obsessed him, and sent his hidden minder talents out of control. It was his most dangerous set of talent-driven memories, etched in horror and blood and the restless ghosts of dozens of doomed children. He felt his body temperature start to leach away.

Desperately, he focused on running, the memory of running with Mairwen that morning, the impact of the pavement, the heave of his lungs, the rhythm of Mairwen's breath, the trickle of sweat on his skin. His unruly talent-driven memory slowly subsided. He had no idea how long he'd been in his struggle. "Sorry," he said, and attempted a smile. "I get distracted sometimes."

Sòng looked surprised. "Are you a minder?"

Luka smiled with practiced ease and shook his head. "No, not according to both rounds of CPS testing." He'd often been accused of it in his career, but usually for his intuition, not for the real talents. His talents were benign to everyone but himself, but even ordinary minder talents were suspect, and his were unique.

"So your records say." He crossed his legs. "Mine say I am a sifter and a twister, and do not say I am also a telepath."

Luka felt his eyebrows raise at the careful statement. He recollected that sifters could detect truth and lies, and could feel when another minder's talent energized. Sòng's combination of talents would make for one hell of an interrogator. Another piece of the puzzle fell into place. "That sensational book from three years ago was right. That pedophile didn't escape, the CPS let him go."

Sòng shook his head. "Funds had been changing hands in a certain unit for years, to influence favorable outcomes. The employees were acting for themselves, not the organization."

"The corrupt trade office, you mean." The scandal that only one person—Sòng—came away from unscathed, if Sojaire's research was right.

Sòng met Luka's gaze squarely. "Newstrends are so unreliable."

Luka had to admire a man who could lie with the truth, or in this case, tell the truth with a lie. "So you weren't involved in the, uhm, extracurricular activities, but feel guilty you didn't know about them." Luka crossed his arms and shook his head. "You don't owe me anything. I was just doing my job."

"I do owe you, because I wasn't doing mine." He planted his feet and put his hands on his thighs. "My parents sent me to the CPS Academy when I was twelve, and to the CPS Minder Institute after that. It was a safe place for minders like me, given that I had enough raw talent that I could hurt someone badly if I didn't learn to control it. The most important tenet of their instruction was that we bear as much responsibility for our inaction as for our action." He frowned. "Once, the CPS was doing the right things for the Central Galactic Concordance, both minders and non-minders alike. Even if they've lost sight of it, the mission still needs doing."

Luka kept a rein on his temper. "I think we'll have to agree to disagree on that. I doubt I'll ever have a lot of respect for the CPS. You probably already know my mother washed out of the Minder Corps because the enhancement drugs were killing her." He tilted his head a little, wondering what Sòng's opinion was. "Does everyone have to take them?"

An unintelligible expression flitted across Sòng's face before he smoothed it away. "They're mostly used for telepath or telekinetic talents. Patterners don't seem to benefit from them." He took a drink of water and held onto the glass. "The CPS contracts with pharmas to develop new drugs and dispensaries to tailor them. It can be difficult to find the right formulation."

Luka nodded, remembering the various combinations they'd tried on his mother, some worse than others. Sòng probably had similar experiences, considering his talent mix.

Right as he was about to ask Sòng another question, his percomp tingled against his skin, signaling an incoming ping from Mairwen. A moment later, a synth voice repeated the message in his earwire. *"Bad air traffic coming."* He loved the woman, but she conserved words like they were an endangered species, and it made her communications particularly cryptic.

"Problem?" asked Sòng.

"Just a traffic alert." But a good reminder that he needed to move the meeting along. If he was going to use his "essence" talent on Sòng, he needed the man relaxed and not paying attention. Luka smiled. "So what does a diplomatic liaison do on a frontier planet?"

"I represent the CPS, and make its services available to the government and individuals. I supervise four minder clinics, which we've combined with local medical clinics, and in one case, with a body shop. I also coordinate CPS cooperation in emergency response." Though his tone was quiet, a thread of pride ran through it.

"No minder testing?" Luka reached for his water glass, as a cover for snaking out a tendril of his talent toward the man in front of him. Luka didn't practice with it as often as he should, but regular use had helped tame it.

He smiled. "No, and no Jumpers, either." He'd apparently fielded the question often. "The CPS is a guest on Abasarran, and the government hasn't expressed an interest in hosting a testing center or a Jumper base. Individuals may request testing through my office, and we arrange free interstellar transit to the nearest testing center."

Luka was ambivalent about minder testing. It helped kids with measurable talents to know that they weren't going crazy, but it also stigmatized them. "Is that why you're here on Nila Marbela?" He extended another tendril.

"No, my wife and I were traveling on family business. My contact said you would be here, and I took a chance that you would be willing to meet. Officially, I'm taking my desert-planet bride for a brief vacation on a water-planet paradise." Sòng frowned and set down his water. "Please stop what you're doing."

Luka froze his talent and assumed an expression of puzzlement. "What am I doing?"

"Activating another minder talent you don't have. The first one was some variant of patterner, but this one is on the edge of telepathy, and yet not. You're very subtle."

Luka took a chance he'd never contemplated, and trusted a man from the CPS. "You're the first person who's ever noticed. I meant no harm."

"I'm a top-level sifter with a lot of training, or I might not have noticed, either." Sòng was silent a moment. "It feels like a unique. What does your talent do?"

"It gives me a holistic impression of who someone is, their essence. I've only ever told a few people about it, because only my telepath mother believed me. If I tried to claim either of my talents now, thousands of criminal cases I worked on would be called into question." Luka twirled his water glass in his hand. "After the Collector case, both my talents went wild, and were eating away at my sanity, until I met someone who could help me find a way to control them." Luka shook his head. "I got lucky."

"Trauma and minder talents can be a difficult combination. After I nearly died in an accident, it took months working with another minder for me to recover, and you didn't even have that advantage." He picked up his water glass again. "Does your essence talent work on everyone?"

"Almost." It was a novel experience, being able to discuss his talent openly, and with someone who understood. "I don't get much from top-level shielders, and nothing from the one or two non-minder natural shielders I've met. I think I tried it on a Kameleon once." He barely suppressed a shudder. "It wasn't pleasant."

Sòng nodded sympathetically. "I can't say that I've ever worked with them."

Which Luka took to mean that since the CPS had never publicly acknowledged the Kameleon program, Sòng wasn't allowed to, either. The CPS was monstrously big, and doubtless had three times more secret programs than public ones.

"I've never met a twister before," Luka said. "I know cleaners erase memories, and they're gone for good."

"Twisters can't erase them, but we can change them, and leave no trace. If the twister is good enough, the real memory can be left intact, leaving two versions of the truth." He smiled crookedly. "Most people think we're dangerous."

Because Luka had hidden his talents, he'd never had bigotry directed at him, but he'd seen it everywhere, once he'd left his home on the comparatively tolerant planet of Lumi Silta. "In my experience, angry, jealous, greedy, or scared people are the most dangerous, and they use the tools they have."

Sòng sipped his water. "Please forgive me if I am too blunt, but I believe you would not have used your talent on me if you hadn't been asked to do so by the person you trusted to arrange this meeting."

Luka felt his eyes widen. "Yes," he conceded. "It feels… unfair."

"Then I think you should do as you've been asked. The person I trusted to arrange my introduction to you specifically said I should be 'open to new experiences.'"

Luka's intuition sparked. "To forecasters, the rest of us are all n-dimensional chess pieces."

Sòng looked startled, then amused. "Indeed." He finished his water and placed the glass on the makeshift table. "What will make your task easier?"

Luka had only had one fully cooperative target before. Usually they were distracted or busy. "Tell me about life on a frontier planet."

As Sòng described a continent with a forest so vast, the locals were still finding new resources to catalog, and of the growing town where his wife was the new manager of infrastructure, Luka opened his talent and let the tangle of impressions come. A strong sense of ethics, and a respect for tradition… deeply held love intertwined with unworthiness… a deep and abiding anger at betrayal of him and the people he loved… twinges of loneliness and fear of rejection… a reverence of peace and justice.

Luka allowed his tendrils to withdraw, one by one, until his talent was quiet once more.

Sòng was looking at him expectantly. Luka hastily replayed the man's question in his head, about whether he'd been to Spires, the Central Galactic Concordance's gleaming showcase of a capital city. "Yes, I have to go in person every year to renew my High Court certification."

"I can recommend a hotel and bar, the next time you're there. You stayed there once, during the Collector case trial." A smile played about Sòng's lips. "My wife was a bartender at the time and remembers you."

Luka shook his head. "I'm sorry, but I met so many people then, and my memory from that time is poor." He'd been hounded like a nova-class star by the press at the time, and he'd hated it.

"I, too, have a poor memory of certain things." The statement seemed to amuse Sòng. "So, did you learn what you needed from me? If I hadn't known what to watch for, I wouldn't have felt it. It's like a phantom breeze."

Luka nodded. "I would hire you for any position of trust. I'm guessing that's what our respective chess masters want to know."

"Very likely." Sòng snorted. "I hope I have a few more years of unworthiness before being singled out for such an honor."

Luka chuckled. "I sync that." He felt some of his tension draining away, and had an idea. "I'm working on a case right now that you might be able to help me with, if you're willing. That can fulfill the favor you think you owe me."

Sòng shook his head regretfully. "I'm afraid I know nothing about forensic investigation."

"No, but I'm betting you know more than most about what pharmas and the CPS do for each other."

* * * * *

Lièrén made a deprecating gesture. "Of course, he also believes aliens from the Andromeda galaxy walk among us and meddle in our politics."

Luka laughed, as Lièrén had intended. He genuinely liked the older man, which was an unexpected bonus. When Luka was reserved, he was sharp, but when he was relaxed, and allowing his intellect free rein, he was a force to be reckoned with.

"Your great-grandfather sounds like he's, uhm, interesting to live with."

"Yes. Luckily, Abasarran doesn't yet have the civilized amenities he prefers." Sòng Tiān Cì's only visit in the last two years had delighted his wife Imara and her son, but had given Lièrén a sudden desire for strong drink.

A subtle flash from Luka's hand caught his eye. "I appreciate your courtesy, but I don't mind if you respond to the ping that came in earlier."

"Ping?" Luka activated the elegant wearable percomp on the back of his hand that had been subtly blinking. "I didn't even notice." He tapped his earwire, looking sheepish. "My partner will be unhappy…" He trailed off as he listened, worry spreading across his expressive face. He tapped his earwire again, then his percomp. "I'm not getting any signal."

Lièrén frowned and activated his own very powerful wristcomp. "Nor am I." That was unusual. Very little could stop CPS communications.

"My partner's message said five mercenary gunships landed on the Chemistry building's airpad. One of them shot at something in the Chemistry building. She wanted us to leave." His lips thinned with tension. "That was thirty-five minutes ago, and now we don't have comms."

Luka stood, and Lièrén stood with him. Luka sketched a bow. "It's been a delight, Mr. Sòng, and I hope we can meet again, but I have to get to Mairwen." He smiled briefly through his worry. "She thinks I'm a magnet for trouble."

Lièrén followed Luka as he walked quickly toward the door and entered the code to unseal it. "Can you find your own way up?"

"Yes, of course." Lièrén had been using his talents to check for people approaching the construction area since he arrived, but now he extended his talents as far as they would go. He'd been training his top-level sifter talent to detect synaptic signatures from increasing distances. "There's an activated ramper coming up… the lifts, I think, not the stairs. Only one other person is on the floor at the moment. A shielder, maybe, moving fast." He pointed toward the front of the building, where the stairs and lifts let passengers out into a widened balcony that joined both wings. "That way."

Luka gave him a startled look. "That's some talent."

Lièrén shrugged. "We use the tools we have."

Luka opened the door and was already keying the lock sequence by the time Lièrén cleared the iris doorway.

A high-energy weapon blast and high-pitched cry of pain sent Luka off like a shot down the hallway. Lièrén trotted behind, seeing that he could never match the pace. He focused on the ramper, who was both fully activated and giving off a haze of violence. The shielder was giving off nothing. Except it wasn't the void he felt from other shielders; it was more like the sound of static. Lièrén sensed Luka's anxiety spike, and sped up to see what the trouble was.

Twelve meters away, in the widest, circular area of the balcony, two women fought each other at astonishing speed. The smaller, very slender blonde in long-sleeved patterned dark green was bleeding from a scorched plasma wound on her right calf. Lièrén couldn't imagine how she was even managing to limp. The taller, broad-shouldered, black-skinned woman, the ramper, was in a tourist shirt, shorts, and running shoes. She was full of angry tension and blurry-fast, vocalizing with each strike she gave and hit she took. The blonde, who he recognized as Mairwen Morganthur, Luka's partner, was equally blurry-fast, silent, and almost relaxed by comparison. Her speed had to be the result of chems, but chemical rampers usually had exaggerated musculature.

The ramper tried to kick Morganthur's wounded calf, but Mairwen narrowly avoided it by lifting and bending her knee, then lunging forward, under the ramper's guard, and landing a punishing blow to the woman's diaphragm and an uppercut to the woman's jaw. Morganthur danced out of the way of a powerful roundhouse fist the ramper threw to cover her retreat.

Lièrén knew from experience that his sifter skills wouldn't work on an activated ramper, and his telepathy was too low-level to work from that distance. He could reach Luka, though.

Luka, do you want me to stay? He sent an image packet of what he could do.

Luka jerked a little in surprise, either from the telepathy or the offer. *Yes.*

Suddenly, in a blur of motion too fast for Lièrén to follow, the black woman was down, stunned, as if she didn't know how it happened. Mairwen was kneeling on the woman's heaving chest, two slender knives in her hands, just piercing the skin of the woman's throat. "Stay still, or die," Mairwen said, low and clear. She repeated it in Russian. She was breathing deeply, but not gasping for air like her opponent was, her lungs compressed by Mairwen's weight.

Luka had already closed half the distance, and Lièrén ran to catch up. He felt the ramper try to activate again, but she was nearly flatlined. Lièrén reached out with his sifter talent and slowed the mu receptors in her brain, which were essential to the ramper process for minders. He gave her a gentle boost of serotonin and gently nudged her delta receptors, enough to make her slightly euphoric and detached.

He knelt and closed his hand around her outstretched bare ankle, then used his telepathy to take control over her body. It was a skill he'd practiced, after nearly being killed by a rogue agent on Spires. Because she was already under his influence, she didn't fight him, although part of her mind knew she should.

Lièrén looked up at Luka and nodded.

Luka put his hand gently on Mairwen's shoulder. "*Ástin mín. Þetta er búið.*" His expression was full of concern and love.

Lièrén directed the ramper's eyes to close. Mairwen got to her feet, then leaned into Luka to let him help her limp a few steps away. She turned around to look at Lièrén, glancing at his hand on the ramper's ankle.

154 Carol Van Natta

Her expression was unreadable to him, but apparently not to Luka. "I'll explain in a minute," Luka said. "I trust him."

Mairwen looked to her partner, then nodded. "Her plasma beamer went flying." She tilted her head toward the south hallway.

"We'll look together," Luka said firmly, as if he was worried she'd take off without him.

Lièrén turned his attention to the ramper, making sure she didn't drift off to sleep with the blowback from overusing her talent. He riffled through her memories and picked up the gist without having to force much of anything. "She's an independent," he told Luka. "Anonymous contract to disable or kill either principal of your firm, with a bonus for both. Her hired surveillance help said Foxe was unreachable at the police station, so she targeted Morganthur as the easier mark. She's been following for two days, and sending progress updates every few hours. Earlier, when Morganthur suddenly left the roof of the other building and went downstairs at a speed only possible for another ramper, this woman decided to test her mettle first. She's very competitive, especially against women. She shot Morganthur to slow her down, to get her to fight instead of run. Payment is to be made to an anonymous escrow account, once the police get an accident or death report with either of your names."

Luka's lips pursed in thought. "Get the contact instructions and the account, if you can. Maybe they're traceable."

"I can do that. What do you want her to remember?"

Luka's expression darkened angrily for a moment, as his eyes flicked to the woman at his side. He took a deep breath and let it out slowly. "Make her think Mairwen was too fast for her, and vanished. Give her an explanation for her injuries, though."

Lièrén nodded and went to work. First he entered the contract and payment details in his percomp, so he wouldn't forget them. While his memory was vastly improved over what it used to be, when he'd been on disabling enhancement drugs and assaulted by a cleaner on a regular basis, he was far from the filer that his beloved wife, Imara, was.

For twisting, it was easier to find previous memories and adapt them to his purpose than invent new ones, so he traced hers until he found one of two mercs who had jumped her outside a bar because she'd killed one of their company. He wove her a blended memory of losing sight of Mairwen on the third floor, then being blindsided by two mercs. She got a shot off at one of them, but one was a fighting ramper, and they knocked her cold and left her where she lay. He also twisted an old memory that he hoped would give her a strong desire to rescind the current contract.

He used his sifter talent to dope her thoroughly, then stood. Rampers, he'd learned the hard way when rescuing Imara's son from one, recovered more quickly than anyone else. "She'll be out for perhaps twenty minutes, maybe more." He activated his percomp, then stopped. "I'll have to send the contract details once we have comms again."

Luka shook his head and smiled. "Thank you, Mr. Sòng. I'd say your debt is paid."

Lièrén returned the smile. "I would be honored if you would call me Lièrén." He bowed his head respectfully, then waved toward the downed ramper. "This one is for free. I dislike hired killers." He looked at the time. It was nearly one-thirty. "I believe my bride will be wondering about me. May I offer you a lift, perhaps to a medical center?"

Luka and Mairwen exchanged a look, and he briefly tightened his hold on her waist.

"No," said Luka at last, "we have our own flitter, and our only employee is still around here somewhere." He heaved a long-suffering sigh, but his eyes twinkled. "Good help is so hard to find."

CHAPTER 20

MOST DAYS, SOJAIRE Celeyron was half-convinced the universe hated him, but today, he had no doubt. His only objective when he'd gotten up that morning had been to get Pico to listen long enough for him to explain, well, everything.

Since then, he'd become the cover story for a clandestine meeting, with instructions to keep an eye out for anything suspicious; introduced to the energetic lot that was the Domestic Launch team, plus a dozen other mischief-makers from her Practical Applications class; and watched an improvised rocket narrowly miss a startled airsled pilot and self-destruct. After that, he'd been introduced to more of the children Valenia cared for, and said hello to the budding empath Miguel and his shy sister Celia, then met several more of Pico's friends as they walked across the commons to the tall Chemistry building. She was popular, and didn't seem to notice or care.

When she'd finally led him by the hand to an out-of-the-way alcove near the curving walkway that she said went to the Materials Science building, he'd suddenly become tongue-tied, not knowing where to start. The beginning was as good as any, since that's where his apologies had to start.

"Remember at space camp, when you found me trapped in the airlock?" When she nodded, he continued. "Do you know *why* you found me?"

"Sure. Insomnia," she answered. "The induced gravity felt weird. I know you're not supposed to be able to tell the difference, but I can." She shrugged one shoulder. "Plus dumb luck."

"Not luck. Well, it was that, too, but when–"

A priority ping sounded from the pendant-style percomp he wore around his neck. It went better with the nice suit he'd worn for Pico's launch. Since he was nominally on duty, he'd stopped to read the message from Mairwen that warned of "bad air traffic coming." He showed it to Pico. "She's with our flitter. Any idea what she might be seeing?"

"Nope, but we could go see." Before he could object, she'd turned and dragged him out another door and back out to the center of the commons.

They'd looked up at clear blue skies with wisps of clouds and seen nothing for several minutes.

"So, at camp, when I was in the airlock…" He trailed off as five red-and-gold flitters with lethal-looking energy weapons rose over the top of the Chemistry building. "Maybe they're just late for class," he'd said hopefully, but knew they weren't. Once again, the "interesting times" curse had come to call.

Pico had grabbed his hand and tugged. "Come on!" She pulled him under the nearest tree. They'd dashed for the round doorway in the shortest building on the floater, which she'd said housed shared labs. As he followed her winding path through more doors and into a curving hallway, he'd hastily pinged a message to tell Mairwen about the gunships, if she hadn't already seen them, and where he and Pico had gone.

Moments later, they'd heard a distant explosion, and hurried to a window. They were just in time to see a gunship pulling up, and smoke and flames coming from the third floor of the Chemistry building. Whether the gunship was investigating or had been the cause of the destruction was unknown.

"This is the opposite of good," muttered Pico. "We need to get out of here while we still can."

They'd almost made it, too, except they were caught at the east exit and detained by a lanky, dyspeptic professor and his twitchy assistant. "Didn't you hear the announcement? Attendance is mandatory," said the professor. "Everyone has to report to the large Chemistry lecture hall immediately."

Short of assaulting the pair, they'd had no choice but to join a group of resigned students, faculty, and staff as they walked through what Pico had referred to as the donut to the Chemistry building. He and Pico both turned around to look when the emergency doors closed behind them, sealing off the Chem building from the shared labs.

The lecture hall was filling up, with at least a hundred people milling around. Being surrounded by crowds put pressure on Sojaire's talents and made his head hurt, so he'd been glad when Pico had found a knot of her friends standing in a corner near some cleared windows. He recognized several from the rocket launch, and gathered they were all in something called the "Practical Applications" class. They'd all heard the explosion, but none of them knew what caused it until Pico had described what they'd seen.

A loud announcement boomed through the lecture hall, ordering them to find a seat, and sit quietly until the speaker arrived. The crowd shifted so the automatic risers with chairs could arrange themselves in the standard lecture format. Pico and her friends ignored them, and stood casually in the back corner, hidden somewhat by the chair risers. The windows opaqued and darkened.

Sojaire could see why Pico liked this group. Just like her, none of them accepted fate lying down. After speculation as to who the speaker might be, with the shortest odds on a politician looking for a full audience hall as a publicity backdrop, they began scheming a way to get out of the hall, since the consensus was that whatever caused the explosion would keep them in lockdown for hours. They were hungry, had better things to do, and the tiny fresher intended for VIP use already had a line at the door.

Their planning turned earnest when they discovered all comms were down, and soon after, when a security detail of six mercenaries—their uniforms matched the gunship color scheme—entered the hall. The mercs made up for being a small contingent by carrying enough firepower to reenact the Last Fall of the Central League, if they were of a mind, and they looked ready to demonstrate. Pico impressed her friends by naming the make, model, and type of most of the weapons. All of the group thought the mercs meant trouble, the kind that sent newstrend ratings soaring.

"You know what I want?" asked Grien, the body-modded woman with blue skin and gills. "Ten minutes in the main Mat Sci lab. I bet that's where my brother is hiding out, the lucky stiff." She hid her worry well.

"Hell," said a tall boy, with classic northern Euro looks and a slight German accent, "I'd settle for my rocket propellant supplies in De Luna's office. There's enough there for ten launches."

"Sure," said short, sharp-eyed Truòng, his South Asian heritage plain, "but no more rockets, unless Adams's roommate has killed another kaffa machine." He flashed a grin at Pico, who returned his smile. Sojaire knew it was ridiculous, but he felt a flare of jealousy.

Grien grabbed the elbow of a short, muscular woman and drew her closer. "Hey, Dortief, I don't suppose you've fixed Doomreaper, yet?"

"I did, actually, and upgraded her with optics, but she's locked in project storage." Her eyes widened. "But I based her design on the cleaning bots, and there are fleets of them in each building. I, uh, kind of borrowed one when I was building Doomreaper." When the tall boy snorted, she jutted her chin out in challenge. "What? I needed the human-avoidance logic cube. That's what failed, you know, when we all got foamed."

"Foamed?" asked Sojaire quietly of Pico.

"Interesting times," she said. He used to think it was only his life that was eventful, until he'd met Pico. He'd never told her how much he admired her for rolling with the punches, instead of letting them stop her, which was another thing he needed to apologize for. It was a depressingly long list.

Dortief crouched down and looked under the risers, then pointed. "See? There are two under here. They get trapped."

Grien crouched down next to her. "How do you catch them if they avoid humans?"

"Cover them with a cold blanket," said Dortief. "They respond to infrared movement."

Truòng leaned against the window nonchalantly, which hid his tapping on the glass with his knuckles. "Typhoon-rated. Need more than a pocketknife to get through. Too bad there's not a door back here."

"There's always the north door," said a pretty, dark-haired boy of maybe nineteen. He was pale, as if he'd been away from the sun too long. Sojaire tamped down his healer talent. It wasn't his business if the boy was anemic from a vitamin deficiency.

"Yeah, and only two mercs with a lot of guns between us and freedom," said a curvy Chinese girl who'd also been leaning against the windows. "Call me warped, but I'd rather not be shot."

The pretty boy put his arm around her shoulders. "Ah, Zee, how would you know if you've never tried?" He lathered on the sexual innuendo with his tone.

Zee rolled her eyes. "Lodkar, you need to see a medic about that hormone imbalance." She poked his ribs, then ducked out from under his arm and moved closer to Pico. Lodkar laughed, but there was a flash of hurt underneath. For all that his good looks probably got him attention, he apparently didn't know how to talk to girls. Sojaire sympathized.

When he was being a professional medic, he could talk to anyone, but when it was just him in a social setting, he stumbled. He didn't have many friends because he didn't know how to make them—his father had viewed them either as competition or a corrupting influence. The fleeting girlfriends he'd had after leaving his father's house had wanted him to loosen up and share, but it wasn't safe, not with his father still trying to control him any way he could. Pico had been one of the few constants, because the universe kept throwing them together in the middle of "interesting times."

When Arsène Celeyron had cohabbed with a beautiful female gymnast for the purpose of having children, he'd wanted a copy of himself, a big, phenomenally gifted athlete with a stubborn will to succeed and a rabidly territorial possessiveness of the winner's circle. When the cohab dissolved, he'd kept the five-year-old son and allowed his cohab to keep the ten-year-old daughter, with the condition that they cut all ties, and never claim the Celeyron name.

It was one of his few losses, because instead of another Arsène, he'd gotten a small boy more interested in musical scores than sports scores, and more interested in knowing how muscles worked instead of building them. Meanwhile, Sojaire's estranged older sister became the youngest athlete to medal in the '36 Galactic Games. At age twenty-eight, one-third of her father's age, she'd already surpassed her father's lifetime net fame quotient, and in grav ball, a sport he hated because it rewarded nimble speed, adaptable thinking, and spatial awareness.

It didn't stop Arsène from doing his damnedest to turn his loss into a win by whatever means necessary, including dragging eleven-year-old Sojaire to an exclusive body shop on Mabingion and demanding they make him taller, muscled, and a brown-eyed brunette, to match his father. Fortunately, the body shop had refused because he was too young.

It had been one of the few times the universe had smiled on him, because he'd also met a therapist telepath-sifter that day who'd changed his life. Saved it, actually. The body shop's policy was to make sure patients were mentally stable enough to undergo extreme body mods, so they'd sent him to their staff counselor, Yanish, before learning how young he was. Yanish, an older Arabic man with warm, kindly eyes, had been astonishingly blunt.

"Your father has a persuasive public persona," he'd said, "but once the medics get over their awe of having a star in their midst, they'll turn him down." Sojaire didn't get to enjoy the relief long, because the therapist startled him with a telepathic connection, his first. It was against standard therapeutic practice, but Yanish was pressed for time. *"Your father is also deeply warped. At least he doesn't abuse you physically, but he's inflicting emotional damage every day. He'll continue to get away with it as long as he's on the top of his game. The best you can do is survive. Weather the storm and plan for the day you can walk out. Don't tell him you're a minder, or he'll use it against you."*

"I'm a what?" Sojaire had asked.

"A healer, and a strong one. I'm a sifter, so I can sense it, even if you can't yet. I see you're already interested in medicine. Use it as a cover—become a medic, or he'll figure it out." Behind the words was a well of complex emotion, as if Yanish knew all too well what abusive parents could do.

"One more thing. Make sure you fail minder testing. The CPS is infinitely worse than your father." The kaleidoscopic packet of images that accompanied that warning had nearly brought him to his knees. Yanish had seen far too many minders destroyed by the control drugs, or what they'd done in the name of the CPS.

"Sojaire, are you okay?"

Disoriented from his side trip down well-worn memory lane, he looked around. Most of the people he recognized were gone, and Pico was standing in front of him looking up, so close that all it would take was tilting his head down, and he'd be kissing her. She was so heart-stoppingly vibrant. His rational mind ordered him to back away, but his body rebelled and refused to budge. "Yes." His voice sounded hoarse. "Where did everyone go?"

"I *knew* you weren't listening." She sighed and stepped back. "Trường noticed the mercs made a mistake, and we're going to exploit it." She tilted toward the front of the room with her head. "The line for the fresher was making it hard for the two at the north door to see, so they moved past them into the hall. Which means an intrepid band of daring corsairs can use the fresher line as cover." She put her hand on the inside of his elbow and bent his forearm to support it. "It's our turn to go stand in line."

She tugged, and he gladly followed. He sure as hell wasn't letting her go without him. For one thing, he'd get lost, and for another, her father would kill him.

Astonishingly, their plan had worked. Not only had Pico's "corsairs" gotten away, but a sizable number of other students had sneaked out the north door before the mercs noticed their problem. Pico's friends had split up into groups, each with a plan as to how to visit mayhem upon the invading force.

Pico, maddeningly, had refused to go to the Mat Sci building where their flitters were stacked, and where Mairwen would be, and probably Luka. "Personal rental flitters are no match for gunships," she'd argued. "I'd like to save getting shot out of the sky for some future date." He'd been so distracted by the hope that he hadn't totally blown his last chance with Pico that he hadn't protested when she insisted on skulking through the lush foliage surrounding the central commons, and slipping into the Math building to check on the kids in the childcare center.

They made it halfway through the lobby, to a large rounded atrium, only to see a group that could only be theft crew entering at the far end of the south hall. Four of the six sported tall mohawks, and all had major glowing body art. The only reason the crew didn't find them in the atrium was because quick-thinking Pico pushed Sojaire behind the long, heavy construction panels stored there and crammed herself in with him. The cramped space put her in his arms, with her back up against his chest. The full contact meant he couldn't help but feel her lungs working and sense the adrenalin that had her heart pumping. She smelled of plants and sweat, and it reminded him of their frantic run through the hydroponics section of the space station. He used a tiny bit of his healer talent to share some of his energy reserves with her. It had always been his silent, secret gift to her when in the midst of "interesting times."

"Thank you," she breathed. It startled him, until he realized she meant the crew had gone out the door, not that she'd noticed what he'd done. She moved out of his arms, leaving him feeling achingly empty. He eased out after her.

"I think we just saw why the mercs are here," she said quietly. "I bet the university called in mercs instead of the police because they didn't want the publicity. Now I'm *really* worried about the kids."

She led him to a lit but closed door frame, where she palmed her biometric and entered a code. The door irised open, and as soon as they stepped in, she used the wallcomp to seal the door as closed for business.

The toys and play areas looked pretty much as they had the night before, but he couldn't see the children. He could feel them, six... no, seven of them, but they weren't visible.

After a quick dash through the kitchen and the nap room, she came back to the playroom. "Thank the constant stars, the staff got them out," said Pico. Her relief was almost palpable, then turned to fear. "Or maybe they didn't. What if they're hostages?" she whispered.

"They're not," he said. "I... that is–"

"You don't know that," she interrupted. "We have to find–"

He cut her off by grabbing her arm. "The children are still here. Seven of them. Including Miguel, Celia, and Lyssi. They're scared and angry, and feeling abandoned, but none are hurt." He put his hand to his sternum. "I'm an empath. I can feel them." It was a heartless way to reveal his secret empath talent, one of the things he'd wanted to explain, but she'd been as close to panic as he'd ever seen her.

Her mouth gaped in astonishment. She looked around, then looked at him. He could see the wheels turning in her sharp mind, and sensed the first breezes of complex emotion from her. He tried to pull into his shell, but couldn't, because he'd connected with her only minutes ago and was touching her now.

"You and I," she hissed, "will have words, but not now." She exerted the strength of mind he so admired in her by pulling away from him and turning to face the seemingly empty play room. "Hi, kids, remember me? Peregrine of the Pirate Clan?"

Sojaire gave up trying to contain his empath talent. He reached out to the ball of emotional energy that was Miguel. He sent soothing waves to the rest of the children, or tried to. He was far better at bottling up his talent than using it.

Because he knew where to look, he saw Miguel's dark head appear from under a twisting slide before Pico did. He nudged her and pointed. Pico ran to the boy. A scrape of fabric from the playhouse behind her brought Lyssi out from under what looked like a wadded up blanket. Pico opened her arms, and both children slammed into her embrace. Within a few moments, she was enveloped in a knot of children, all chattering at once.

"The new teachers went to lunch and didn't come back."

"They said they'd bring us candy if we didn't tell."

"Miguel said there were hunters."

"I'm hungry."

Pico caught Sojaire's eye. "Could you see if there's something to eat?" She tilted her head toward the kitchen. He nodded and started to cross the room, only to be intercepted by solemn Miguel.

"*Éramos zorros.*"

"Mairwen's game?" Sojaire remembered when Miguel had mentioned it last night. "What did she teach you?"

"How to search like a hunter, and how to hide like a fox." His English was softened by his Spanish accent. "After the teachers left, some men wanted in, but they didn't have the code. They were... *muy enojados?*"

"Angry," translated Pico.

"One had red hair like mine, but straight up, like this," said Lyssi, holding splayed fingers on top of her head, where a mohawk would be.

"Yes," said Miguel. "Mairwen said hunters forget how small foxes are. She showed us how to hide in spaces where they wouldn't look. *Éramos zorros.* We were foxes."

The boy's face held quiet pride. "You did exactly right," Sojaire said. "Come on, let's see what's in the kitchen." Miguel's hand slipping into his was a surprise, but shouldn't have been. Empaths found comfort in physical contact.

They brought out plates with hastily assembled sandwiches, assorted fruits, and some bite-sized carrots and served them to Pico and the kids.

Sojaire positioned himself by the door, like he'd seen Mairwen do when she was pretending to be a dimwitted nightshift guard. It was safer than being so close to Pico.

"Children," Pico said as she stood up, "quick like bunni… like foxes, take your plates to the kitchen and put them on the counter, then use the fresher to wash your face and hands. Sojaire and I need to talk about what to do next."

They obligingly scampered into the kitchen while Pico brushed crumbs off her pants as she walked toward him. He slammed his containment down as tight as he could. His stupid empath talent had never been anything but trouble.

"Oh, stop looking like I'm going to eviscerate you with a force blade. It's too messy." She put her hands on her hips. "The irresponsible ziftbrains who are supposed to be here probably got caught up in the same sweep we did, and are stuck in the lecture hall. None of the parents will be coming for the kids for hours–"

They both jumped when the door behind him chimed.

"Oh, frelling hell," grumbled Pico. "What now?" She slammed her palm on the wallcomp just past his ear. The display showed the grim face of Luka Foxe, and he was carrying Mairwen in his arms.

However badly the childcare center was managed, its facilities were adequate and secure, and the suite's medic kit was comprehensive. While marshaling the children into setting up a makeshift treatment area, Pico watched Sojaire slip into his professional healer mode and take charge. It was what had attracted her to him in the first place, at space camp. While Valenia had drooled over the several cute boys at camp, Pico thought they were all lopars, but she was drawn to the young and handsome blond medic, especially when he showed far more compassion for the campers than the leaders had.

To keep the children out of the way while Sojaire worked, she took them into the nap room and got them to lie down and read or watch vids quietly. It would have to make up for their regular post-meal nap. Unsurprisingly, Lyssi crawled into her lap and fell asleep. Eleven-year-old Miguel, too old for a nap, asked permission to go see if Sojaire needed help.

"Yes," she said, "and tell Mairwen how you were all foxes."

She tried the comms again and got nowhere. That left her alone with her thoughts, which weren't very restful company. She hoped her dad was far away, but wished he was there with her. She was concerned about Professor De Luna, because she wasn't the type to sit idly by while mercenaries traipsed through the hallways, but she didn't know about the crew. She wanted to thank Mairwen for empowering the children. She was sorry Mairwen had been hurt, and glad she'd accept help from Sojaire. She worried about her friends, who could also get hurt if they pissed off the mercenaries or the crew. She wanted to kill the childcare center's manager and owners for hiring selfish, good-for-nothing staff who deserved to be stranded on a barren island where the only drinkable water was infested with starving piranhas.

And then there was Sojaire's revelation that he was an empath. It cast the last three years in an infinitely more painful light. She'd assumed he hadn't known what she felt for him, how her crush had matured into a full-blown, unrequited love, that she wanted him with an intensity that flamed her skin and stole her breath. But since he was an empath, he'd known all along. Therefore, each time he'd ignored her, each time he'd put people or distance between them, he'd done it deliberately because he didn't return her feelings. She was pretty sure he liked her as a friend, but that was it. She was hurt and angry that he'd lied to her, but mostly, she was just embarrassed that she'd spent three years pining for a man who would never want her. She was going to have a long cry about it, and probably rend a few garments in the process, just as soon as this frelling day from black-hole hell was over.

She carried the totally boneless Lyssi to a cot and kissed her forehead as she covered her with a thin sheet, then went back to the main playroom.

Luka was pacing, although he was having a hard time navigating around the toys, and talking to himself. "...have to assume the crew were in the labs, so the question is, why?" Mairwen and Miguel were focused on repairing the scorched hole in the back of her pant leg with medical tape.

Sojaire looked up from putting medical supplies back in their cases. "Pico, Mairwen said when your dad saw the five gunships, he landed his flitter on the Mat Sci airpad and took his gun bag into the building. She also said one of the gun ships shot up the third-floor Chemistry lab."

"Dad will be looking for me." She knew that with the certainty that she knew the planet orbited the sun. "I hope he finds Professor De Luna, too. I expect she's causing trouble."

CHAPTER 21

SWEAT POURED DOWN Jerzi's neck like he was in a sauna, but he ignored it. His vantage point behind the large arrow-leafed plant under the bent trunk of a tree was safe enough, as long as he didn't move. A nearby fountain made to look like a tiny freshwater pond provided moisture and attracted mosquitoes and other insects, which kept the orange-specked fish near the surface. His camouflage vest and cap took on the green color near him, but movements from his dark pants and muddy, but still tan-skinned, arms would be more obvious. Another group of the theft crew came into view with yet another cart full of crates and boxes. They'd taken to using the wheeled carts that worked better over the permaturf walkways than the finicky grav carts.

He was close enough to hear loud voices, but not the quiet muttering that was often more useful. Still, he'd gotten the picture that the crew was sneaking their stolen goods out the Materials Science building's loading dock, just west of where he was, while fighting the mercs in the top of the Chemistry building. They'd been feeling pretty smug about it, too, until one of the crew had brought the news that the mercs had landed more gunships and personnel. They'd begun transferring the goods to the low-profile powered barge a lot faster after that.

An hour earlier, when he'd been in the third-floor Materials Science laboratory, he'd heard an all-floor announcement by Department Leader Vestering to report to the big Chemistry lecture hall. If Jerzi was going to be useful to anyone, he couldn't afford to be bottled up in the lecture hall, so he'd used the nearby stairs to slip down to the first floor of the Mat Sci building with the idea of finding Andra. When he'd imagined Pico stuck in the lecture hall, however, he decided he needed to see what was going on for himself.

He reviewed his mental map of the lecture hall, from when the entire POGS Day fair had been stuffed into it because of the rain, and remembered the walkabout ledge at the top northeast corner. While accompanying Mairwen on her assessment, he'd noted the small, rectangular access door behind the second-floor chemistry lab, and Lavong had said it was a closet for audio-visual use.

Slow, careful slinking got him and his gun bag past the mercenaries and well-meaning staff who were collecting people to send to the hall, and into the closet, which, as he'd hoped, gave him access to the ledge. He could have really used Andra's ocular implants at that moment, but he could at least recognize faces when they looked up. His vantage point gave him a bird's-eye view of the seating arranging itself, the swelling knot of people in line for the fresher, the loaded-for-war but inattentive mercs, and the clever group of students who were using the fresher line as cover to escape out the north door. His heart leapt when he recognized Pico's distinctive white-and-red jumpsuit, and saw that she was escaping with Sojaire. His daughter was smart enough to get somewhere safe.

He stayed long enough to determine that Andra wasn't in the hall, which meant she was still free, and likely in the thick of things, or soon would be. He slithered back into the A/V closet and tried comms again, but no luck. He'd heard the mercenaries complaining about it, too, and relaying orders to look for tech suppressors. Like the military, mercs needed constant, real-time communication for peak efficiency.

The Chemistry building became too dangerous when more mercs arrived on the roof, so he'd gone to the ground floor and slipped outside, only to realize he'd traded one hot zone for another. A large theft crew was hauling equipment out of the building wholesale, and he only avoided getting caught because he dove for a thicket and curled himself tightly around his gun bag. The presence of the crew explained the tech suppressors, which gave their hands-on, analog methods an advantage.

He'd made his way east, on the water side of the conjoined buildings, one natural outgrowth and engineered landscape feature at a time. Most of the crew looked typical, with extreme body art and metal implants, and an apparent fondness for mohawk hairstyles, but some looked more like students or staff. Which, once he had time to think about it, made sense for a daylight heist. People were much less likely to question ordinary workers in lab coats directing a grav cart full of lab equipment.

The chatter he heard suggested a central crew had contracted other, smaller crews to help. He decided his initial theory, that the mercs had been called in to protect the Chemistry building, might be incomplete. The theft crew believed the mercs were trying to effect a theft of their own. Jerzi doubted mercs needed lab equipment for themselves, but he couldn't imagine who had hired them. Mercs were better at invasions and takedowns.

He was regretting his choice to get closer to the barge. He hadn't learned much new, other than the crew had already taken anything that wasn't nailed down, judging by the boxes of supplies and shipping crates in the front of the barge, and the barge had a cloaking canopy that used the same technology as his vest and cap. Now he was stuck in the mini-grotto, because the barge was never unattended long enough for him to slip away. If the crew had been more vigilant, they might have noticed the squirrels and birds above his position were vocalizing predator warning calls. Fortunately, the loadmaster was loud and voluble, and the crew was more attuned to urban threats.

Since he was there, he'd really like to see what was in the shipping crates. Once again, he wished for Andra's oculars, but he had the next best thing. Ever so slowly, centimeter by centimeter, he unsealed his gun bag, then patiently oozed his hand inside, constantly conscious of his visible movements. The contents were jumbled because he'd become lazy about snapping everything in place since leaving the military. Finally, his questing fingers found the spotter's scope case. With exaggerated care, he pulled it closer to the opening, freezing every time someone looked his direction. He opened the case and extracted the scope, then powered it on. He'd long ago put tape over its flashy startup lights, which kind of ruined the stealth concept. At least it didn't play a merry little tune.

The trick to slow movements was using just enough muscle tension for control, and to keep other big muscles from tensing up in sympathy. He was a little out of practice, so it helped that the crew expected trouble from the sky or the building, not the overgrown landscape. Out of habit, he engaged the recording feature. It wouldn't be ultra-res, but it was good enough for most loss auditors. He did an overall sweep first, then zoomed in on the crates. The closeup view was unhelpful until he found a crate that had cracked open, revealing what looked like packs of hypojets for delivering subcutaneous drugs. He'd seen enough of them in the past couple of days to recognize them by now. Lavong, the labs manager, had pointedly made the distinction between the physical chemistry done in his buildings, and the organic chemistry and pharma labs in the university's medical department, so the jets were puzzling.

He was just putting his scope back in its case when the loadmaster shut the barge's gates and signaled to the pilot. The five crew left on the dock decided it was too hot to stay outside, so they trudged back up the path to the Mat Sci building's mid-section doorway. Not wasting any time, Jerzi sealed his bag and crawled out of his den, grateful to finally be able to make progress toward his goal of the east end of the building. After he quickly rounded the exposed northeast corner, with only eight or ten meters between him and the sea, and between him and the deserted public transport stop, the undergrowth revealed a grisly tableau.

Two dead men from the theft crew were attracting flies. One had his pants around his ankles and a phase knife in his right hand. Both died of perfectly targeted flechette wounds to the neck, back, and throat. It looked like Andra's handiwork, and she'd have had a good reason for killing them.

Jerzi confiscated the phase knife and two hand-beamers, amused to note that none of them had biometric locks. He'd have thought thieves would be more inclined to protect their weapons from theft. He wasn't a forensic specialist like Luka, but logic said the bodies couldn't have been there very long, maybe thirty minutes. It was long enough for Andra to have gone almost anywhere.

He eyed the Math building to the south, and decided she'd reject it. The action was in the Mat Sci-Chemistry-labs complex, so that's where she'd be.

Another fifteen minutes of recon skulking got him to the second floor, where her office was. His long-shot gamble paid off when he saw she'd taped a note to her door. *"Lightning grades posted in the big lab. Hope you crushed it!"* She'd always been clever.

He left the note where it was, in case one of the warring parties noticed its absence. Considering the number of combatants he'd seen so far, he'd been damn lucky not to run into them in the corridors earlier. Whatever they were fighting over had to be valuable, to make it worth the personnel cost. Deciding that lifts were for the suicidal, he chose the east stairs as the best of a bad lot, and vowed to make it up to his already sore legs when this was all over by booking an hour-long massage and spa-tub soak.

He didn't like the look of the plasma-scorched doors that led to Department Leader Vestering's office, but he didn't have the time to investigate. The artfully curved corridors, which he'd privately thought were pretentious, turned out to be surprisingly helpful in making him less immediately visible to anyone else in the corridor. The classroom doorways he passed were all closed and dark, and he hoped they'd stay that way. He slowed and listened intently, then peeked for a quick view of the top of the mid-building stairs and lifts. He saw a scorch mark and congealed blood on the floor, but no people. He was cheered by the fact that, outside of the dead crew in the bushes, it was the first blood he'd seen in the school. He edged closer, controlling his foot sounds on the textured floor, but the juncture appeared deserted. He walked quickly and quietly past it, using all his senses to maintain environmental awareness. It was a trick he'd learned watching Mairwen. He'd never match her phenomenal skill, but the technique had proved useful in the physical security business.

The next problem, what to do about the closed and dark laboratory entrance, was solved by luck, when Truòng, from the rocket launch team, appeared from the other direction. He was wearing a lab coat and carrying what looked like a cleaning bot wrapped in clearpack. He palmed the biometric reader and the doorway irised open. Jerzi ran toward the entrance, startling poor Truòng into yelping and dropping his prize, which Jerzi caught by sliding in on his knees. His gun bag's forward momentum knocked Truòng's legs out from under him. The door irised closed behind them.

"Nice entrance, Crush." Some of the worry he'd been carrying melted away at the sound of Andra's amused voice.

He turned around in time to see her putting her Lipara flechette gun in her pocket. He handed the surprisingly cold cleaning bot back to Truòng, then stood and grinned at her. "Did I miss the fireworks display?"

Twenty minutes later, Jerzi was sitting next to Andra on a lab bench, holding one of the cleaning bots steady while she used his confiscated phase knife as an improvised spot welder to attach a bead-like camera eye to its side. The launch team of Grien, Truòng, and Dortief, plus Grien's older brother, were all working on devices and compounds that were mostly designed to frighten, distract, or mislead. They couldn't take the chance on hurting innocent students or staff.

When he could get away with it, he looked for hidden injuries Andra might have sustained. She'd given him what he suspected was an extremely sanitized account of what had happened after he'd left her in her office two hours before. He didn't blame her for not wanting to scare the students, but he suspected the "brief interlude spent in the company of some mercs" had caused the bruise on her jaw. He'd been luckier, with only a few scrapes and bug bites.

She'd caught the students trying to break into her office, so she'd let them in to get their rocket propellant ingredients, plus she took her own backpack and bag. She hadn't known he was on the floater—in fact, had hoped he was somewhere safe—when she'd posted the note, which she'd intended for Pico.

Based on their pooled intel and knowledge, their working theory was that the theft crew was stealing from the university, and the mercs were stealing from the crew. None of them could come up with an idea on what was worth stealing, except maybe a commercial project, but none of them used more than one lab. The hypojets Jerzi had seen were suggestive of illicit chems, but the organic chem labs would be a much easier place to make them. The comms were still out, and the public transport harbor was still blockaded, so unless Vestering had made good his escape and contacted the authorities, it was likely no one off the floater knew there was trouble.

Some of the other escapees had headed toward the shared labs building, and Pico and Sojaire had last been seen heading for the Math building.

"Checking on the kids, I expect," Andra guessed. His worry must have been showing, because she'd patted his shoulder. "It's as safe a place as any right now."

Their current plan depended on getting eyes on the mercs and crew, so they'd raided the project vault and cannibalized Dortief's new and improved Doomreaper for the tiny camera eyes. Dortief had sulked until Andra had promised to help build Doomreaper's Daughter. Their hope was that the tech suppressors wouldn't affect the micro-power cameras, and the bots ran on long-life rechargeable batteries. They hastily reprogrammed the bots to think the third-floor lab was their home base, then set them loose.

Andra drew Jerzi aside toward her backpack. "I don't want the students playing with them, but I've got both KemX and RakX, and some home-brew TBY3 gel. I trust you not to blow the floater sky high."

"Wow," he said, remembering how she'd described the contents of her backpack the day before, "sex toys sure have changed since I was a lad."

"*Idiota*," she replied, rolling her eyes. "I was thinking about the big smuggler barge you saw, and that freight flitter Grien's brother says is hogging the Mat Sci airpad. Be a downright shame if something happened to them."

"Oh, yeah," he agreed solemnly. "A crying shame."

Chapter 22

MAIRWEN SAT ON the only available adult-sized chair in the childcare playroom and watched Luka's progress as he threaded a crooked path through the clutter. She knew he needed to pace, or better yet, run, not hop over children's toys and skirt entirely too many pieces of child-sized furniture. He had never been good at waiting, and they'd been in the center for fifty-eight minutes.

Without comms, without information, and with added responsibility of seven young children, waiting was the best option for the time being. The room was thick-walled with no windows and a controlled single point of entry. It was also better for Pico to stay in one place, so Jerzi could find her.

Mairwen's calf was much better after Sojaire applied the wound pack and used his healing talent. She was functional, but stayed seated because it made Luka happier. After Sòng departed, Luka had insisted on carrying her in the lift from the third floor to the first-floor childcare center, and she'd let him. In her old life, no one ever carried trackers, unless it was to dispose of their corpses.

Pico had roused the children from their quiet time five minutes ago and had them scrounging for more food. Miguel, who'd been alternating between her side and Sojaire's, helped his sleepy sister peel a banana. They were the same children that had been there yesterday, with the addition of six-year-old Nico, an olive-skinned boy who spoke a confusing mixture of English and Portuguese.

Luka froze in mid-step and looked at the percomp on the back of his hand. "Incoming ping." He activated it. "It's the data from Sòng, from an hour ago."

"I'll try my dad." Pico activated her percomp quickly, but her face fell. "Nothing."

Luka's fingers danced over the interface. "I'm getting GDAT sync. At a guess, the tech suppressors are down for this building, but not the others.

I'll try an emergency priority to the police. Majeed, if I can get her." He glanced to the children, then switched to subvocalization. Luka had shared his admittedly shaky framework of suppositions about what the crew and mercs were doing, with the key assumption being that the crew weren't just one-shot thieves, they'd been operating in the labs since the first security upgrades had gone in eight months before.

Pico told the children to eat fast, because she and Sojaire were going to teach them a new game called Run Like a Fox. While they'd napped, she'd presented her idea to the rest of the adults that they'd likely have to carry the children out of the building, possibly at a run. The children would be more comfortable and cooperative if they practiced ahead of time. Pico was short and small, so it made sense she'd only carry one child, while the rest of the adults carried two.

Luka was the tallest and strongest of them, and would be carrying Miguel and his sister Celia. Lyssi insisted that Mairwen carry her, along with Nico. Sojaire insisted that Pico should carry tiny Parekh, because only she knew where the boy kept hiding the clothes he so despised. That left Davalia and Isiro to Sojaire, doubtless by his design, because they were both taller and heavier than the others. Mairwen had to consciously consider nurturing objectives; with Sojaire, they were instinctive. His talents were perfectly suited to him.

Lyssi helped Nico figure out where to put his feet so they didn't dig into Lyssi's thigh or Mairwen's ribs. Fortunately, they were each about twenty kilos, so she wouldn't be unbalanced if she had to run. Her half-healed calf wouldn't be happy about it, but she could do it. She walked around the room with them once, then made them practice mounting and dismounting several times. When Luka ended his call, he easily picked up Miguel and Celia and carried them to where she and her charges stood.

"How's the leg?"

"Functional." She smiled briefly, because she'd surprised him by not saying "fine."

Luka put the children down, then motioned Pico and Sojaire closer. "The best Majeed could do was divert an airborne AI for a flyover of the floater. It seems the police are busy with two other laboratory locations in Tremplin that were raided by mercenaries, and the labs fought back." He sighed. "The Tremplin Police magistrate is a lazy ónytjungur who ordered her to stay out of our situation, citing lack of jurisdiction. He didn't tell her she couldn't share the live AI feed, so she's going to send it to me and

Division Colonel Bittman of Military Command."

"What's an *ónytjungur*?" asked Lyssi. She reproduced the pronunciation rather well.

"A tosser," responded Sojaire quickly. Mairwen didn't correct him, although it actually meant "sack of shit." It seemed to upset people when children repeated rude words, even in Icelandic.

Luka kept glancing at his percomp. "Makes me wish ours were like Sòng's. His probably has its own exploration comm relay." He crouched and held out his arms to Miguel and Celia. "Let's practice again." Mairwen suspected there would be new percomps coming for Foxe Investigations after this case.

Six minutes later, the AI feed arrived. Their little floater looked like a war zone, with armed flitters on all airpads and a large collection of boats huddled around the north-side docks. The drone also caught the arrival of a military cruiser as it approached the southwest landing dock. Moments later, the dock exploded, seriously damaging the hull of the cruiser.

Luka whistled. "Well, *that* ought to get their attention."

* * * * *

Jerzi patted the glittery lava-red skin of his rental flitter. He'd be sorry to have to give it up at the end of his vacation. Moving it farther away from the now disabled freight flitter on the Mat Sci building's airpad would make for a safer liftoff. An explosion somewhere to the southwest suggested things were heating up.

When he'd arrived on the airpad with Andra's little package of KemX, he discovered one or more lethal persons had been on the airpad before him, because the mercs who had been guarding the flitter were all dead. The freighter was half off the airpad, probably moved to allow access to the stacker, and its doors were wide open. Any cargo it had carried was gone now.

Jerzi opted to disable the freighter by frying its steering controls using one of the mercs' plasma rifles. No sense wasting perfectly good KemX. He stowed the rifle and the rest of the merc weapons in his flitter's luggage hold.

A loud static crackle in his ear startled the hell out of him. He'd forgotten he was still wearing two earwires, the one on his left jaw pilfered from a merc, and his own on the right, hidden among his earrings. His chirped an incoming ping from Luka with an invitation to a secure conference. He subvocalized the passkey of *Beehive*, the name of a ship only he, Luka, and Mairwen would know, and he was in.

"*Dad, I'm okay. Are you?*" Pico's rapid words made him smile and sigh with relief.

"I'm good. Are comms up everywhere?"

"*For now,*" said Luka. "*I think the mercs found and killed the tech suppressors the crew set up. I'm with Mairwen, Pico, and Sojaire in the childcare center.*"

"I'm on the Mat Sci airpad by my flitter. May I invite Andra De Luna to our little party?"

"*Already here, Crush.*" Jerzi grinned. Even subvocalizing, her distinctive Spanish accent came through. It was amazing what a little real-time communication could do for a man's mood.

Luka quickly brought them up to speed on what the police AI flyover revealed. Andra and Jerzi agreed that the damage to the military ship would be more than enough provocation for them to come in force.

While Andra explained what she and Jerzi had been doing and planning, Jerzi scuttled to the north edge of the building and peeked over the ledge. The big freight barge had returned to the loading dock, but it was now accompanied by three smaller boats and a swarm of crew, hurriedly transferring stolen goods under the direction of the freighter's loadmaster. Her booming voice was audible even from three stories up. Beyond that, he could see watersleds and a racer or two rounding the curve of the floater and heading north.

"I grounded the mercs' freighter," Jerzi subvocalized, "but the crew's freight barge is a problem. Too many people on shore. I could swim from the public transport dock, if I had the right equipment, but the temporary oxygen breather we rigged up is only good for about ten minutes before the membrane clogs."

"*We need exit options,*" said Mairwen. "*I'll go scout.*"

Luka objected, citing a leg injury she'd apparently gotten in a fight with a ramper. They took their discussion offline. Jerzi had never seen them fight, or even raise their voices to one another, but they did disagree from time to time.

Andra broke the silence. "*The Grien siblings are here in the lab and want to help with the barge issue. They said they'd meet you at the third-floor north stairs.*" She sounded unhappy about their choice.

"We could let the barge go," he said.

"I don't care about the barge itself, but we need to keep the crew busy. The launch team and I have come up with a way to get the people out of the big lecture hall."

"Dad, just so you know, we've got seven children who are coming with us."

"We can fit them in my flitter. If Mairwen gives me the code, I can get theirs out of the stacker."

"Sending it to you now," said Sojaire. *"I'll keep the conference open as long as we need it. Mairwen specified high encryption, so it should be secure."*

Jerzi muted his earwire, then ran across the airpad to the cover of the freighter. Now that comms were working, the mercs would soon be sending someone to check on the null response from the freighter. Easing around it, and keeping an eye on the sky, he sprinted to the stacker kiosk and beamed it the code Sojaire sent. He winced at the stacker's noisy machinery, but it couldn't be helped. He ran to the stairway door, opened it, and darted inside, remembering at the last second to leap over the body of the merc who'd had the plasma rifle. He stopped a moment to listen, then descended the stairs to the second floor quietly, glad they were slip-resistant and his all-terrain boots had cushioned soles.

He watched for the Griens, and irised open the door as soon as he saw them.

"Our gills are real, and our skin is enhanced," said Melly Grien quietly. "We can stay underwater as long as we want."

Her brother Trenton nodded. "We checked from the windows in Vestering's office. We can take off from the public transport dock and swim out and around to the back of the barge, and attach the package so it's ready to blow."

"The theft crew will kill you if they catch you," Jerzi said bluntly. "They're under pressure. They won't take time to ask questions."

"Our skin is the same color as the water," said Melly. "We're hard to see from above."

"We'll be careful," said Trent. "We've got friends in that lecture hall. Professor De Luna thinks they'll become hostages if we don't get them out. She needs the crew distracted for her plan to work."

Jerzi nodded. They were adults and knew the risks. "Okay," he said. He pulled their homemade remote-controlled bomb from his gun bag and handed it over. Melly put it in a net bag while they briefly discussed where it should be placed for maximum chaos. He sent them off with a promise to watch for them at the public transport stop, and gave them a final order. "Your ghosts better come back and protect me, because Professor De Luna will definitely shoot me if you get killed."

In the meantime, he had an inspiration about what he could do with his leftover KemX. Be a shame to let it go to waste.

* * * * *

Taliferros Radomir was having one of those days he'd heard the ghosts complaining about, when nothing was going as it should. Dixon announced he'd talked the CPS into letting them stay a few more days in paradise, and clearly expected his staff to be pleased about it. Georgie, in one of his lucid cycles, had discovered news about the experiment on the college girl and reported it to Renner. So far, Renner hadn't reported it to Dixon, which meant it was yet another thing Renner was holding over Taliferros's head.

Then the independent ramper that Taliferros had hired to take care of Foxe Investigations reneged on the contract and returned the retainer with the ten-percent penalty, no questions asked, and no questions answered, either. He had to assume that either Foxe or Morganthur got to her and warned her off, meaning they likely were one step closer to identifying him. He'd used the usual discreet hiring practice, but since he'd used CPS funds, they might be more traceable than if he'd used his own. The only good news was that, if he acted fast, he might be able to catch both Foxe and Morganthur. They were together on the same university floater he'd used for the "accident" job, and he knew it very well. He spun a tale to Dixon about going to a body shop for a biometric modification and left quickly.

He rented a small flitter and entered the floater's coordinates, but the traffic control system refused to route him, citing an "emergency vehicle" priority. He could drop off the TCS and land anyway, but it would report his flitter's rogue behavior immediately and attract the unwanted attention of the enforcement division. As much as time was of the essence, staying out of custody was a higher priority. He changed his destination to a public airpad on the small island that was three miles to the east.

When he got there, his luck temporarily improved when he came across an unattended airsled that had been left unlocked. The humid sea air would probably wrinkle his suit, but it was a small annoyance.

The nature of the "emergency vehicle" priority became apparent as he approached the floater. He snorted in cynical amusement. Doubtless the traffic control system didn't have a preprogrammed condition description for "war."

Taliferros was not risk averse, but conducting a hunt through a combat zone took risk to a whole new level. On the other hand, the circumstances had likely bottled up Foxe and Morganthur, and if he could find one or both, their deaths would be attributed to the war. The chance to get them off his back was too good to pass up.

The Math building, where he'd staged the accident and conducted his experiment, was the best option for landing, since it only had one flitter on top. He could have landed on the dock, but there were too many people—crew, based on their attention-seeking clothing and hairstyles—to make that a viable option.

He eased the airsled down as low as he dared as he approached the north wing of the Math building. At the last second, he pulled up and over the edge, touching down on the gravel-top roof. He controlled the bounce so it took him on top of the rooftop planters. He confirmed both with his eyes and his talent that no one was near. Even ghosts gave off an energy aura if he concentrated.

On the south wing, he sensed two energy sources, neither with enough talent to stop him, and three ghosts. He slipped through the rooftop foliage to get a better view. The three ghosts, well armed, faced the central stairway and lifts. One of the active talents, a mid-level telepath of some sort, sat in the flitter's pilot seat, using the comms. The other talent, another in the telepath class, stood near the rooftop door, rifle at the ready, but facing southwest, looking out to sea. Taliferros ordinarily didn't like to waste energy sources, but he was on a schedule. He took aim with his Davydov plasbeamer and downed them in rapid succession. The high setting of the Davydov didn't so much kill people as bisect them, and he practiced diligently with it to be both fast and accurate.

His talent told him the mercs were concentrated on the third floor, more toward the center. As with most merc companies, they relied heavily on technology to make up for fewer numbers, but twenty at once was more than a lone man with a Davydov could take on. Fortunately, he probably wouldn't have to, since Foxe and Morganthur had no reason to be with them. His talent said the lowest concentration of mercs was in the south wing's stairs, so that was his best bet for getting in. As he crossed the rooftop, keeping his talent actively monitoring the ghosts in the stairway, he spent his spare attention on assuming the look and body language of a harmless, hapless teacher who had stumbled into an armed conflict.

Maybe if he was lucky, he'd run into some energy sources to replenish his reserves along his way to the first floor, where he planned to start his search.

CHAPTER 23

* Planet: Nila Marbela * GDAT 3241.149 *

LUKA WAS HANGING onto his patience by a rapidly thinning thread. Mairwen was out ghosting her way through the building, vulnerable to both mercs and crew. Admittedly, they'd probably be more vulnerable to her, but it didn't stop him from worrying. He wished he'd made her eat more than a banana, because she was probably using tracker mode, which burned through her energy reserves at a prodigious rate.

Pico and Sojaire were keeping the children entertained with an improvised game that coincidentally caused them to move toys and furniture to create a wide, clear circle near the door. On the surface, Sojaire was his usual contained and genial self, but there was a certain brittleness about him whenever he looked at Pico.

For her part, Pico looked just as subtly unhappy when she looked at Sojaire. It reminded him of how lost Jerzi had looked when he'd come home after an assignment to discover Pico alone and Dhorya gone. Luka didn't know what he could do about whatever was going on between Pico and Sojaire, or if he should do anything, other than be a friend when needed.

He glanced at his percomp, willing it to ping with either results of the public data queries he'd launched, updates from Majeed on the other two "entirely coincidental" cases involving merc raids on labs, or anything at all from the rest of the team.

"*Luka,*" said the woman he loved as much as he loved air, "*the crew are massing behind the Math building. They are about to assault the mercs on the third floor and airpad and steal their flitter.*"

Luka snorted. Even he knew it was a bad choice to fight armed mercs who had the high ground. "I guess there's no minimum intelligence needed for joining a crew."

"*Indeed,*" said Mairwen. "*You and the others should leave now. Go through the atrium. The Materials Science building's airpad stairway is unguarded. Jerzi destroyed the lifts and is blocking doorways at each floor of*" *the far east stairway."* Her tone said she approved of Jerzi's initiative.

"Where are you?"

"Keeping the stairway unguarded."

Pico and Sojaire had heard and were already rearranging the child-carrying assignments. Luka would now carry Lyssi and Nico, Miguel would lead his sister Celia by the hand, and carry her if needed.

"We should leave a note for the center's staff," said Sojaire.

Pico looked startled, as if it hadn't occurred to her. "No. *Pieprzyć ich,*" she bit out angrily. "Fuck them. They left the kids." She frowned sourly and sighed. "But I'll send a ping to the manager, because the parents will be frantic."

Pico keyed the wallcomp to send the message, then made it display a view of the hall outside the door to check that it was clear. When everyone was ready, she picked up Parekh, then palmed open the door. Luka picked up Nico and Lyssi, then stood in the threshold to prevent the iris from closing. Sojaire, with quiet Davalia and fretful Isiro, slipped past him and started rapidly down the hallway. Pico was next, carrying a mostly clothed Parekh, with Miguel and Celia holding hands right behind her. Luka gave them a little space, then stepped out with Nico and Lyssi, both of whom were blessedly quiet. He heard the door iris closed as he followed.

They'd only gone a few steps when Miguel stumbled back, as if something had hit him. He scooped up his sister and turned back to Luka with a look of sheer panic on his face.

"¡El hombre malo está allá en el atrio!"

Whatever it meant, it caused Pico to drop Parekh to the floor and start running toward the atrium.

"English," ordered Luka.

"The hunter! Out there!" Miguel pointed toward the atrium. "He's hurting Sojaire!"

Luka put Nico and Lyssi down and pushed them toward the center. "Take them back to the doorway and wait," he ordered Miguel. It was safer than where he was going.

He unmuted his earwire and subvocalized. "Trouble. Valenia's attacker is in the atrium. He has Sojaire. Probably wants Mairwen or me."

"Coming." Mairwen always sounded calm when she was at her deadliest.

Throwing himself headlong into the situation wouldn't help. He walked steadily while setting his earwire to pick up spoken words as well as subvocalized speech and unleashed his essence talent. It briefly caught on Pico, with her bright curiosity and deeply loyal nature, but he forced it forward, past familiar Sojaire, to the man… yes, a man, a shielder, exultant in his power and forgetting to shield himself. The tangle of images that made up the man was horrific, corrupted, stripped of humanity, tortured. Luka fought to pull his talent away. He'd remember those few images for the rest of his life; he didn't need any more. Whether he'd been shaped long ago, or by the CPS, the man was warped beyond redemption.

"…finished with your bosses, my beautiful young man with energy to burn, you and I will play." The man's voice was high and reedy, but the atrium's acoustics made it seem like they were only a few meters away.

Luka was listening so intently, he ran into Pico. He grabbed her shoulders to steady her. Beyond the leaning stacks of heavy wall units in the atrium, about twelve meters away, he saw the tops of two heads, a blond and a medium brown.

"I know someone's there," called out the reedy-voiced man. "I can feel you. Mr. Foxe, I think. Your energy precedes you." He chuckled. "Do come out, or I'll kill your deliciously tasty assistant."

"You'll kill him anyway," said Luka. He felt a tickle in his mind, like a breeze blowing past.

The man chuckled again. It sounded off, like something he'd practiced without understanding it. "Well, it was worth a try," said the man. "My, but your talent is slippery. I know it's there, but I… can't quite…"

Luka heard a child, probably Isiro, start to cry.

"Your Davydov is frightening him," said Sojaire loudly.

"Aren't you the clever boy," said the man, just as loudly. "I know Morganthur is around here somewhere. Is she a minder, too? It would certainly explain how you've managed to track me."

"You have no idea," Luka said. It was curious that the killer, with his obvious sensitivity to minder talent, hadn't noticed Pico. Then Luka remembered she'd fooled the CPS Testing Center, so maybe it fooled the killer, too.

"Pico," he subvocalized, "can you flatline his Davydov? You'll only have one shot, or he'll feel it coming."

"Oh, I think I have a very good idea," said the man. "Apex predators always recognize the talent of another."

"*Yes,*" said Pico, "*but it'll fry your percomps and earwires.*"

Luka needed to keep the man busy. He took a stab in the dark, based on a flash of intuition. "Are you a CPS employee, or just a contractor?"

He heard a quick breath of surprise. "Whatever do you mean, Mr. Foxe?" The innocence was exaggerated.

"Contractor, then," said Luka loudly. "CPS employees are smug about it."

Pico's shoulders tensed as she raised two fists. Luka hastily pulled off his earwire and started peeling off his percomp.

The man laughed genuinely. "You're right–" He screamed in pain. The wall lights in the hall and atrium sparked and went dark.

"Sojaire, run!" yelled Luka, throwing his smoking percomp to the ground.

Luka ran into the atrium, in time to see Sojaire, burdened with two children, trying to kick through the main doors that wouldn't open.

A smallish, thin man with a receding hairline stalked after him. One hand held a knife, ready to throw. The other hand, charred and bloody, was cradled against his stomach.

"Why don't you pick on someone your own size?" snarled Pico. She had a surprisingly big voice, and the atrium amplified it.

The man glanced at her, then did a double-take. "It was you!" He veered toward her and cocked the knife. "I'm going to feast today."

From the north and south hallways, the unmistakable sounds of energy weapons and projectile fire heralded the start of the crew's assault. Behind him, he heard Miguel urging the children to run.

Pico heard it, too. Desperation warred with anger in her expression. She raised her fists. A heavy wall panel suddenly flipped forward and slammed into the man. A second one followed and landed on top of him, flattening him under its weight. Each panel had to weigh a hundred kilos.

Pico wiped at her suddenly bloody nose as she looked at the panels, confusion and wonder on her face.

Luka turned around just in time to see Miguel carrying his sister and herding the other children. Luka scooped up the closest two. Sojaire was turning the manual crank for the front door's iris. Luckily, it opened from the bottom first, so they could crawl through if they had to. A stray energy beam lanced into the atrium from the north hall. They were out of time. He'd have to hope that the crew found and finished off the man under the panels, if he wasn't already dead.

"Pico! Grab the kids, now!"

* * * * *

Andra held her breath until Truòng made it back to the large clump of elephant-leafed plants that Dortief and Vandeerink were hiding under. He'd been fast and efficient at spraying the base compound onto all the windows of the lecture hall he could reach, but she only had one rifle and two flechette guns to protect him with while he worked. She'd given Truòng her shockstick.

The application of the catalyst would start the real fun. With real-time comms restored, the entire self-appointed team had been sending messages to their friends in the lecture hall, directing them to casually move toward the windows. By then, it'd become clear to the lecture hall occupants that the mercs weren't security for a VIP; they were jailers. The idea was to prevent the mercs from immediately noticing the increased light and fresh air until the windows finished melting. She'd gotten the idea from the meltglass tables in Dominar Carlotta's, and Vandeerink, bless his mischief-making heart, had happily contributed his chemistry knowledge to the task. Dortief raided a supply closet for two vertical cleaning nozzles and the bigger cleaning robots they belonged to, and Truòng, with his enviable minder fixer talent, helped her fashion them into manual sprayers attached to canisters.

Ms. Chao and Ms. Hranush, two more of the lecture hall escapees, had raided one of the chemistry supply closets, then holed up in the audio-visual closet that Jerzi had found earlier, making remote-detonated smoke bombs. Their idea had been to make it hard for the combatants to get around on the second floor. Andra talked them into sneaking the bombs into the second-floor chemistry lab near the circulation intake, then waiting until her signal to trigger them all at once. The smoke should pour into the lecture hall, and again set off the fire suppressant system, which should keep the mercs busy.

Mr. Lodkar and Ms. Flaurin from her class, and Mr. Ravlenko from the chemistry program, were in the narrow corridor that was the loading side of the food court's wall of vending machines. Their initial target had been the heating wands and pressure units, for making a bomb they planned to set off in the lifts, but they'd gotten pinned down because the crew had begun using the loading dock, and mercs were in and out of the food court. Andra talked them through using what they had on hand to improvise non-destructive but noisy flash-bangs instead, to cover their exit via the food-court access panel.

Her earwire came to life. *"Professor De Luna,"* said Melly Grien, *"you can blow the barge anytime. We're swimming back now."*

She quickly switched to the secure conference that Foxe Investigations had set up. "Unless anyone objects, I'm blowing the barge in five minutes."

After a moment of silence, Jerzi responded. *"Luka and Pico ran into some trouble, but they're handling it. I'll go meet the Griens at the public transport stop."* Subvocalization flattened intonation, but she knew he was worried.

"Okay. See you up top." Their plan was to meet at the Materials Science airpad, hold it until everyone was safe, and fly off into the sunset. Sadly, the sun wouldn't be setting for another two and a half hours, and a lot could happen between now and then.

She tapped her earwire to switch to the conference net she'd hastily arranged for her students. "Chao and Hranush, smoke bombs, if you please. Everyone, ping your friends."

"Done," said Chao.

Andra resettled herself under the mass of blade-like leaves in the raised vegetation clump under the abstract statue in the center of the commons. It gave her the best vantage for picking off mercs from outside, but had some dangerous blind spots. She swiveled the Hellrim on its monopod toward the windows, then picked up her flechette guns. "Truòng and Vandeerink, the catalyst."

Truòng carried the bulky tank while the taller Vandeerink sprayed the windows, from bottom to top. Both men wore heat- and chemical-resistant gloves. At the end of the darkened windows, they abandoned their equipment and ran back to the first one, where Dortief, also in gloves, was waiting, and the glass was already deforming and slumping into the frame. They pulled the taffy-like glass out and down, before it solidified, then moved onto the second window.

"Ganesh's trunk, but it stinks in here!" said Hranush.

"The smoke?" asked Andra, worried that the young women would have to find a new hiding place if they got smoked out.

Hranush giggled. *"No, Chao farted."*

"Did not," said Chao. *"The smoke is already... there goes the suppression mist!"*

"Stay put, ladies. You're safer where you are. Mr. Lodkar, you and the others get out when you can."

"The mercs in the food court are all getting pinged. Yep, there they go."

"Go now." For Ravlenko, the enthusiastic but careless lopar that he was, she added, "Don't use the flash-bangs until you need them. It's no fun if it's not a surprise."

"Seawater triggered. Foam's away!" said Chao.

Andra was tempted to use her oculars to watch the action at the lecture hall windows, but she couldn't afford to lose the big-picture focus of the area she was supposed to protect. Several people had already escaped through the first few windows. Four muscular students, big enough to be redball or pelotón players, stationed themselves near the compromised windows and started pulling people out as fast as they could.

"Barge blowing in five seconds," she told the student network, then switched briefly to the secure conference and told them the same thing.

She sent the code and mentally counted down. On the sixth second, she heard a deep, chest-vibrating thump and the rush of displaced water. A good explosion was almost as good as sex.

The universe must have heard her thought, because the top floor of the Chemistry building suddenly erupted in a fireball of ear-splitting glory worthy of a centennial celebration display. She willed herself to look away from the smoke and ignore the debris raining down so she could cover people still scrambling out of the windows and the several dozen people who had started running in every direction across the commons, away from the Chemistry building.

"A little gaudy, maybe," said Jerzi, *"but impressive."* She'd forgotten to switch back to her student network.

"I'm flattered, but it wasn't me. Busy. Talk to you soon." She tapped her earwire.

"...been shot!" Lodkar's voice was near panic.

"Say again. Where are you?" She kept her voice calm and deliberate.

"Santé's been shot by a beamer. We're behind the mermaid fountain behind the southwest dock. Rav had a watersled here, but the whole dock is wrecked."

"Can Flaurin move? Where's Ravlenko?"

"She's unconscious. I think one of her lungs has a hole. Rav went to the shared labs for a med kit."

"What can you see? Crew, mercs, ships?"

"Nothing. We're in the fountain's service well."

"Stay there, then, unless you absolutely have to move. Ravlenko, where are you?"

"At labs door, waiting for military point-person to look away. They try

to fix broken boat." His English wasn't nearly as good as his Russian.

She pictured the location in her head. "Lodkar, launch one of your flash-bangs if you have any left, to the southwest. Throw it if you have to."

A merc suddenly appeared on the commons, running from the Materials Science building toward the lecture hall windows. "Stop right now," he yelled, firing warning beamer shots toward the windows. The glass he hit melted even more. He didn't get a third shot because Andra took him down with flechettes to the unprotected knee and throat.

"Shit!" yelled Dortief. Someone from inside the window opening behind her was trying to pull her inside by the hips. Before Andra could trigger her oculars, Dortief pulled free, then turned around and punched whoever had grabbed her. A moment later, a red-uniformed figure slumped into the frame. Dortief dragged him out and punched his head again before tossing his body aside. Someone should have told the merc it wasn't smart to piss off a ramper.

She spared a glance up at the damaged Chem building. She couldn't see any flames, but dense brown smoke was rising to the sky.

"Chao, Hranush, how are you?"

"Good," said Hranush. "Shuyun called her Uncle Huan. He's sending drones for real-time vid." Chao's uncle owned *Zhàomíng Lùjìng*, a very popular news magazine.

"If you can, stay there, where you're safe."

"We scored a huge stash of junk food from the chem lab, so we're good."

The flood of people from the lecture hall windows had reduced to a trickle. "Dortief, Vandeerink, Truòng, you're done. Find a place to hunker down and stay safe. Lodkar? Ravlenko?"

"We're still in the well," said Lodkar. *"Rav put burn and wound packs on Santé, and I put a breather on her. She's stable, but she needs a med evac capsule."*

"Hang tight. Chao, ping your uncle and tell him to get the military to quit fucking around and start doing their jobs. Students are dying."

Chao snorted. *"Oh, he'll love that."*

The university wouldn't, but she'd bet high that they'd interfered with or delayed the emergency response so it wouldn't hit the newstrends. They got what they deserved.

CHAPTER 24

JERZI WAS NO longer enamored of real-time communication because he hated feeling powerless when he heard things he couldn't do anything about. He'd been sealing the third-floor stairway door with more of the waterproof adhesive they'd used for the barge bomb when he'd heard Luka's announcement that they had trouble from the killer. His heart rate climbed when he heard Pico agree to use her talent to flatline a Davydov beamer, and then brief feedback when their comms got fried.

Independent-minded Mairwen would ask if she needed anything from him, so he left her alone. He was about to head to the airpad when he'd remembered Andra's backpack. It still had plenty of explosive contents that he wouldn't want in the hands of merc, crew, or inquisitive students. And because he'd just sealed himself into the stairway, his only choice was to go down three flights, outside, and back up the southeast stairs. He was grateful to whichever university architect had an obsession with multiple stairways for buildings.

He had to hide in an alcove when he heard several voices coming. From what he could hear, four or five crew were hauling an overburdened cart to the center freight elevator. They were antsy and short-tempered. Jerzi counted the seconds and concentrated on even breaths and slowing his heart rate. Adrenalin wasn't helping at the moment.

Once the lift door closed, he listened to the ensuing silence for thirty seconds, then walked quickly down the hall to the lab. He palmed the door lock and it opened. He wondered if a security audit would ever notice the fact that Andra had added his biometric to the "all access" group.

He stuffed a spare lab coat in the backpack to keep the contents from rattling around, then slung it over his shoulders. At least it wasn't as heavy as before. He started to leave, then hesitated when he saw the bone regenerator unit the students had pilfered from the lab's first-aid kit. If anyone else besides Mairwen was injured, more supplies might come in handy. He opened the backpack, removed the lab coat, then stuffed as many med supplies as he could into it. He was sealing it again when the distinctive tone announced Andra had rejoined the secure conference.

"Unless anyone objects, I'm blowing the barge in five minutes."

Jerzi waited for a moment in case Mairwen had something to say, but she was silent. "Luka and Pico ran into some trouble, but they're handling it." He fought to let the worry slip away. "I'll go meet the Griens at the public transport stop."

"Okay. See you up top." She sounded marvelously calm. He was glad she was the one orchestrating multiple amateur teams of students, not him. Gunnin, and now students, followed her because they knew she'd have their backs.

He re-slung the backpack on his shoulders, grabbed his gun bag, and repeated his careful run down the hall toward the southeast stairs. He ran down them quickly, eased out of the building, and headed northeast toward the public transport stop, using the overgrown vegetation as cover. In the humid undergrowth, the odor of rotting flesh made him grimace. Apparently, no one had yet found the two dead crew Andra told him she'd killed before they could rape an unconscious merc.

"Jerzi, we're coming from the Math building entrance. We need help getting to the far east stairway," said Mairwen.

He peered out to the empty public transport stop, but saw nothing. "When? The Grien siblings aren't back yet."

"Now. We have the children. Crew and mercs are fighting in the Math building. Crowds are coming."

"On my way," he said.

He high-stepped out of the vegetation and crossed the permaturf walkway to the artful clumps of flowering plants that hugged the Math building, and followed its wall west. Up ahead where the building rounded, a head peeked out fast. A moment later, Luka came around the corner fast, carrying a tense older boy and a frightened younger girl. Jerzi picked up his forward speed.

"Help Sojaire and Pico behind me. They have five kids. Mairwen is covering our exit."

Jerzi nodded and slipped past Luka. A shout from the commons made him cast an uneasy eye toward the west. If Andra's plan worked, at least a hundred and fifty people would soon be loose on the commons, and some would head straight for the Mat Sci building's airpad.

Andra's tone sounded in his earwire. *"Barge blowing in five seconds."*

Jerzi got four more steps father before a muffled explosion and a splash meant the barge bomb had blown. He hoped the Griens were far away.

A second, much louder explosion came from the east. Jerzi cleared a tree and saw that the top floor of the Chemistry building was engulfed in a rising ball of red flame and black smoke. He didn't think it was Andra's doing, but he couldn't resist teasing her. "A little gaudy, maybe, but impressive."

"I'm flattered, but it wasn't me. Busy. Talk to you soon."

Jerzi broke into a run when he saw Sojaire carrying three children, and Pico carrying two.

"Take Pico's," said Sojaire. "I'll give her Parekh."

The children, a dark-skinned girl and a pale red-haired girl, tightened their grip until Pico said, "It's okay, he's my dad." She pried them off and handed them to Jerzi. He took them together in his left arm, leaving his right free in case he needed to grab the beamer in his pocket. His camouflage vest was dithering, trying to decide what background colors it should be matching.

Sojaire handed the littlest boy to Pico, then resettled the other two boys he carried and started forward.

As Pico was encouraging Parekh to wrap his legs around her waist, Jerzi asked, "What happened to your nose?"

"Blowback," she said. "Sojaire will fix me. Mairwen's still at the door, I think."

"You go on. I'll wait."

She nodded and took off. He turned his attention to the commons. He thought he saw movement.

"I'm Lyssi," said the red-haired girl.

"I'm Jerzi," he said. He switched to subvocalization. "Mairwen, we're at the corner."

"I see you. Go."

He turned and followed the path his friends had taken. With his longer legs, he soon caught up to Pico. She looked emotionally spent and physically exhausted, but he'd save his concern for later, once they got off the floater.

He tried to get a glimpse of the public transport stop as they headed for the far east door, but the vegetation that had given him cover also prevented him from seeing anything but distant water.

"Jerzi, down!" Mairwen ordered.

He dove onto his right side, cradling the girls' heads with both hands. His hip landed hard on his gun bag, and he heard something crunch that sounded like glass.

About eight meters away, a mohawk-wearing woman staggered into view, then fell to her knees, blood pouring down her front from her throat, where two matching knives protruded.

Mairwen vaulted in to kick the woman sideways, grabbing her Hellrim rifle as she fell. Ice formed in his veins, until he realized the rifle was almost brand new, not old and battered like Andra's. Mairwen retrieved her knives and wiped them on the dead woman's leather pants.

Jerzi climbed to his feet, his overworked thigh and butt muscles screeching complaints about the strain. Two hot soaks and massages, he told them.

"Thanks," he told Mairwen as he half-ran to the doorway to the east stairway. He took a deep breath, promised his protesting thighs three hot soaks, and started up.

Andra's tone pinged in his earwire. *"Hi, again. What did I miss?"* Her teasing voice, even subvocalized, was somehow soothing.

"A little trouble getting out of the Math building. We're going up top now, with seven children. You?"

"Oh, you know me. Sowing a little chaos and distraction. The news media will be here soon, if their drones aren't already, which ought to speed up the military's response. As soon as I make sure there's a med evac capsule on the way for one of my people who got shot, I'll be coming your way."

"Could you get the Griens? I said I'd meet them at the public transport stop any minute now."

"Copy. See you soon."

"Wait! I have your backpack. And be sure to take the far east stairs." He hoped she'd heard him, or if she hadn't, that she was out of flechettes by the time she found him.

* * * * *

Andra used the reflection in the Math building's windows to tell her when the coast was clear enough to pull her gun bag out of the mud. Its bright colors afforded good camouflage from thieves, but not so good when she was trying to hide in a crowd. She slung it over her back like a gym bag, not caring if the mud smeared her clothes. After today, they'd probably have to be incinerated. The reflection told her she had grease on her pants, a singe from a too-close beamer shot, leaves tangled in her hair, and a torn sleeve from when she'd been escaping the custody of the mercs who'd caught her in the hall a couple of hours ago.

According to the live feed that Ms. Chao's uncle was live-streaming on all the news bands, the military had arrived with four heavy cruisers. They were in the process of clamping a temporary dock to the south edge of the floater, next to the destroyed dock that had damaged their light cruiser earlier. She'd rather not be rounded up for containment and questioning until after her friends got off safely, and after she'd found a safe place for her gun bag, which wouldn't go with her professorial image. Thank the universe Jerzi had already thought of her backpack, because the military took an especially dim view of civilians, even ex-military civilians, carrying a veritable sample case of modern explosives.

Chao's uncle had also come through with the med evac capsule, and Ravlenko and Lodkar had locked themselves into one of the shared labs' storage rooms. She'd strongly hinted to all of her students that discretion would be better than pride when it came to describing what they'd been doing, even though it had probably saved lives. She wouldn't put it past Vestering to use their exploits as an excuse to shut down the Practical Applications class, but she wouldn't apologize for teaching them to apply their knowledge to the real world, where brains could prevail over brute force.

She stepped onto the permaturf walkway that led to the public transport stop and walked quickly. The sooner she got the Grien siblings to safety, the sooner she could get up top and, if the universe loved her, long gone before the military brought in air support and Jumpers to lock the floater down.

She was surprised to see at least twenty people milling around, and a few more seated on the faux sandy beach that marked the floater's rim. The crew must have abandoned control of the area. A mid-sized boat was pulling away from the second berth.

"Professor De Luna, where were you?" Andra looked around for the speaker, and finally saw one of her Materials Science students, who had been in the second wave of escapees. He looked sweaty and wrinkled, but otherwise unharmed.

"Just hanging around, watching the fun. Have you seen Ms. Grien or her brother?"

"Sure, you just missed them. They're with Mr. Lavong. I think Trenton got hurt."

"Where?"

Severin pointed out to sea. "On the boat."

Andra used her oculars to zoom in on the boat. It was an emergency dock boat, like the one she'd told Vestering to use. Lavong was at the controls, and Melly and her brother were seated close to him. One blink closer revealed that Trenton was leaning on Melly, and his head was bleeding. Lavong was piloting with one hand and holding a beamer on the pair with the other.

Swearing in Spanish, she started to pull out her Hellrim, but realized she'd never make the shot. She knew someone who could. She turned and sprinted for all she was worth toward the east stairway.

She tapped her earwire. "Jerzi. Lavong has the Griens in the boat that's leaving the transport stop. He'll kill them."

"*On it,*" said Jerzi. His unquestioning trust was a balm.

"*Why would he do that?*" asked Pico.

Andra hit the stairway door and slammed it open. "I think he's crew, or they bought him." She took the stairs two at a time. "Explains the tech suppressors in all the buildings. I should have seen it. I don't know where the profit is, though." She was out of practice at subvocalizing while panting for breath.

She grabbed the handrail to help control her swing to the second-floor set of stairs. She wasn't going to need a gym visit this week. Maybe this month.

"*I do,*" said Luka. "*Blackmarket pharma clones. My police contact said mercs punched two more labs today, and they both belong to crew in that line of business. The university's isolated physical chemistry labs were a perfect setup. Much easier than the organic chemistry labs in the medical area.*"

"*I have a general lock on the target,*" said Jerzi, "*but no eyes. Scopes got cracked. I need you.*"

The third floor landing was wet, and she almost wrenched her shoulder, trying to stay upright. "Aw, gunnin," she puffed out between gasps for air, "you say... the sweetest... things."

"*Kiss me later. Watch out for the blood at the top of the stairs.*"

The rooftop door opened ahead of her, like the proverbial door into light. She pulled herself up the last couple of steps and splashed heedlessly through the pool of blood that came from the body of a dead merc. Pico stood at the doorway and pointed north. "He's set up on the wall."

Andra dropped her fifteen-kilo gun bag at Pico's feet and felt momentarily like she could fly, but she shook it off, knowing it to be euphoria caused by exhaustion. She could collapse later.

She skirted around the flitter stacker, still mostly full of airborne vehicles, and sprinted straight for Jerzi's familiar broad shoulders. His camo vest had matched the color of the retaining wall, making his bare arms look like an organic architectural detail.

"Lift me up on the ledge," she said.

He turned from his railgun and caught her by the waist as she jumped, then swung her around so she was seated facing out. She found the boat and locked in on it, then blinked to activate her oculars. She twitched her left eye sideways to connect to the railgun's onboard systems.

From her peripheral vision, she saw Jerzi adjusted a control on his gun. "Best place is near the gate," he said. "He'll be distracted. The flags give me wind direction, at least there."

She read off the numbers from her oculars. "Distance to the gate is… nineteen eighty-seven, which is about the end of my range. Target is twelve hundred twelve meters. Angle is forty-one, maybe forty-two. He's stuck in the traffic lane, but once he hits that gate, he's free to turn. Top speed for the emergency evacuation boats is twenty-nine KPH, and he's pushing it."

Jerzi swore. "This targeting system is *gówno*. " He turned to yell over his shoulder. "Pico, I need your brain."

"My eyes, her brain. What are you, Crush, an illegal cloner?" She didn't want to lose the target, so she didn't look when she heard Pico's footsteps.

"He's building a Frankenstein monster." Pico sounded exhausted, but at least she still had her sense of humor.

"Numbers?" he asked.

"Distance sixteen twenty-seven. Speed twenty eight. Angle thirty-eight."

"Pico, the gate is nineteen eighty-seven. When will he hit it?"

"Nine seconds."

"Count it down for me," he ordered.

"Eight… seven…"

Andra blocked out the distraction and kept her eyes on the boat. "No change. Lavong is leaning forward. Ear or throat?"

"Yes," said Jerzi. He sounded cool and calm, like she remembered so well.

"Five…" said Pico.

The railgun beside her whispered, and the projectile went subsonic, drowning out Pico's voice.

"…three…"

The railgun whispered again.

"…one…"

Lavong's head jerked, and blood exploded on the far side, spattering the windscreen. He started to topple, then jerked as the second projectile plowed through his neck like butter and shattered the windscreen altogether. With no one at the helm, the boat's safety systems flashed bright blue and took control. The boat slowed to a stop and began drifting.

Melly Grien dragged her brother away from the carnage, so she could cradle him in the middle of the boat.

The wall under Andra began to vibrate. Because she'd grown up on a seismically active continent, she knew to get off the edges of high buildings. She spun around to get off the ledge. Jerzi caught her as the vibration got more intense and threw her forward. He staggered with suddenly unstable footing, but managed to grab his railgun even as he let her down. Pico picked up his gun bag and stumbled toward the airpad. Sojaire came from around the stacker and ran to meet Pico, helping her stay upright on the bouncing gravel.

"The flitters!" Jerzi shouted as they all staggered toward the airpad.

Sojaire got Pico to the less treacherous airpad surface. Jerzi and Andra caught up with them, and Jerzi scooped up his daughter.

"Sojaire," yelled Luka.

Sojaire hesitated, then ran toward Mairwen's small, dull purple-gray flitter. Luka had just scrambled into the passenger area behind her and was reaching out a hand.

Andra veered away from Jerzi's side and ran to get her gun bag. Jerzi growled but kept running straight for his flitter, parked on the gravel beyond the edge of the airpad. Andra didn't care how unhappy it made Jerzi, she wasn't leaving her gun bag, and its entirely-too-interesting contents, for just anyone to find. The tremors nearly tripped her as she scooped up her bag. She turned and tried to concentrate on the movement of the ground under her feet. She counted herself lucky that she only fell once before throwing her bag in, narrowly missing Pico, and scrambling through the door. Pico slammed the door shut manually and scrambled into the front passenger seat as Jerzi lifted off.

"Fly north!" ordered Andra. She tapped her earwire and subvocalized. "Go north! If that shaking is what I think it is, someone sabotaged the floater's short-axis anchors. Once they fail, the heavier buildings will sink this side of the floater."

The eyes of all seven children were on her as she got to her knees. They were all sitting beside and on top of one another in the wide rear seat. "Having fun, *hijitos*?" She grinned at them. Miguel, the oldest boy, gave her a tentative smile.

"Acknowledged," said Mairwen.

"Will it flip?" asked Sojaire.

"Not unless we get a tsunami," said Pico. "Otherwise, it'll raise about twenty-one meters at the south center point, and the first floor of the Materials Science building's north side will get swamped."

"How do you know that?" he asked.

"Class exercise," Andra offered over the comm. "Vestering's approved scenario was too theoretical." She crawled awkwardly to the side window and looked down. The Griens out at sea were probably safe enough in the emergency boat, if the floater tilted slowly enough. The military weren't going to be thrilled that their new, temporary dock was twenty meters in the air. "Forget you heard that last bit, Ms. Adams."

"Where to now?" asked Jerzi.

"Majeed's office would be safest," said Luka. *"The last thing we need is to become casualties of a political pie fight. The police can deal with the university on notifying the children's parents."*

Andra stretched out her rapidly stiffening legs as best as she could over her and Jerzi's gun bags, and leaned her back against the flitter door.

"In that case," Andra subvocalized, "fly east three miles to Île de L'Espoir and pick up the traffic system and let it route you. Police stations get priority."

"You should know," said Jerzi, "that if the police get a look at what's in my flitter's hold, they'll detain me for days. I've got enough confiscated weapons to start another small war, and that's not counting Andra's sex toy collection."

Andra snorted, which made her sore ribs complain. She foresaw a visit to a minor medical care center, to get some of her deeper bruises taken care of, especially the ones in her side and hip where she'd taken a few shots from the merc who hadn't wanted her to leave.

"They have no reason to ask," said Luka. *"But if they do, we'll take up a*

collection for bail."

Jerzi laughed, but he winced. Andra wondered what kind of damage Jerzi, of the "think of something that doesn't hurt" school, was hiding under his clothes, beyond the mostly healed flechette wounds from yesterday. Which led her, of the "hormones with rotten timing" school, to want to be the one to examine him. She groaned and closed her eyes.

"If Mr. Vestering says anything, I have the perfect way to distract him," said Pico with studied innocence.

Andra opened one eye. "Tell me."

"I'll thank him for organizing our first Merc and Crew Recruiting Day."

Andra was too tired to do anything more than smile, but Jerzi laughed enough for them both.

CHAPTER 25

"PEREGRINE ADAMS?"

Pico nodded, but didn't even bother straightening up from her slump. The lobby chair was only slightly less uncomfortable than the interrogation room chairs. She'd been asked her name about sixteen times, sometimes ordered to move to another room, or asked if she wanted water, but mostly just asked her name by a succession of police and military personnel. Didn't anyone talk to anyone else?

During their twenty-minute flight, Luka Foxe had advised them all to have a simple, clear story, and not add extraneous details. She and Sojaire sneaked out of the lecture hall, went to the childcare center in the Math building, and stayed. She was surprised when her dad's friends Mairwen and Luka showed up to use the first-aid kit, and had no idea how Mairwen had gotten hurt.

When they ran into the crazy man with the Davydov plasbeamer, Luka and Sojaire would claim the power blew, probably from something the crew did, and used the distraction to throw a wall panel at the crazy man. They'd dropped the second one on him just to be sure, then ran to get away from the fighting. They took the children off site for their safety.

Yes, they'd been very lucky not to get shot by the mercs or the crew, and doubly lucky to leave before the floater foundation became unstable. Pico ruthlessly used her small size and best imitation of Melly Grien's wide-eyed innocence to encourage the questioners to underestimate her.

The gold-haired woman standing in front of her said, "Come with me, please."

She was the same officer who had taken charge of the children and asked Pico to verify that she recognized the various parents when they came to claim their children. She appreciated their diligence, which was more than she could say about the childcare center. Miguel and Celia's dads had both hugged and kissed their children, then hugged and kissed her, too. Lyssi's mother was subdued and polite, and had even thanked her.

Sometimes it took extraordinary events to make people quit wallowing in their own personal drama.

Pico stood and trudged after the officer. She practically had the layout of the place memorized, and she didn't even work there. This trip took her to a nicer office than before. The name on the door read "Captain Rana Majeed." The gold-haired woman opened the door and ushered Pico inside, then left, closing the door behind her.

She was apparently last to the party, because her dad, Sojaire, Luka, Mairwen, and Professor De Luna were all sitting or standing in an attitude of waiting.

"Hey, long time no see," she said to her dad, who was leaning against the wall, a meter or so from where Professor De Luna was sitting. Mairwen stood at something like parade-rest behind Luka's chair.

"Hours, at least." He smiled. He was probably relieved to see her. She felt the same.

The only place to sit was on a couch next to Sojaire. Her feet took her there before her mind could catch up and stop her. She'd just pretend he was the illegal clone version, and face cold reality in the morning. He made the illusion seem more real when he took her hand in his once she sat.

"Door," said Mairwen softly. Pico suppressed a smile. She'd overheard grumbling from one of the military interrogators, whom she suspected might be a telepath, that Mairwen might be deaf.

A few seconds later, an Arabic woman strode into the room, shut the door, then crossed to behind the desk, but didn't sit. She was tall enough to be a Jumper, and she had an aura of command.

"I'm Captain Majeed. It's nearly midnight, past my bedtime, so I'll get straight to the point. I know, and the military probably guesses, that you've left out some key facts. I also know Foxe well enough to know I'm not going to get them out of you, because he chooses his friends well. I could tie you offworlders up here for days, but it would likely piss you off, and I'd rather have your cooperation." She put her hands on the back of her executive chair. "Here's my offer. I let you all go now, in exchange for your promise to faithfully answer any pings from me on specifics. Don't make me hunt you down across the galaxy, because it won't be me, it'll be the military. They lost three boats when the floater anchors failed, and took heavy fire from the crew, so they'd be easy to motivate."

"What about us locals?" asked Professor De Luna.

Majeed frowned. "Optimal Polytechnic is being a pain in the ass.

They're calling in every political favor they can, trying to get you and Ms. Adams released, or at least in protective custody, and the whole case shielded from journalists. Their security people are sticking their chopsticks in my rice bowl. They'll exert pressure on you both to stop cooperating, but I hope you can find ways to help us. At least three students and four faculty are dead, so far, and who knows how many are hurt. I'd like to go after the people who are responsible."

Pico hadn't known about the casualties, and it distressed her to think of her friends being shot. Frustration and anger boiled up in her. "The university can eat hot death as far as I'm concerned. They care more about their reputation than anything else. The only thing they can do to me is expel me."

She noticed she was squeezing Sojaire's hand hard and tried to let go, but he wouldn't let her. Exhaustion coursed through her, then a trickle of something else, small and subtle. She finally recognized it as healing energy from Sojaire, like when he'd healed her nose after they'd gotten the children to the airpad. She squeezed his hand once, briefly.

"As much as I might agree with Ms. Adams's sentiments," said Professor De Luna, "my contract has a comprehensive nondisclosure clause and lawsuit-happy lawyers to back it up. However, the university regents have to specifically invoke it." She sighed. "I can't tell you how much it pains me to say this, because there are about a half-dozen beers, a shower, and a soft bed calling to me, but your only chance at me is tonight, while I'm still in your tender care."

Pico turned to her dad when he cleared his throat. "You may as well keep me, too," he said. "I'll be in seven days of transit back to Rekoria, starting the day after tomorrow. Your pings might not reach me for days, and I don't want to be spread-eagled on the pavement at the Etonver spaceport by some overeager ranker bucking for promotion."

The corner of Majeed's mouth quirked in a brief smile. "Thank you both. I'll try not to waste your time. I'll get you something to eat, and maybe a chance at a shower. The rest of you can pick up your comps and comms at the front."

Pico was glad her dad was staying with Professor De Luna. She deserved a friend in her corner, and there was no one better than her dad.

Luka stood, which was the cue for her and Sojaire to stand, as well, and addressed Majeed. "I'll ping you tomorrow, after we've all had a few hours of sleep." He caught Jerzi's eye. "We'll take care of Pico." He started to leave, then turned back to Majeed. "You might want to get a medic in for your guests. I think her ribs are cracked, and he's probably bruised from head to toe."

Pico couldn't resist a glance at Sojaire, who'd suddenly found great fascination with his scuffed boots. He'd probably told Luka about what he sensed with his hidden healer talent.

Majeed said she would take care of it and opened the office door for them using a control on her desk.

Once they retrieved their flitter, Mairwen took the controls, and Luka slid his seat up close to hers. He was engrossed with her percomp, the only one that had survived Pico's microteke blast. Mairwen took flying seriously, but Pico noticed she put a hand on Luka's thigh and kept it there.

The flitter's narrower back passenger section forced Pico to practically sit in Sojaire's lap, and she couldn't find it in herself to mind.

"Thanks for telling Luka about the medic for my dad and Professor De Luna. Gunnin don't like to admit weakness."

"You're welcome," Sojaire said softly. "Where is Valenia tonight?"

"I don't know," she said. "Being pampered in her parents' luxury hotel, I expect. Wait until she hears about today's 'interesting times.'"

Sojaire chuckled. "We'll never live it down."

The feel of his warm breath on the side of her face sent a tingle through her. She looked out the window at the city lights to distract herself. "Hey, where are we going? This isn't the bay."

"Our hotel," said Luka. "Sojaire can take you home if you insist, but I'm guessing the news media will have found your address by now. A lot of names are trending, and yours is on the list. Since none of us have been answering incoming pings, they're probably already knocking on your door."

Pico sighed. "Shuyun Chao. She's in my Materials Science class. Her uncle owns the top investigative news magazine on the planet. She's probably given him every name she knows." She frowned and looked at Sojaire. "I didn't introduce you to her, did I? Could she find you?"

"No. We're booked under the company, not individual names."

She relaxed a little. "Can I borrow some funds for a room, Mr. Foxe? My percomp… I guess I owe you and Sojaire new percomps, huh?"

"I think saving our lives makes up for it," said Luka. "Besides, Mairwen wanted us all to buy better ones anyway." He patted her hand on his thigh. Mairwen spared him a quick glance. Whatever he saw in her face made him laugh.

The couch in Sojaire's "reception suite"—meaning it had two rooms and a fresher—was compact, but comfortable and firm, which was a good thing, because Pico was sleeping on it for the night. The hotel was booked solid, so it was either that, or search for another hotel in the dead of night. Waves of exhaustion were beating her down, and yet she was still keyed up from the day's events. She had yet to process the fact that her teke talent was more than she'd imagined. She was also distracted by the sight of Sojaire in low-slung sleep pants and nothing else as he opened the bag of warmed candied nuts into a bowl, which he handed to her. "This will fix your low blood sugar better than I can."

She sat on one end of the couch, hugging a pillow between her knees and her chest. At least she was clean and dry for the moment. Sojaire had kindly lent her one of his knit shirts to sleep in, since her poor jumpsuit was sadly in need of cleaning. The borrowed shirt was plenty long enough, but a little clingier than she was comfortable with. She was already so hopelessly vulnerable to Sojaire right then, without revealing her body's response to him.

When he pulled up the room's overstuffed chair and sat facing her, she waved him away. "Shoo. Bedtime." She pointed to him. "Work." She pointed to herself. "Class."

He pointed to himself. "Understanding boss." He pointed to her. "Underwater campus."

She snorted, and her eyes started to fill. She put the bowl down beside her and sighed shakily. "Don't mind me. I'm an emotional train wreck."

"I know," he said. "It's okay." His solid presence and sympathy felt so real, so personal. And not real.

"You *do* know, don't you? You knew all along." Tears spilled down her checks. "Why didn't you tell me? I'd have understood." She'd have quit bothering him, and quit finding ways to meet him again. Maybe she could have found someone who could love her.

"Because I assaulted you, and I was too ashamed to admit it." His voice was raw.

She blinked. "Assaulted me? When?" He'd healed her a few times, but it never hurt.

He squared his shoulders, but it didn't erase the vulnerable look on his face. "On the space station, when I was stuck in the sabotaged airlock, I was desperate. I reached out with my empath talent. I twisted your emotions so you'd think you loved me and would want to help me."

She thought back to that night, three years ago. She remembered waking because she'd dreamed gravity was pulsing again. Valenia's blue nightlight made it easy to find her plush warm robe and soft, grippy slippers in the slick-floored, darkened habitat. A quick visit to the fresher and a pouch of water and she'd be fine. Sleeping on cots in temporary domes had been fun for one night, but by the fifth night, they'd grown old.

"Bring me some water, too," said Valenia sleepily. "Next summer, we'll go to room service camp."

On the way from the fresher to the cold box where the water was kept, she noticed a diagnostic percomp on the edge of the communal dining table, just like the one Medic Celeyron used. She picked it up to move it to a safer place, and learned his first name, Sojaire, from its property tag. Very French. Valenia was teaching her the language, so maybe older, sophisticated, sexy Sojaire would practice with her. She smiled and put the percomp in her pocket, then pulled two pouches of water from the cold box.

Something unknown—a sound, a breeze, a whiff of sour acid—made her think she wasn't alone. It made her nervous enough to freeze and listen. She knew Medic Celeyron often stayed up studying for his B-level certificate, and she had a sudden wave of longing to find him, to see him, to give him the percomp, to have him laugh with her and tell her she was imagining things.

The door to his makeshift clinic was wide open and the light was on, but no one was there. A rising sense of panic told her she needed to find him, because he could save her the way he'd saved the boy who had broken his neck just that afternoon.

A faint tapping sound to the left of the clinic door sent her in that direction, toward the sealed and locked camp entrance. Farther to the left was the camp's very own practice airlock, which led to the rigid cage in space where they practiced in exosuits and learned zero-G skills. The airlock felt wrong, like a bad circuit or a leaking power source. She'd never told anyone she could feel such things, because maybe she just had an overactive imagination and read too many adventure stories. Still, she edged closer to it, going slow enough so she wouldn't slip. Her grippy slippers weren't up to the micro-smooth threshold intended for gravity boots. She stood on her tiptoes and looked through the airlock's view window.

Sojaire's desperate and anguished face on the other side scared the life out of her.

Pico looked up at the real man in front of her. "When did you assault me? I found your comp, I found you in the airlock, I got you out, those three wastes of carbon chased us, you flatlined the phase-knife jerk with your talent, I flatlined the tech with mine. Was it when you stopped me from bleeding out and healed me?"

"No, earlier. I saw you standing at the cold box, getting water. I knew you liked me, and I breached your shell and pumped you with as much love as I could, so you'd want to see me, want to be with me, and find me."

"I admit I liked you, maybe even already had a crush on you, but I was more terrified than anything else," she said.

He hung his head. "That was my fault, too. Once I connected us, I didn't know how to let it go. I was scared to die, and I thought they'd kill you, too, because you found my percomp with the evidence. You couldn't help but feel it, too."

Chaos, she was tired, but she needed to hear this. "Let's say it's all true, that for as long as we were in that stupid space station, you played my emotions like a tesla harp. Not buying it, but nonetheless." She took a deep breath and glared at him. "How does that explain how I felt—how you *knew* I felt—for the last three years?"

He flinched, distressed. "I *didn't* know. I never used my empathy talent. It hurt." He pushed his hair back from his forehead, then leaned forward to rest his elbows on his knees, his fingers barely touching. "I knew about my healer talent early on. It's strong, and it's who I am. My empathy talent didn't even show up until I was about sixteen, and I thought I was just cracking under the pressure of living with my bastard father. He no longer had to tell me he hated me, I could feel it. The household staff was terrified of him. His manager felt sorry for me. His hordes of women were jealous. Finally, a friend at school, and empath herself, told me what I was, and showed me how to contain my talent."

He looked so forlorn, she wanted to touch him, to at least hold his hand like he'd held hers in the police captain's office. She didn't know how to close the distance. "But you got out, didn't you? You left."

"The day I turned seventeen. He'd been counting planetary years, not GDAT years—he thought he had another year to 'fix' me. I filed a severance declaration at the stroke of GDAT midnight and left with only the clothes on my back. I moved in with a friend and took an emergency response job so I could eat. For the next two years, my father got me evicted, fired, or expelled, each time he found me." He smiled lopsidedly for a moment. "I thought space camp would be safe."

She returned his smile. "I thought it would just be boring."

His smile faded. "Remember when you told me you were leaving Rekoria to come here?"

She sighed. "Yes." He'd been at his careless, distant worst. It still hurt.

His shoulders hunched. "Luka and Mairwen had dug up the evidence that exonerated me and exposed my father's lies. They testified for the injunction. A week before you told me the news, the day my medic license was restored, a couple of freelance enforcers tried to jump Mairwen. They were supposed to hurt her and tell her that if she and Luka continued to corrupt me, their business wouldn't last another year."

"Corrupt you?"

"An obsession of my father's. I was afraid that since he was brazen enough to send someone after my bosses, despite the injunction, he'd go after you. You were the only constant friend I had through all the schools, and jobs, and living situations. If you were on another planet, I thought you'd be safe."

"There's that word again. I think we should ban it from our vocabulary, so the universe doesn't keep trying to prove us wrong." She dropped her feet to the floor, but kept the pillow close. "Why didn't you tell me all this at the time? I'd have understood."

"Because I fucked up. I used my empath talent on you again."

"You manipulated my emotions?" He'd purposefully made her feel sad and abandoned?

He shook his head vehemently. "No, no, I just read them." He took a deep breath and let it out. He caught her gaze and held it. "I found out you loved me as much as I loved you. If I'd said anything at all, you'd have stayed. You're a fighter, Pico. He'd have destroyed you."

Her jaw and the pillow dropped at the same time. "You love me? Since when?"

"Since… I don't know when." He pushed his hair back again. "When we met, you were underage, and I was in a position of trust. I liked you too much even then. Then you were an adult, and your mom shredded you and your dad, and still you laughed with me and kept me from getting lost. Not just in the 'interesting times' moments, but in my head. In my self-pity. And we kept running into each other, and I didn't know how to talk to you, so I didn't. I just soaked up your sunlight."

The sweet, earnest look on his face was mesmerizing. And his "interesting times" reference made her smile. She so much wanted to believe him, that this was real, that the baseline version and the illegal clone were one and the same man. "What was going on at the restaurant, then?"

"Sensory overload. Mairwen's been pushing… Well, no, she doesn't push anyone. She just becomes an immovable object. She's been encouraging me to learn to use my empathy talent instead of fighting it. She said a friend used to fight his, and it didn't go well." He flattened his hands on his thighs. "But now I'm not so good in crowds, and the restaurant was packed, and I was having to keep healing myself of a headache. And then there you were, gorgeous and sexy, and I was tongue-tied, and I owed you three years' worth of apologies. Then those idiots behind us started fighting, and it overwhelmed my containment." He smiled ruefully. "The best I could do was try to help Valenia, and she was calmer than I was."

"So are you containing now?" She wished she could tell. Maybe she could learn.

"As best I can around you." He sighed. Even exhausted and wrung out, he was impossibly handsome.

"Well, stop it. You already know all my secrets. And now, I know all yours." She raised an eyebrow. "I do, don't I?"

He held up his hands. "Honest as the stars."

She slid the pillow aside and stood up. "Then tell me again that you love me."

One step put her in front of his knees. "Let me feel you."

She grabbed his hands and pulled him gently to his feet, pressing her aching, tingling body against the hot, hard, muscular planes of his, and sliding her arms around his neck. She felt his arms wrap around her and hold her like the sun was going nova tomorrow. She looked up at him. "Let me feel all of you."

He tilted his head down and she met him halfway, with her soft lips and inquisitive tongue. The feel of him, in her head and in her heart, sent her up in flames. Tears began to flow. Three years of dreams paled in comparison to the real man in her arms.

He shuddered and deepened the kiss, thrusting his hips against hers, letting her feel how much he wanted her. Loved her. Burned for her. His warm hands palmed her butt and lifted her. She wrapped her legs around his slender hips and broke the kiss to gasp for air and wipe away the tears from both their faces.

She nibbled on his ear. "Take me to your bed and ravish me, my brave corsair Sojaire, that I may return the favor soon after."

She felt him smile as he pivoted and carried her through the doorway to his bedroom.

"As my lady Captain commands, so it is my pleasure to obey."

She sighed against his neck. "I really loved that show."

CHAPTER 26

ANDRA HELD HER head over the solardry in Luka and Mairwen's hotel suite and toed the unit on. She ran her fingers through her hair to encourage it to dry. She'd deal with the frizz later.

A minute later, she gathered it in a barrette, while grimacing in the mirror at her clean but still bruised body, especially over the newly repaired ribs. Another visit to the medical center was high on her agenda. She pulled on her stained but clean exercise pants and loose top and thanked the cosmos for upscale hotel freshers with oversized, multi-head showers and built-in clothes sanitizers. She opened the fresher door and padded barefoot into the reception area of their suite, where everyone else was waiting for her.

Jerzi, hair and skin still damp, wearing his torn tank top and stained cargo pants, sprawled on the small couch. While she'd been washing off the smells of war zones and the police station, he'd done the same in the fresher in Sojaire's room. Jerzi was obviously torn between staring at and avoiding the overstuffed chair, where contented Sojaire cradled a blissful Pico in his lap. Andra couldn't help but smile. She didn't think she'd ever seen two people more in love, and it had to be shaking Jerzi's worldview.

Luka looked up from the percomp in his hand, just like the other two on the tiny table in front of him. "Breakfast is on its way." He'd apparently convinced—or bribed—the hotel to acquire replacement comps and deliver them to their room. He'd been using his to query the newstrends while waiting for her and Jerzi.

She sketched a slight bow. "My hollow stomach thanks you. They never got around to feeding us last night." While the room suite was pleasant, luxurious even, it had no windows, which was rare in Tremplin, where the constant view of a tropical wonderland was one of its main selling points. "What time is it?"

She and Jerzi had stumbled out of the police station sometime before dawn. Majeed had offered junk food scrounged from various desks, had the staff medic treat them, and allowed them short naps in between interview sessions. Jerzi had pinged Mairwen, who he was confident would be awake, and she'd invited them to the hotel for food and the use of their freshers. Since Andra was still temporarily homeless, it was too good an offer to pass up.

"Six thirty-seven," said Mairwen, standing near the door, feet slightly apart, hands clasped behind her back. She was wearing the solid gray tunic and pants she'd worn five nights ago in the restaurant in the sky. So much had happened since then that it felt like that was weeks ago. Mairwen turned her head a little. "The cart is here."

The suite's wallcomp lit up and chimed a moment later. Mairwen opened the door to reveal the automated cart full of food. Andra cast a look at Jerzi telling him to stay put, then crossed to help Mairwen unload the stack-locked plates and carry them into the miniature kitchen area with its narrow sink and token counter. They quickly distributed the plates all around. Mairwen sat next to Luka, leaving Andra's only option to sit on the couch next to Jerzi.

Ten minutes later, she and Jerzi finished their omelets and pastries almost simultaneously, as if they'd been in a race. She laughed to herself as she leaned back on the couch, reveling in the first comfortable place she'd been for the last two days. It was like a post-mission wind-down in the military, but better, because all these people genuinely cared about one another.

Luka cleared his throat. "While you two were entertaining Captain Majeed, the 'floater war' story reached critical mass in the newstrends. So far, they know crew and mercs are dead or detained by the military, and the floater is damaged. The prevailing narrative is that an upstart crew was using the labs to make illegal recreational chems, and that a rival crew hired the mercs to steal their product and punish them by sabotaging the floater." He waved a fork with a bite of sausage on it. "I think the 'rival crew' is actually a pharma company, and the 'recreational chems' were actually blackmarket clones of minder enhancement drugs made specifically for the Citizen Protection Service's use in the Minder Corps. It's the most logical reason for their involvement."

"So, did Manager Lavong work for the crew or the pharma?" asked Pico, brushing flakes of croissant off the front of Sojaire's shirt. He thumbed a smear of jam off her cheek, then gently pulled her off the arm of the chair and willingly back into his lap.

"Crew, I'll bet," said Andra. "He had the expertise, and months to install the tech suppressor network, under the cover of the security upgrades." A thought struck her, and she looked to Mairwen. "What did your security assessment say? Did you send it?"

"Yes. It said the labs had noticeably higher security than their value warranted."

Andra snorted. Knowing the university, they'd assume it was high praise. Until the floater war, they'd probably been planning to give Lavong a commendation. "Romila, a chemistry professor who's also a friend, and a data finder, said Lavong had been trying to get transferred to the Human Medical Department labs for years, and blamed the regents for blocking him. From what I saw, he was a vindictive bully, so maybe he thought it served the university right." She shrugged. "Or maybe he just liked money."

Jerzi nudged her knee with his. "Have you heard from Romila yet?"

Andra nodded. "Her townhouse got damaged by the same type of explosive micro-array that took out my apartment. She was across town at a party. It spooked her, so she burned flux to the other side of the planet, where some friends have a mountain resort, and holed up. She says by the time she got to thinking she should warn me, the floater war story was already trending."

"Hmph," said Jerzi quietly. She agreed, and yet didn't, because civilians couldn't be expected to act like a gunnin.

Luka pointed to the percomps. "The news says both short-axis floater anchors were sabotaged, but the north side went first. That's a drastic way to protect your laboratory investment, so I like Andra's theory. Hurting the university was justice. Money was his reward. What did the police ask you about him?"

"Nothing," said Jerzi. "I overheard one of the military interrogators ask for a media blackout, and mention the Griens."

Luka smiled sardonically. "That's because they gave an exclusive interview to *Zhàomíng Lùjìng*, the planet's top news outlet, and described how Lavong kidnapped them because they tried to stop him from taking the emergency evacuation boat from the dock, and that a stray crew bullet killed him. The interviewer made a point to ask where the military was while these poor students were being terrorized in their school."

Andra sat up. "Majeed said the new fifth-floor lab in the Chem building, or what's left of it, had a hidden security room, which was the origin of the explosion that took off the top of the building. She asked if I thought Lavong knew about it. I ducked the question, because I didn't want any questions about his death, but I think the crew had secret working comms during the tech blackout, or they'd have never been able to avoid the mercs when they were hauling out their investments. Lavong would have enjoyed orchestrating the crew's activities from his spider hole."

"Mr. Foxe, why do you think the CPS is involved?" asked Pico.

"Call me Luka. The man you stopped in the Math building's atrium all but admitted he was a CPS contractor. I still don't know his name." A troubled expression settled on his face, and he looked at Mairwen. She nodded so slightly that Andra almost missed it.

"The CPS protects pharmas they do business with, so when Medithera complained about the blackmarket clones undercutting their market, the CPS looked into the problem. It turns out Medithera has a subsidiary here on Nila Marbela that manufactures enhancement drug 'overdose antidotes' and sells them to anyone, not just the CPS. I think the CPS saw the opportunity to both help their partner and punish it, so they had their killer arrange 'accidents' for the crew chief and the pharma rep. I think a covert CPS unit had a prolific serial killer on a leash, and used him to do their dirty work. I doubt they expected it would start a war."

"But why was he chasing you? He knew your name. He knew who Sojaire was." Her hold tightened convulsively on Sojaire.

Luka slid his fingers through Mairwen's. "We've been tracking him for the last four planets. I don't know how the covert units are organized, or how much autonomy their contractors have, but I think the killer knew we were closing in, and saw the war as the opportunity to rid himself of us. He tried something new this trip, and hadn't perfected his technique."

Pico looked puzzled, until Sojaire said, "Valenia."

Her expression turned thunderous. "I already wasn't sorry to have hurt him, but now I hope each and every one of his molecules eats hot death."

Andra had the flash of an idea, and was too tired to lead the others to it gently. "You need to distract the CPS, or they'll be looking where you don't want them to."

That got their attention. "Me, I'm just a simple gunnin," she said, ignoring Jerzi's soft snort, "but the rest of you have secrets. So does the CPS, in this case." She looked at Luka. "Individually, they could destroy you, so you need allies. Connect the dots for your rich client on how the killer of their relative was protected by 'someone in the CPS.'" She made air quotes around the phrase. "Tell them your hands are tied. Even better, do the same with any other rich or powerful families who lost someone to him."

"But he's dead," said Sojaire.

Andra shook her head. "We can hope, but there's no corpse to point to. That ought to be enough to shine some spotlights on a dark corner or two. If the CPS does anything to Foxe Investigations, it will confirm the suspicions of motivated people with money. The CPS is big and powerful, but they have the same public relations problem as the university. They fucked up, and will be willing to make certain sacrifices so they don't have to admit it. Has to be fast, though, before they can fortify their defenses and tie up loose ends."

She cast a sidelong glance at Jerzi, wondering if he thought her proposal sounded ridiculous now that she'd said it out loud. His secrets were minor, outside of the extra-judicial takedown of Lavong, but his daughter's were significant. The CPS Minder Corps would love to get control of a multi-weight teke like Pico. It had happened to a squad mate of theirs from Forward Intelligence days, and the results had been ugly.

"For what it's worth," said Jerzi, "I think it's a good idea. Sting a bear on the nose a few times, and it'll leave the honeycomb alone."

Luka stood, restlessly, then took a deep breath and sat back down. "I like it, but I want to think about it." He gave Jerzi a crooked smile. "Always good to know who your friends are."

"And to have more than one way off the planet," he agreed with a return smile.

Andra snorted. She'd like nothing more than to stay and find out what it meant, but she got to her feet instead. "The real world beckons, or in this case," she said, showing them her frantically blinking percomp, "sends priority pings every five minutes. Once I answer, I'll have to play by their rules, so I need to buy some clothes and get a hotel room while I'm still free."

"I'm sorry," said Luka, "I should have mentioned it sooner. While you were in the shower, we, Foxe Investigations, decided we're leaving early. Today, in fact. Would you like to take over one of our suites?"

Andra turned to look suspiciously down at Jerzi. He held up his hands in surrender. "Not my idea."

"It was mine," said Pico. "I was going to invite you to stay in my flat while they repair your apartment, because Valenia's withdrawing from the university and going back to Rekoria."

Andra was both touched and annoyed at the same time, because Pico should know better. "You are kind to worry about me, but I'd have to decline. Students and professors–"

Pico laughed. "I'm not a student. Or I won't be about five minutes after my interview with *Zhàomíng Lùjìng* goes live at eight o'clock."

"Why, what did you say?"

She held up fingers to enumerate her points. "Zero university security staff on the floater to protect the students. Seven children abandoned to the mercy of a vicious crew. The university didn't address the glaring, single point of failure in the floater's anchor system that our regent-prize-winning class project warned them about, and the incident brought to light the insufficient number of emergency evac boats on hand, unable to accommodate even half the school's student population."

Andra whistled. "Well, Ms. Adams, that's an impressive boom-down of your bridges." She smiled and crossed her arms. "I'd say you chose your career field well."

* * * * *

Jerzi switched on the last candle and checked the time. Andra was either going to thank him or shoot him. Or maybe both.

Since he couldn't cook for her, he'd done the next best thing and ordered takeout from her favorite restaurant, Blue Clouds in Sky. He filled every available table and counter in her hotel suite's reception room with small plates and appetizers that she liked, at least according to the restaurant's manager.

Pico was back at her apartment, where both she and Valenia were packing. As she'd predicted, Optimal Polytechnic had expelled her, though it had taken them half a day to come up with a plausible reason, some vague accusation about the "domestic rocket launch" damaging the Math building's dock. Pico was quite certain any university in Etonver would be happy to take a new student with high marks and money, because that was where she was going.

Jerzi's introduction to the upcoming changes in Pico's life was through her startling announcement when he'd walked in the door of Sojaire's hotel suite after returning from the police station. "Hi, Dad," she'd said.

"I'm desperately in love with Sojaire Celeyron, and we had glorious sex last night. I'm moving back to Etonver to go to school, and we're going to live together. The fresher's right through there."

While in the shower, he considered all sorts of responses, but in the end, he settled on quietly telling Sojaire to keep her safe. The worry in Jerzi's heart eased a little with Sojaire's reply. "We'll keep each other safe, sir." Seeing them happy together, clinging to each other like *papużki nierozłączki*, inseparable parrots, made him smile.

Andra had given in and taken over Sojaire's room when he, Luka, and Mairwen left for the spaceport at ten. He knew she didn't like owing favors, and hated being cosseted, but it made perfect sense, especially since her name was peak-trending and journalists had their best finders out looking for her. She'd insisted on reimbursing Foxe Investigations for the cost.

She hadn't been joking when she'd implied O-Poly would shut her down. They'd invoked every clause in her contract to keep her from talking to anyone about anything, up to and including the weather. Her boss had tried unsuccessfully to pressure her into moving into a different hotel at the university's expense "for her safety," in between giving her coordinates and room numbers for the temporary classrooms where she'd be teaching Materials Science starting in three days, and oh-so-regretfully informing her the Practical Applications class was suspended for the session owing to lack of suitable laboratory space.

Jerzi had hung around long enough to make sure she didn't need a ride, then left, because he knew she needed to be alone. In between packing for his trip home tomorrow, helping Pico and Valenia get ready for the movers, and yet another visit to a medical center to get better treatment for the deep, massive bruise on his hip, he'd contemplated what to do about his friendship with Andra. All things being equal, he wanted Andra in his life, but all things weren't equal. She had a career on Nila Marbela, doing something she loved, on a paradise destination planet. She didn't just teach students, she inspired them. He had a successful career on Rekoria, doing something he was good at, with a great boss and friends. And soon, his daughter.

Knowing Andra had a hundred details to sort out, he'd decided he'd surprise her with a quiet dinner, and hope the universe had run out of any more surprises for the time being. She was smarter than he was, so maybe she could figure out how they could keep their re-established connection alive, assuming that's what she wanted.

Looking around, he had second thoughts about the candle-shaped light sticks, which suddenly seemed too romantic. He grabbed four of them and turned up the general lighting. He was just putting the candles in the bottom drawer of the pretend kitchen when the hotel room door slid open.

Andra entered carrying several bags, saw him, then looked around. She was wearing new, bright casual clothes and sandals, and her hair in a loose ponytail. She shook her head and smiled ruefully. "I should have checked with the hotel on who still had access to this suite."

"I figured you'd be busy today, so…" He waved his hand to indicate the food.

"Good thing I didn't already order room service." She shook her head, then crossed toward the bedroom. "I'll be back."

She reappeared a few moments later. "So, does this catered meal include any beer?"

"It does." He opened the tiny cold box and pulled out two and handed her one.

She took it, opened it, and drank a healthy couple of swallows. "Did Pico put you up to this?"

"Nope, my idea. She and Valenia are packing the stuff they don't trust the movers with. Valenia's parents are paying for them both to go back to Rekoria the day after tomorrow, which saves Pico the cost of separate freight."

Andra picked up an empty plate and began loading it with selected appetizers. He finally relaxed a little, glad she didn't appear to want to shoot him, and began filling his own plate.

Seated on the couch, they'd eaten their fill and were enjoying the last two beers. "So, are you okay with Pico and Sojaire?"

"He makes her happy. What father wouldn't want that for his kid?" He smiled. "Besides, it's bringing her back to Etonver, and I like Sojaire."

"You really like family, don't you? I don't think I ever knew that about you." She set her beer down on the table and turned to face him on the couch, curling her legs up under her. "I'm ambivalent. My biological family doesn't know what to do with me. They're big and successful, but they still have frontier-planet values—produce more offspring, acquire more land, loyalty above the law. I wanted to see the galaxy, learn new skills. The first time I really felt at home was in Forward Intelligence. By marrying Da'vin, I was really marrying into the unit. Da'vin's death devastated the whole unit, and the colonel blamed herself. I couldn't stay, because the memories were too much for me, but I miss that family, the one we made."

"I do, too." He never talked about his past much, because he didn't want the pity, but he thought Andra might understand. "My family was tiny. My mother was a casino game master, and my father was a watership crewman with serious cases of wanderlust and claustrophobia. He'd put up with domestic tranquility for all of about three weeks before taking another job on a new planet that put him out to sea for months at a time, and we followed. When I was eight, he took a job on another planet, but didn't send for us. My mother dragged me and my baby brother around from planet to planet, one step behind my dad each time he took off."

Her eyes widened with surprise. "You have a brother? Where is he?"

"No idea. My mother left with him when I was sixteen. She lined up a new job where my father was and wanted us to move again, and I didn't want to go." Jerzi shrugged. It was water under the bridge. "She never pinged, and never answered mine. I don't blame her, though. Paweł was still too young to take care of himself. I wasn't." He took a long pull on his beer. "I think part of what attracted me to Dhorya was that she had a large, stable family that wasn't going anywhere. Of course, as it turned out, 'stable' didn't mean 'pleasant,' much less loving or welcoming."

A ripple of laugher went through Andra. "I think all big families are wobbly, if you look past the genealogy lines and award plaques. Da'vin had two great aunts who believed they were secret aliens from the Mirach's Ghost galaxy, stranded here. My family is littered with crew chiefs and con artists. Half my great uncles are probably wanted criminals on a dozen planets."

Jerzi smiled. "No wonder they didn't approve of your military career. Conflict of interest."

"I believe the phrase used was 'fraternizing with the enemy.'"

A comfortable silence stretched between them, and he cherished it, but time was slipping away. "I had an ulterior motive in bringing dinner."

"Getting out of helping two young women pack their extensive wardrobes?"

"That, too, but mostly I wanted to thank you for being my friend, and I hope we can keep the connection." He snorted. "Sorry, that sounded like a greeting card. You have a life here, and I have one on Rekoria, but maybe we can meet in the middle every once in a while. Preferably not in a war zone." Some quiet place where they could relax and get to know one another again, and maybe more.

"I'd like that," she said. "But based on empirical data over the last week, there's something about the Adams clan that attracts extraordinary events, so we should probably come prepared for them, anyway."

He didn't know if he believed that, but he felt like he should apologize. "Uhm, sorry?"

"I don't mind, Jerzi. *Es lo que hace la vida interesante.*" She unfolded her legs and stood up. "That's what makes life interesting."

She started gathering the mostly empty plates, and he got to his feet to help. The small kitchen's recycler was thankfully normal size, and able to handle the debris.

"What's next for you?" she asked. "Once you get home, I mean."

"Help Pico and Sojaire find an apartment in a decent neighborhood. Plot with my boss how to take over the company with our little division. Help Pico get a handle on her teke talent, if she'll let me."

"Ask her to help you with yours." She gave him a cheeky grin. "Tell her you want to rank me in flechettes at the gun range."

"Sneaky." She really was a born teacher. "What's next for you?"

"Improve the Materials Science program. Vestering will need all the help he can get to save his department and cover his ass, so he'll have to quit bothering me for a year or two. Buy a new shockstick, in case he doesn't. Find out when I can move back into my apartment."

"That reminds me, I was supposed to tell you that Pico and Valenia's flat is prepaid for another six months, nonrefundable. They want you to have it until yours is repaired. It's not as nice a view, and the tenants on the floor above practice tap dance or something at all hours, but it'd be cheaper than a hotel room."

"It's a handsome offer. I'll consider it." She took him by the hand and led him to the door, then turned to face him. "I'm glad we met again, and if I have to be in a war again, I hope you're there with me."

He shoved the swell of longing into a corner of his mind. "Likewise." He gave her a teasing smile. "If you're ever in the mood for action, Etonver is renowned for street fights and riots. I'm sure we could scare one up if you're in town."

"Funny man." She smiled and slid her hands into her pockets. It made him smile, because only Andra would insist even form-fitting pants had pockets.

He needed to get out of her presence before he did something really stupid. He reached for the door.

"Before you go, what was that bit between you and Luka, about knowing who your friends are, and having more than one way off the planet?"

"Advice from… a friend, I guess I'd call her. She's not the kind you have a beer with. She's the president of La Plata. Luka and Mairwen used to work there, too, before they went off on their own. She's a forecaster, so you have to take what she says with a grain of salt, but she called us all together one night for GDAT New Year's and told us there was trouble on the horizon, and gave us advice."

She looked thoughtful. "Trouble where—Rekoria?"

"That's what I thought at the time, but I've come to believe she meant the whole Concordance."

"What was her advice?"

"She told us to know who our friends are and keep them close, and to have more than one way out of the city and off the planet, and have safe places to land. Luka thinks her advice was more metaphorical, but I'm just a simple gunnin, so I just take it to mean what it says." He shrugged. "Her third piece of advice was not to trust the CPS, but we already knew that. Minders need schools and places where we can be safe, but with the CPS, the price is too high."

"What time does your shuttle leave?"

"One, but I have to drop off the Pazorbaal. I'll miss it." He took a deep breath and held it. "I'll miss you, too."

She sighed, then took a step closer. "I thought I could, but I can't let you go like this."

"Like what?"

"Without kissing you, for a start." She took a tiny step closer.

He blinked in surprise. "Why?" His body said to stop talking.

"If you have to ask, Commander Crush, then it's been way too long since you've done it." She slowly closed the distance between them, as if giving him time to get used to the idea. "Because it's killing me not to."

He didn't know why he was hesitating, because kissing her, and a lot more, was the deepest secret fantasy that he'd never admitted, but he disciplined himself to think. "I can't stay friends." Hell, that sounded like primer school. He tried again. "If I touch you, if you touch me, we'll never be 'just friends' again."

That stopped her. "Is that all you want? Friendship?" Her dark brown eyes held a vulnerability he'd rarely seen from her. He had a feeling he'd hurt her, somehow. He wanted to fix it.

He shoved his hands into his pockets and made fists. "Sex fucks up friendships. As much as I want you, have always wanted you, even when I shouldn't have, I value what we have between us more. We're... What's the Spanish word you used?"

"*Simpatizamos*," she said. "We sympathize with each other."

"Yes. *That's* what lasts. Not impulses, not hormones." He rocked back on his heels once and almost hit the door. "I have a lot of friends because I get along with people. But damn few of them are good friends, and I don't want to lose even one of them. You most of all."

She reached out to pull his hands from his pockets and coaxed his fists open. Her fingers felt warm and capable. Her deep brown eyes were shining. "Tell me that part again about how you always wanted me, and I'll tell you how that first year in the unit, you were the star of my fantasies. I all but posed naked on your bed to get you to see me as something more than your teammate."

"I did see you," he said softly. "I saw you as the woman who ranked me by four grades at the time, and could and would kick my ass if I disrespected you. Asking if you wanted a hot-connect seemed damned disrespectful to me."

"You have a point." She quirked a smile at him and squeezed his fingers. "I still had a lot to prove back then."

"Is this," he pointed to her chest and his, "just a one-time wish fulfillment, then?" His body wanted him to stop talking and start kissing, but he couldn't do that without knowing where it was going. It would be too easy to fall hard and fast for Andra, and he'd barely regrown his heart from the last woman he'd given it to.

"I certainly hope it's more than once," she said with a suggestive smile that caused a wave of desire to course through him. "We have all night."

He fought not to drown in the depths of her warm brown eyes. "And how will we make this work when we're seven transit days apart? Trust me when I tell you that long distances are hell on relationships." Even as he said the word, he realized he wanted that with her. A relationship. Love. It made the breath freeze in his lungs.

She was silent for a long moment. "I'm scared, too."

He started to deny it, but realized she was right. He was terrified. She was strong and smart, and hot enough to ignite a star, and he was already caught in her gravity well. He didn't know what was right for them anymore. He felt dizzy.

"But you know what scares me more?" She crept closer to him, to where he could feel the heat of her body searing his. "Letting you go, and always wondering what we could have had." She caressed his jaw, stroking his beard, then put her warm hand on his shoulder. "Life is so short, *querido*. It can be snuffed out between one heartbeat and the next."

Tears welled in her eyes, and it was more than he could stand. He lowered his head and kissed her, then wrapped her in his arms. He touched her lips with his tongue, and she opened for him. The taste of her was as instantly addictive as he'd always suspected it would be.

She moaned in his mouth and arched into him, igniting sparks across his skin. He slid his hands down the sides of her generous breasts, down to her glorious, muscular ass, and pulled her hard against his arousal. He broke the kiss to gasp for a breath of desperately needed air.

"Bed," he growled into her sweet-smelling hair. That sounded too far away. "Couch." He nuzzled her ear, touched a tongue to the lobe, and was rewarded with her shiver of delight. "Nearest flat surface."

"Bed," she said firmly. "Soft, comfortable, big bed."

CHAPTER 27

ONLY BECAUSE THE wall display clock said so did Andra know it was dawn. She'd been awake for a while, contemplating the years and months and days behind her, and considering her options for the future. Half wrapped around her, warm and comforting, Jerzi stirred in his sleep. They hadn't been able to get enough of each other in the night as they'd each learned what made the other tremble and shudder with pleasure. She wished they had more time, but he had to get over to Pico's for his belongings and to say goodbye to his daughter, and she had a to-do list that kept getting longer.

Andra couldn't remember if he liked coffee or kaffa in the mornings, but she did, and the hotel room had a built-in kaffa dispenser. She untangled her legs from his and rolled to the edge of the bed. Muscles she hadn't used in a while were deliciously sore.

After a visit to the fresher, she drew a mug full of the fragrant, hot kaffa and took it back to the bedroom. She stood a moment in the doorway and stared at the man in her bed. Jerzi in clothes was good-looking, but without them, he was a work of art. His light gold skin was a clean canvas, except for the small, deep-inked peregrine falcon on the curve of his hipbone. No need to ask what that represented. All the other colorful body art he'd acquired during his time in service was gone, as were the wrist studs that had symbolized his marriage to Dhorya, even though they hadn't actually married until much later.

"A gorgeous naked woman with kaffa," Jerzi mumbled sleepily. "I must be dreaming."

"Want some?" She angled her hip provocatively and thrust her breasts forward a little.

He raised his head and grinned. "You have no idea."

She let her gaze travel down his chest to his sculpted stomach and the juncture of his thighs. "Oh, I think I do." She smiled, then sighed. "But the kaffa will have to do. I'll get you a cup. Straight, or flavored?"

"Straight. The flavors all taste like cheap air fresheners."

She heard him stumble into the fresher while she found and filled another cup. She found the controls for the bed and made it provide a backrest. She unashamedly enjoyed the view when he came back and got into bed next to her.

"I've been thinking," she began.

"Pleasant thoughts, I hope." She didn't miss the undercurrent of worry in his light words.

"Let's clear that up first." She set her mug down behind her on the headrest, then kissed him deeply and thoroughly. "I don't regret a single second of last night, and I want more as soon as possible, but you have schedules to keep, and so do I."

"Okay, so what were you thinking?"

She should have waited until the kaffa had time to work its magic, but she'd just have to push on. "I wish we had time for a slow tango, learning to trust each other, but that damn clock keeps marching forward." She retrieved her mug and held it in front of her with both hands. "Are you worried that I might not be able to love you because Da'vin was a woman, and you're a man?"

He was silent a long moment, then shook his head. "No, you're too honest—you'd have told me that up front. I'm more worried that you're smart and beautiful and sexy and educated, and I'm just an A-level gunnin who tanks at relationships."

"Who also has a heart the size of the Andromeda galaxy." She dropped her hand to rest on his relaxed thigh. "I'm no prize, *querido*. I'm moody and independent, and I need time alone. I won't put up with being treated like a princess. I have opinions."

His eyes widened. "I'm shocked. You? Opinions?"

"*Burro*," she said. "But I'll always try to listen to yours."

"I'm … thank you."

"So, what really got me thinking was the advice from your forecaster friend, about knowing your friends and having exit strategies. I've been plotting how to rebuild the Materials Science program for Optimal Polytechnic, and for Vestering, but the O-P regents won't care if it's good, just that it's in the catalog, and I'll have to fight Vestering and his like-minded minions. They're not my friends."

Jerzi snorted. "They're flaming idiots."

"Which brings me to my point. If I'm going to put my energy and heart into building a Materials Science program, I'd rather do it someplace where I *do* have friends. For a start, one sexy, good friend, and his amazing daughter, and two new friends who I'd like to know better. Someplace like, say, Etonver, where there are, so I've been given to understand, plenty of professionals interested in studying better ways to achieve destructive objectives."

"You're thinking of starting your own school for teaching explosives?"

"Not right away. I think I'll try for a teaching job first, so I can get to know the area. But I have this idea. Explosives would be the sizzle, the distraction. What I really want is to teach more people like Pico, or the Practical Applications students, how to think for themselves, how to use science and ingenuity to solve problems." She laughed, because it sounded so idealistic. "And I'd have an excuse to operate my own lab, because what's life without a little boom-down?"

He put his empty kaffa cup on the bedside table, then sat up and turned to face her. "I would be the happiest man on the planet if you could come to Etonver, and I'd help you in whatever way I can. But... I still tank at relationships, and I don't want you to regret moving to Etonver because of me."

"You tanked at *one* relationship. You haven't let yourself have another since. I've had a few since Da'vin died, but they failed because my heart wasn't engaged, and because I was terrified of loss. I still am, but you make me want to take that chance."

He pulled the mug from her hands and set it aside, then took her in his arms for a long, sense-drenching kiss. "Thank you for not shooting me last night when I brought dinner."

"I would have, if Pico hadn't warned me. She was afraid I'd call the police." She kissed his nose and grinned. "You know me better than she does."

She couldn't resist running light fingers over his chest until she found his flat nipples, which were surprisingly sensitive.

"What's your timetable for this new venture of yours?" His questing hand found the tip of the raised phoenix design that started on the bottom half of her right breast. "What can I do to help?"

"A few months... oh, yes, like that, with your tongue," she gasped, arching into him. "I'll ping you..."

The capacity for words dissolved in her brain as she gave herself over to the man who tasted of kaffa and love.

Epilogue

RENNER STOOD STATUE-STILL in the corner of the luxury room that Dixon Davidro had made into his office while in Tremplin, glowering at the bank of nine windows that overlooked the beach. The hotel had safer, less exposed rooms, but the tropical air on Nila Marbela had put Dixon in a pleasure-seeking mood, and he'd insisted on a view of paradise. Furthermore, he refused to darken them at night and left the lights blazing, meaning anyone could see whatever Dixon was doing.

Which in this case, was receiving expert oral sex from one of the exciters on the hotel room service menu. Dixon liked being watched. And heard. Usually Renner got stuck being the audience, but tonight, anyone flying by in a flitter or airsled would see the show.

Renner knew without looking at a clock display that the collar on his neck would be ratcheting in the next minute. After eight years with the bloody thing, he could almost feel it. He twitched a lip in sour humor at his own joke. Dixon was distracted by his new project, who was turning out to be more of a challenge than Dixon anticipated, and the man loved new challenges. However, his distraction meant he'd forgotten to loosen the collar more often lately, meaning Renner's neck was often bloody. He used to wear high-necked shirts to absorb it, but he'd noticed that it bothered Dixon's other staff more if they could see the red rivulets running down. Besides, sleeveless tank shirts made his scarred muscular arms and chest more intimidating. Vicious guard dogs should look the part.

While Dixon was shouting about his impending second orgasm, Renner took the chance to send his talent out to nudge the switch that controlled the morphglass. Fortunately, it was a slider instead of a step control, so he could darken the windows bit by bit. As Dixon pointed out with almost the same regularity as the collar ratcheted, if Dixon died, Renner would soon follow, since only a live, cooperative Dixon could loosen the collar. To reinforce the lesson, Dixon occasionally let the collar tighten on purpose, once to the point that Renner was in a hypoxic delirium. Regardless of whatever lesson Dixon thought he'd been imparting, Renner's takeaway had been to come up with several contingencies for killing himself before he'd let himself die like that.

Renner's collar ratcheted tighter. Blood dripped.

Dixon yelled his release, and the exciter sat back on her heels with a look of professional satisfaction. Dixon praised her skill and sent her on her way, then used the fresher to clean up. When Renner was seventeen, and newly conscripted into Dixon's menagerie, the near-daily sex displays had aroused him, and made him angry that his body reacted the way Dixon wanted. After nineteen years, it was no more titillating than seeing the man blow his nose.

Dixon was at his most mellow at times like these, so now was the time to strike.

"You have a problem," Renner said. The scar tissue buildup on his throat made his voice gravelly, and painful for long speeches. Pain was Renner's old and most reliable friend. Well, second most, but his most reliable friend was gone.

"What problem is that, Rexium?" It amused Dixon to call Renner by common names for pet dogs. Renner didn't care, since he'd had quite a few names in his youth before being captured and collared by Dixon. Renner pretended that it annoyed him, because Dixon liked predictable responses.

"Radomir."

Dixon sighed. "What's he done now?"

"Georgie says the families of his personal kills on Sanangerel, Funlun Aiye, and Terakhir are all talking to a prominent journalist about an interstellar serial killer. Georgie forecasts that more will be talking soon, once the details trend."

Dixon stood and stretched, angling his naked torso toward the windows for maximum exposure. The man spent a small fortune in body shops and parlors to look young and fit. "What do they think they know?"

"That he's protected by the CPS." Dixon jerked in surprise and wrenched his back. Renner laughed inside, but kept it off his face.

Dixon sat and frowned. "You're feeling smug." He gave Renner a narrow-eyed look. "There's more, isn't there?"

"Two days ago, he told you he was going to the body shop and got 'stuck in traffic.' Instead, he went to the floater war and killed at least eleven mercenaries and crew. Then he went to the body shop, where he paid them extremely well with his own funds to secretly treat him for a burned hand, broken bones, and crush injuries."

Dixon crossed his arms. "Perhaps he went after the independent investigators."

"Assuming the 'investigators' aren't just a cover for him wanting to kill again, you told him to keep them busy, and no more deaths." Renner twitched an eyebrow. "Have you looked at your Davydov lately?"

Dixon looked at him expectantly. "What will I find when I do?"

"Fried. Not by me." Whoever had done it had less finesse than he did, but he had no equal, as far as he knew.

"Wounds can't be traced to a specific energy weapon." Dixon's tone was mild, but his fingers twitched, a subtle sign that he was irritated.

Renner allowed himself the hint of a smile. "Five-prong burn marks can."

"Mr. Radomir's homemade stunner?"

"This afternoon's local newstrends have a story of two accident victims and a mutilated college girl with the exact same upper-spine burn marks." His throat was burning from so much talking, but it was worth it.

Dixon frowned. "What college girl?" His fingers began curling as if they wanted to be fists.

Renner bared his teeth in a caricature of a smile. "The girl he attacked hours after the crew leader job, in the same building. He made her bleed. You'd recognize the pattern."

Dixon was silent for a long moment. Renner was afraid he'd have to spell it out for him, but as careless as the man was with details, he wasn't stupid.

Dixon took a breath in slowly, then blew it out fast. "It would be inconvenient if the various police departments compared notes on sanctioned accidents and the reward outings. I think we need another reinforcement session with Mr. Radomir. We'll have to train him to use different techniques, and supervise him more closely. And perhaps look for the investigators. They might be the source of our newstrend trouble."

Renner went for the prize. "Will you have time to do that again, and work with the new subject? Can you trust Radomir?" He knew Dixon was banking on the success of the project to get promoted, and relied on his staff for daily supervision to keep the subject in line. Radomir could do considerable damage to Dixon's plans, if he was feeling desperate or vindictive.

Dixon launched himself from his chair to stalk to the windows. "I dislike greedy people, always wanting more." He turned to glare at Renner. "I protect you all, and give you what you need. You'll have to take on enforcement duties again. Where am I going to get another shielder?"

Renner kept his mouth shut and met Dixon's gaze with his usual glower. Renner had done Dixon's wet-work on and off for years, so it was nothing new. Dixon always had ways to collect new pets, as all his independent contractors could attest.

"Bah," said Dixon in disgust. He turned back toward the windows. "Mr. Radomir has outlived his usefulness."

"Tonight?"

"Yes, yes," growled Dixon, flapping his hand in dismissal. "You know what to do with the remains. Oh, and send Lamis in. I need her to arrange travel. I've found the perfect location for our special project."

As Renner walked down the hall toward Radomir's suite, he opened a gate to his anger and let it build. His talent worked without it, but his perpetual rage needed the outlet. He used to think that's all he was, a murderous rage generator, until Dixon's oldest pet had healed him and taught him friendship.

When Radomir had hurt Neirra, she'd extracted promises from Renner not to tell Dixon, and not to sign his own death warrant by going after Radomir. Neirra's steady decline had given Renner daily motivation to catch Radomir's mistakes and give him pain, as a cover for his true goal of getting Dixon to order Radomir's destruction. It was the first long-term plan Renner had ever come up with. He owed Neirra sanity, friendship, and comfort. He couldn't give her any of those, but he could give her the gift of retribution. She'd done her own damage to the warped twist, making him depend on the drugs daily, for life, but the ultimate revenge would now be Renner's. Power crackled along his skin.

Neirra had taught him the value of having something to look forward to, something to live for. He decided his new plan would be to find a way to thank her before she died, and tell her about Radomir. After that, he'd start on the most dangerous plan of all, figuring out how to get free. It would probably kill him, but it would be a hell of a ride.

ABOUT THIS BOOK

Thank you for reading *Pico's Crush*. I hope you had as much fun reading it as I had writing it. By the way, if you haven't already read them, *Overload Flux* (Book 1) introduces Luka, Mairwen, and the Central Galactic Concordance universe, and *Minder Rising* (Book 2) introduces Lièrén Sòng, his wife Imara, and delves into the Citizen Protection Service. The short novella, *Zero Flux* (Book 2.5) returns to Luka and Mairwen for an adventure and mystery. Book 4, *Jumper's Hope*, has new characters on the run from whoever wants them dead, this time for real.

I'd be thrilled if you'd post a review of *Pico's Crush* at the retailer where you found this book. Even if it's short and sweet, it really helps. Reviews are what get books noticed and read by others. Think of it as paying forward for the last time someone recommended a book you really liked.

For news of upcoming releases, and to find out what's next in the Central Galactic Concordance series, please sign up for my newsletter at http://bit.ly/CVN-news. I promise not to send photos of my cats or vacations (unless it's somewhere off-planet).

I'd love to know what you think about the story and what you'd like to see in the future books. You can visit my website and blog at the cleverly named Author.CarolVanNatta.com and drop me a line, or connect with me on Facebook at CarolVanNattaAuthor.

I owe a deep debt of gratitude to Mirek, who helped make Jerzi's and Pico's Polish excellent, and to Jaime, who helped make Andra's Spanish shine. Thanks to my beta readers, Jill, T3, Melisse, Merry, Roger, and Ann, who kindly pointed out myriad ways to improve, well, everything. I am also grateful for the professional editing services provided by Shelley Holloway of Holloway House, and the stunning cover design by Gene Mollica Studio.

ABOUT THE AUTHOR

Carol Van Natta is a science fiction and fantasy author. She shares her home in Fort Collins, Colorado with a sometime-mad scientist and various cats. Any violations of the laws of physics in her books are the fault of the cats, not the mad scientist.

Sign up for her newsletter at her website, http://Author.CarolVanNatta.com.

BOOKS BY CAROL VAN NATTA

Space Opera

Overload Flux (Central Galactic Concordance, Book 1)
Minder Rising (CGC Book 2)
Zero Flux (CGC Novella 2.5)
Pico's Crush (CGC Book 3)
Jumper's Hope (CGC Book 4)

Fantasy

In Graves Below
Shift of Destiny

Retro Science Fiction Comedy

Hooray for Holopticon (with Ann Harbour)